OTTO
ECKHART'S
ORDEAL

OTTO ECKHART'S ORDEAL

SHORTLISTED
FOR THE 2021 WILBUR SMITH
ADVENTURE WRITING PRIZE

THE
WILBUR & NISO SMITH
FOUNDATION

NIALL EDWORTHY

Publisher: Badger Books Ltd, 2024
First published by Universe, an imprint of the Unicorn
Publishing Group LLP, 2020
5 Newburgh Street
London W1F 7RG

ISBN 978-1-738452-28-6 (Print)
ISBN 978-1-738452-29-3 (Ebook)

Cover Design by Izzy Barrett Insta:@izustrations
Book Design by Principal Publishing
Author website: nialledworthy.com
Email: niall@nialledworthy.com
Insta: @nialledworthybooks

CONTENTS

AUTHOR'S NOTE ••• 7

CHAPTER ONE ••• 11

CHAPTER TWO ••• 46

CHAPTER THREE ••• 76

CHAPTER FOUR ••• 98

CHAPTER FIVE ••• 120

CHAPTER SIX ••• 148

CHAPTER SEVEN ••• 180

CHAPTER EIGHT ••• 206

CHAPTER NINE ••• 238

CHAPTER TEN ••• 254

CHAPTER ELEVEN ••• 267

CHAPTER TWELVE ••• 298

CHAPTER THIRTEEN ••• 315

CHAPTER FOURTEEN ••• 338

ALSO BY THE AUTHOR ••• 348

ACKNOWLEDGEMENTS ••• 349

DEDICATION

To Charlie, Alfie and Eliza

AUTHOR'S NOTE

Otto Eckhart's Ordeal is a work of historical fiction based on a true premise. A young medievalist – Otto Rahn – was dispatched to find the Holy Grail by the Ahnenerbe, a pseudoscientific branch of the SS established in 1935. The Ahnenerbe (meaning 'ancestral heritage') was the ugly brainchild of SS leader Heinrich Himmler, ever eager to provide evidence of Aryan superiority and validate the perverse racial doctrines of the Nazi Party.

The real 'Otto' met a mysterious death on an Alpine mountainside in 1939, the story of his plight soon buried under the events of the Second World War. I can only hope the fictitious 'Otto' fares better. Both Ottos were born in Michelstadt in the central German region of Hesse, both were experts in the legends of the Holy Grail, in the Nordic myths and in the Cathar movement and both lived for a time in the Pyrenean village of Montségur. But that is where the resemblance of their stories ends, and fiction takes the baton from fact.

ABOUT THE AUTHOR

Niall Edworthy has written over forty books in a variety of genres on a wide range of subjects, some under his own name, some under pseudonyms and a great many under those for whom he has ghosted.

CHAPTER ONE

The letter instructed me to present myself at Prinz-Albrecht Strasse, 8. I knew the grand old building well. It was in the heart of Berlin, home to the School of Industrial Arts and Crafts where my cousin Max had studied. But that was what? Seven, eight, nine years ago, another time, another world.

The day I returned, well, I remember it as if it all happened this morning, every detail. You don't forget that day, the one that changes your life forever, when nothing again will be even remotely the same as the life you knew previously, when you end up wholly altered by the experiences that flow from it. Mine was the sixth of May 1937, and oh God, what a naïve dolt I was. I didn't even have the excuse of heedless youth on my side. I was almost thirty.

Father did warn me, in his gentle way. The letter was unheaded and unsigned – secrecy was paramount it said – but it was stamped with the official Reichsadler imperial eagle and swastika. When I showed it to him, his face and shoulders dropped. He tapped the envelope, put his hand on my shoulder and said: 'Careful, son.' Had Mother warned me against it, it may have turned out differently. She was all for me making the trip to Berlin and getting a 'proper' job. But really, did I ever have a choice in it? Did any of us have the slightest control over our fates then? They were going to get us all in the end, one way or another. We were all of us being swept along by the surging torrent of events, and the moment to resist the flow had long since passed.

But I knew none of this that fresh Spring day. I was full of hope, twitchy for sure, but excited and curious by what lay in store. The mystery of it! In any event, I'm still here, looking over my shoulder but safe again, for the time being at least, ready to put it all down straight off the top of my head, no notes, no diary. I don't need them. It's all stamped on my mind as if with a branding iron. The way it all seems to be heading, my story will likely prove to be no more than a microscopic footnote in the history of the times, but you can make up your own mind about that.

Prinz-Albrecht-Strasse was no more than a five-minute walk from Anhalter Station. That much at least was the same. But the giant station clock read twenty-five to three and the meeting was not until four. I had taken the early train from Frankfurt. I was not going to risk being late, not with the letter's promise of travel and adventure – and the hint of some Reichsmarks into the bargain. This was one opportunity I was not going to mess up.

Holy hell, how I needed the money then. The ratcatcher's dog back in Michelstadt had more in the bank than I did. I would have taken any job, anything to avoid joining the Reichswehr – the Wehrmacht, I beg your pardon – and anything to escape the tedium of provincial life and my mother's ceaseless disappointment in me; anything to be carefree and on my travels again. Wandering Europe for five years, ducking my responsibilities, writing a book no one wanted to publish, I only had myself to blame for being penniless and as good as unemployable. I had been home for a month, written two dozen letters seeking work – research and minor academic posts mainly – but nothing doing, just plenty of polite replies wishing me well in my hunt.

So it had been with my manuscript as well. The drawer of my kneehole desk was full of courteous rejections from publishers, all along the lines of… '*Dear Herr Eckhart, We were flattered to receive your manuscript of* **Parzifal, the Cathars and the Search for The Holy Grail**, *a most fascinating field of study of which you are evidently its master. Unfortunately, these are difficult times for books. After careful consideration we are sorry to inform you of our belief that your book will fail to appeal to a broad enough section of the reading public to justify itself in the marketplace…*'

To be fair, it is a truly awful book, a re-hash of my university thesis padded out with even more nonsense about Nordic Gods, Teutonic Knights and the mystery of the chalice from which Jesus and his disciples were said to have drunk at the Last Supper. The annihilation of the Cathars in the thirteenth century by the Church is terrible and fascinating certainly. If only I had stuck to that!

Parzifal – no, I certainly wouldn't buy it, but I had to justify my travels somehow and I liked the idea of being a published author. Most people don't read books, they just like having them on their shelves to show how clever they are. I was gambling on some fool out there who might get behind it, throw me some Reichsmarks and sell into that growing market of Nordic myth cranks and fuming patriots. So Mother was right about me, about my prospects. She had taken me to task again just the other night – before, that is, the arrival of the letter, and all of a sudden I was her little Goldilocks again. I was 'idle as a bed of potatoes' she had thundered.

I have never quite understood that expression of hers and, emboldened by Father's shy smile, I dared to have a bit of sport with her, pointing out that from its unpromising beginnings as a small seed bud, the potato will grow into an impressive and useful form of life. I even held up a potato from my plate to prove my point. Father found it funny at least. Mother shot back, spittle flying:: 'But a potato needs the right conditions in which to flourish! Lying around in France and heaven knows wherever else, trying to write a daft book about Norse myths and French heretics is hardly the ideal growing conditions for a man. Damn your idleness and damn the French!'

Anyhow, there I was on the sixth of May, letter in

my pocket, hope in my heart, standing on platform 4, buffeted by a torrent of passengers, steam pouring from beneath the train. I was holding onto my fedora and staring up at the vast glass-and-iron arched roof of Anhalter Station, surely the grandest in the world, majestic as any palace or cathedral, my eyes slowly drawn down the platform to the great red and black swastika banners, fifty feet high and more, draped on the interior of the red-brick facade. Of course, I had seen these flags in Frankfurt and even in little Michelstadt – they were as plentiful as leaves on a tree – but nothing on this scale. I was dumbfounded and, I must confess, a little impressed too. It's hard not to feel some sort of thrill at the sight of them – the red and black, the colours of power, and the swastika, that mesmerising rune with its ancient promise of good fortune. I know about the power of symbols and you have to hand it to the National Socialists – they have chosen a mighty potent one in the hooked cross.

I went through Anhalter's magnificent lobby into the square outside the station on Saarland Strasse (that's what they are calling it now), straight into a man on a bicycle with a basket full of giant brezls, steaming lightly in the chill Spring air. I was famished, and with no more than a few Reichsmarks in my pocket to last me until I got home long after midnight, I bought two to see me through the day. My mother won't speak to people who eat in public, and ordinarily I would never, but I was almost dizzy with hunger.

By the time I had descended the stairs, bought my 10-pfennig ticket and felt the warm rush of the oncoming S-Bahn train, I was halfway through one of them. It was just two stops to the new station on the Unter den Linden, and I was chewing the last of it as I made my way up the steps back into the sunshine. My first thought on emerging into the great boulevard of Imperial Berlin was that I must have missed my stop. I looked to my left and there was the Brandenburg Gate just as it was meant to be. I looked to the right and there in the far distance was the Berliner Dom, resting place of a thousand Hohenzollerns, the pale green dome of the cathedral just visible on the skyline.

I turned around and there was the Hotel Bristol, one of Germany's finest, just as it always was when Max and I used to take tea and watch the wealthy promenading along the avenue in all their finery. Whenever I had grown tired of my own studies in Heidelberg – which was quite often, because I was reading Medieval German literature – I used to jump on the train and meet him at the end of classes on the steps of Prinz-Albrecht-Strasse. We'd skip off to the cafés on the Linden and the jazz bars in Ku'damm, see and do things we'd never dream of telling our mothers about. You could watch naked dancers in the afternoon while enjoying tea and cake and, if you were really in luck, get to kiss a girl before nightfall. Imagine that in little Michelstadt!

This wasn't the world I remembered. But yes, for sure, this was the Unter den Linden. All the lovely sweet-smelling lime trees from which the grand old street takes its name had vanished, replaced by a few weedy saplings no taller or more robust than me. What a plain thoroughfare it had become since my last visit seven years ago; grand still, yes of course, but sulking over its Spartan starkness, like a child after an overly severe haircut knowing it was going to take an age to grow out. The double carriageways had been widened but there was barely any traffic, just a few black cars and a couple of cream twin-deck buses. But no rustling foliage to soften the austere grandeur, no shade, no promenaders, no joy.

I pulled out my Murattis, fired up my first cigarette of the day and blew out my cheeks, looking up and down into a swaying forest of swastika flags and banners and a blur of uniforms. In my baggy double-breasted suit, scuffed brogues and floppy threadbare fedora, I was that guest who had not been informed the party was a fancy-dress affair. I had never seen so many different uniforms, dozens of them whichever way you looked; black ones of the SS, brown ones of the SA, field grey ones of the Wehrmacht, the green ones of the street police, swankier than Prussian generals...

The familiar white costume of the traffic policeman outside the Bristol, comic and Italian, was comfort of sorts, a throwback, waving his gloved hands and blowing his whistle at what traffic there was. But if I hadn't known better, you'd have forgiven me for thinking that, in my time away, the country had fallen under foreign occupation.

A troop of SA, the *Sturmabteilung*, was milling around the news kiosk outside the S-Bahn entrance, reeking of beer, jostling and barging each other, a few of them tearing at brezls like dogs stripping meat from a bone, their mates queuing for the newspapers. I had heard a great deal about the 'brown shirts' while in France and I stared at them, engrossed, from beneath the lowered brim of my hat. The papers, especially the foreign titles, were full of headlines about the Spanish Civil War but the SA men were interested only in copies of *Der Sturmer* and the afternoon edition of *Der Angriff*, each one thrusting out his arm and Heil Hitler-ing the vendor before handing over their coins. The poor old man in the kiosk must have been exhausted, dutifully lifting his arm in response to each bark of his customers. Side-on to the kiosk, I couldn't see his face, just his bony hand shooting out every few moments, each time a little lower than the last.

Some of the SA men rolled up their papers like truncheons and slapped them in their palms, one with his chum in a headlock, beating him with his. I had to assume this had become an everyday sight for Berliners, because no passer-by batted an eyelid, just kept walking, eyes front.

You have to know this was all new and strange to me and I felt a sudden and acute awareness of my age, gawping and thinking: don't they all look exactly the same, these big boy scouts? The short-cropped hair, the olive-brown shirts and caps, riding breeches flared at the side, the knee-high boots, shoulder cross-belts, the chests puffed out, faces glistening with beery sweat – from only a short distance, all indistinguishable from one another, just a mass of roiling brown shirts. *Ein volk! Ein Reich! Ein Führer!* – the slogan *du jour*. I had heard it endlessly on the wireless and seen it on all the posters. And there it was in the flesh right before me, a newsreel come to life.

The most drunk among them, and that was a notable achievement, strode my way, standing so close I felt and smelt his hot, beery breath. When he began *heiling* everyone emerging up from the S-Bahn, I backed away a couple of steps. He span on a heel and, stabbing his arm and flat palm at me, I confess I felt intimidated and returned the gesture, my effort rather feeble, more of a muscle spasm.

I walked on, head down through the brown shirts, crossing the Wilhelmstrasse, and made towards the Brandenburg Gate, returning the nod and smile from the porter in his big top hat, under the burgundy awning of the Hotel Adlon. I passed under the great arch of the Brandenburg Gate into the Tiergarten, a group of ten-year-old schoolboys on an excursion *heiling* each other and passers-by, laughing and shoving.

It was quite exhausting just to witness this new craze. I sat on a bench, the sun on my neck, facing the smoke-blackened, roofless shell of the Reichstag and lit a cigarette. A squirrel raced over and stood up on its back legs, casting me a sinister eye, begging for the brezl sticking out of my suit pocket. I took out the letter from my inside pocket and read it again, looking for clues.

'Sehr Geehrter Herr Eckhart, Your name has been passed to my department through the official channels. Our Darmstadt office informs me that you are now back in the Reich following your latest endeavours in the realm of historical research. I do hope the expedition, to the Cathar heartlands of Languedoc I understand, was both fruitful and enlightening.

On reading your work, with great interest and admiration I must add, I am persuaded that your knowledge and expertise could prove to be an invaluable asset to the Reich and, in particular, to a new institution established during the period of your absence. For reasons which will become clear at our meeting, the work and aims of this institution are best left undisclosed here lest they should fall into the wrong hands.

I have a foreign assignment in mind that may be of interest to you. Were an arrangement to be reached, satisfactory to both sides, you will of course be well remunerated for your important efforts. I thank you in advance for presenting yourself at Prinz-Albrecht-Strasse, 8 at 1600Uhr on Thursday, 6 May.
Heil Hitler!

My expedition! If only they knew. *My work!* Were they confusing me with another Otto Eckhart? But then how did they know where I lived, that I had been abroad, that

I had written a book? *My knowledge and expertise! Invaluable asset!* Thank heavens they hadn't consulted Mother or Professor Gebhardt at Heidelberg University. *Foreign assignment! Well remunerated!*

I can barely bring myself to admit to those feelings of exhilaration now. But I must remind you that I had only been back in Germany a very short while, that I didn't have two pfennigs to rub together, I had no prospects but a life of idle provincial tedium ahead of me and I longed to be back on the road, a free spirit once more. You see it, don't you? I do hope you will forgive me my naivety when you discover what was about to happen.

In fact, what happened first was that I finished another Muratti, saw that it was gone half past three, and shot to my feet. I hurried back to the Linden and, at the corner of the Adlon, trotted right into the Wilhelmstrasse, the street of German power that runs all the way down to Belle Allianz Platz on the Landwehr Canal, a street so clean you could happily lick it. This is the government quarter – and good heavens does the place want to impress its authority upon you.

I paced beneath the giant Union flag of the British Embassy, past the old Presidential Palace and Foreign Ministry, through a procession of uniforms, under banners so pristine they might have been laundered overnight, past brass plaques polished into mirrors and doorknobs into Christmas tree baubles.

By the time I reached the Reich Chancellery in Wilhemplatz, I had broken into a canter, my watch telling me it was gone a quarter to four, my heart thumping, the heat steaming under my fedora. I ran across Leipziger Strasse, dashing between two trams crammed with shoppers, cigarette clenched between my teeth, the smoke stinging my eyes. I stopped to get my breath back, wiped my brow with my pocket handkerchief and set off again, Hermann Goering's famous Air Ministry to my right, Europe's largest office building, taking up an entire block and every bit as monumental as he boasted. (Now, Goering I had heard of. How could I not, even living in a remote village in the foothills of the Pyrenees so long? Goering and Goebbels, the 'Laurel and Hardy of Germany', as my landlord Raymond there liked to say.)

I was blowing hard by the time I reached Prinz-Albrecht-Strasse, coughing like a consumptive. It was almost five to the hour now and I took a moment to compose myself outside the little walled garden that abutted the School of Industrial Arts and Crafts. It was a relief to see that there was at least one building in the city left unadorned by giant banners and flags. I smoothed down my hair, brushed down my lapels and, balancing like a flamingo, wiped each shoe on the calf of the other leg.

I jogged towards the School, hat down, swung left up the steps and straight into a wall of ink-black uniforms topped with helmets and tailed with gleaming knee-length boots. I fell back to the pavement, adjusting my hat. Cut-down machine guns hung from their broad shoulders, long daggers from their belts. They stared down at me, me up at them.

Hand still on my hat, I wondered whether this section of the building had been commandeered for a military conference, and the entrance to the school had been moved further up the street or to the side door up from the little garden. I looked for the old brass plaque to the right of the arch but there was only the pale imprint of where it had once been. I took out my letter and was about to ask for directions when the soldier closest to me, holding a clipboard, pulled it from my hand and said:

'Herr Eckhart, yes?'

I stammered an affirmative.

He said: 'You will need one of these,' and he handed me a ticket.

He paused, staring at my shoes, an honest pair of brogues, and said, 'The ticket is not so that you can get into the building, Herr Eckhart, it is so that you can get out.'

I was expecting a laugh, a smile at least, to follow on the coat-tails of his humorous remark, but none was forthcoming. The others stood aside for me, lowering their heads as one, and they joined their colleague in staring at my shoes like I had arrived barefoot. The great iron door was pushed open. I stepped inside, and it shut fast, a heavy clunk echoing around the vaulted stone ceiling. I brushed my shoes on the fitted doormat, rubbed them on the back of my calves again, took two deep breaths and made my way up the broad split-level staircase into the central hall.

Not for the last time that day, I had the disorientating sensation of having arrived in the wrong place. When I had last stood in that hall, it had been adorned with paintings, posters, exhibits and notice boards, alive with the bustle and happy chatter of students streaming up and down the stairs, eddying and chirping in little clusters. Now, stripped of its decorations and information boards, the only sounds were the metallic click of heels on flagstones and the murmur of low voices from a small group of peak-capped officers by the wall over to my right.

The entire space had been painted a dirty cream, giving the impression, in the quiet and the dim light, of an overcast windless day. Three long bench pews of solid wood sat below high latticework windows facing to the sunless north. On either side of them, the only works of art – two busts on plinths, one of the Führer and one of Goering. The hall narrowed to a broad corridor and at the far end of it, a shallow staircase of about six long steps. An oblong of fading afternoon light, refracted by a high-arched glass partition, cut through the gloom.

A telephone rang and my eyes were drawn to the desk at the foot of the staircase. I made my way over, relieved I had never got around to replacing the metal heel protectors, for I was starting to feel distinctly apprehensive. This building was no longer the Industrial School of Arts and Crafts, of that much I was now utterly certain. (Father's warnings were starting to stir in the well of my mind, but at that stage, in my excitement, I was still happy to believe that the building was an academic or research institution. Why else would I have been summoned to it?)

I took off my hat and, clutching it to my chest, I made a small bow to the woman seated behind the desk as she was replacing the telephone handset. She was an attractive woman of middle years, so blonde she may just as well have walked out of one of those hair-dye posters I had seen plastered everywhere since my return. Her eyes were ice-blue and they came with a manner to match. When I handed her the letter and smiled, she tried to return the gesture, but gave up halfway through, as though the effort had hurt her cheek muscles. She gave me a quick up-and-down, her eyes lingering on my ill-polished shoes. Or were they? With a cough and a rapid wiggle of the index finger, she summoned one of the two soldiers stationed at the foot of the grand flight of steps that ran through the heart of the building.

'To the chief,' she said to him, and handed me back my letter.

I went to take the stairs along the stone bannister, but the guard took me by the elbow and steered me into the middle so that he was on the inside. I threw him a quizzical look and after a few steps, he pointed up the stairwell and said: 'It's a long way to fall.' I was encouraged to make a small joke of my own, nervous I suppose, and eager to connect with someone.

'I can assure you, sir, that my days of sliding down bannisters are over. I am almost thirty years old.'

His laugh emerged in the form of a rapid expulsion of breath through the nostrils and I was pleased to have amused him. We walked on in silence, flight after flight, twisting left and left and left again. By the time we reached the fifth and final floor, my chest was heaving, and I tapped it to show that I needed a moment to recover. When I opened the palm of my hand to show I was ready to proceed, he pushed open a door to a long, narrow corridor and I followed him through.

We were in a warren of offices, rushing by the porthole windows of the doors, secretaries jabbing at typewriters within, uniformed men bent over files or telephones pressed to the cheek. We passed through another stairwell into another corridor, then another, through door after door, landing after landing, turning this way then that, past armed guards bolt upright like statues of black marble, a bust or portrait of the Führer in every corridor, a fearful row taking place behind one door, accusation and denial merging as a howl. I was sweating from the effort of keeping pace and from my rising discomfort.

We halted in a hallway between two corridors, and I had a strong sense that we were back close to where we had started. My escort disappeared with the guard on the door into the passageway behind. I walked to the window, rocked on my heels, hands in pockets fingering my Murattis. Over the rooftops of southern Berlin, I could make out the green swathe of Viktoriapark and the pinprick of the Kreuzberg memorial on the hill at its heart. My mind drifted back to those happy days picnicking and carousing in the woodland clearings of its slopes.

Beyond, there lay what must have been Tempelhof airfield, half-encircled by a bow of vast hangars and buildings. An aircraft pulled off the far end of the grass runway and went into a steepling ascent, appearing almost stationary at that distance. I have never been on an aircraft, and I am not sure I ever want to – but oh how I wished I was aboard that one! My hands were trembling, and I put them inside my hat to hide them when the others returned.

My escort held open the door and flicked his head back. Stooping a little as if under a low beam, I went in. A woman, lit by a shaft of sun, was standing in an open doorway immediately to the right, a phone ringing from within.

She said: 'Herr Eckhart, please. He'll be with you shortly.' She made a gesture with her hand encouraging me to step on it, and I hurried in after her. She pointed to three wooden chairs along the wall to the right and tore the phone from its cradle. 'Yes?'

It was a small, non-descript room, an Underwood typewriter on her desk, flanked by stacks of papers, and a bank of filing cabinets on the wall behind her.

The small window faced north, overlooking a block of rooftops and then the dark expanse of the Tiergarten woodland and the soaring Victory Column.

'Yes, I understand that perfectly. It will be done at once… and yes I have sent the files… yes, the table is booked… yes, the corner one away from the piano… no, I didn't tell Marga… yes, I have arranged the delivery of the stilts and the tortoise… tomorrow, or Monday at the latest… no, he assures me it's not Russian, it's a red-footed species from Central America… yes, very good.'

She replaced the receiver with some force and pulled out a cigarette with her teeth, flicked open her lighter and swept the flint wheel across her thigh. She put the flame to the tip, taking a deep draw and exhaling a long stream of smoke in my direction, the other hand on her hip. She was extremely beautiful – even with her pitch-black hair in a bun, her cornflower blue eyes raging behind her thick-rimmed work glasses.

She said: 'Well, I hope you're having a better day than I am. You're here to discuss unicorns and Holy Grails and such like I understand. He thinks your book is a masterpiece so you should find him in good spirits. Sorry, I'm Ingrid, one of his overworked secretaries. I hope he goes easier on you. What does he have in mind for you?'

She dropped her shoulders, broke into a warm smile and walked towards me. I stood up and shook her hand and exchanged how-do-you-dos. She smelt of lavender. My God she was beautiful. With her easy manner, it was as though we had known each other for years.

'I haven't the faintest idea, I'm afraid. I don't even know who I am meeting.'

'What?' She blurted it out in a cloud of smoke. 'You don't know who *he* is? He's – '

The phone rang and she apologised with her hand, lifting the receiver with her other. 'Yes, sir. Right away.'

And to me, with a mischievous smile, reaching for the door handle, '*He* is ready to receive you. You should be alright. He sounds calmer now. Probably had a pill or two. Pleasure meeting you. I am quite certain we will be meeting again.'

We shook hands once more, a little longer this time and I could have sworn she gave it an extra squeeze.

'Well, yes, a pleasure and maybe, well, who knows, thank you, goodbye…'

The door at the far end, about thirty yards away, opened slowly, filling the end of the passageway with light and revealing the silhouette of a slight figure in flared breeches – either that, or someone with unusually developed quadricep muscles.

'Hurry along, I promise not to bite you! Don't listen to Ingrid.' The voice was deep and mellow and there was the gurgle of a chuckle. I quickened my stride and found myself clutching an outstretched hand and looking into a boyish face with a broad smile, light toothbrush moustache and warm, hazel eyes behind a pair of round, rimless glasses. His head was at least two sizes too small for his body, its brown hair shaved at the side and, what remained of it, flattened with pomade and sitting on his crown like a large skull cap. His rounded cheeks put you in mind of a squirrel with an acorn lodged in each cheek.

He pushed his face closer, tilting his head a little and stared deep into my eyes. The cheeks were shiny and dark and he was close enough for me to smell that he had eaten fairly recently and that he shaved with sandalwood products. For an awful moment, I thought he was going to kiss me, as men will do in France, but he pulled back, exclaiming, 'Good! Good! Excellent!' and threw a hand upwards like it was being yanked by a piece of string.

'Heil Hitler! Well done, well done! You made it. I can see from your shoes you have had a long walk. I hope you haven't walked all the way from Michelstadt!'

I Heil-Hitlered him back, shooting my hand up quickly and looking to my shoes at the same time. These were English shoes of very good quality – Crockett & Jones no less! I swallowed my grievance and muttered an apology about a long walk in the Tiergarten.

'Anyhow, enough of your footwear. Your mind is probably on higher matters. I am quite sure they will enjoy a good polish when you get home. In fact, there's a very good shoeshine boy just outside the entrance to Potsdamer Platz U-Bahn station. Please – ' and he thrust out an arm. I thrust my arm out again, but realised he was showing me to a wooden chair right in front of his desk and I put my arm away and sat down.

He sat down too, leaning on his forearms, craning his

neck towards me, and continued rolling his head from side to side. He did that long enough to make me break eye contact and look back down at the brogues that had fallen under so much suspicion since arriving in Berlin.

It was some time before he said: 'I have been greatly looking forward to making your acquaintance.'

I stammered, I fear, in that reedy voice I get when jumpy: 'And I yours, even though – '

'You are a member of the Party, yes?'

'Well, no, not quite yet, I have only just returned and you can't join in France – ' I had put on my deep voice to sound more important and confident.

'Not yet! Not yet!' And he threw back his head and roared with laughter. And I threw back my head and roared with laughter. I didn't have a damned clue why we were laughing but I kept it up all the same until he stopped abruptly and I stopped abruptly; then his smile vanished, and my smile vanished, his face snapped into a look of gravity, my face snapped into a look of gravity, and then we were staring at each other again in silence.

Once more, the stare was long enough for me to turn my eyes, first to the left, then to the right, then round and round the room not knowing where to look. They settled on the wall in the alcove behind him where there hung a portrait of Adolf Hitler as a medieval knight, wearing armour, sitting on a black horse and holding a swastika banner.

To the right, tucked into the corner, there was a turquoise two-seater sofa – curious place for a sofa, I

was thinking – and to the left, a huge floor-to-ceiling bookcase built into the right angle of the walls, each shelf crammed tight with volumes; most of an historical nature, as far as I could tell at a glance. Unsure what to say or what to do in the silence, I leant forward and ran my eyes over the spines: *The Struggle & Death of Karl XII…
The Myth of the Twentieth Century… Tacitus's Germania…
Wolfram von Eschenbach's Parzival* (my subject!), *Henry the Fowler*, several about Wagner and, grabbing the eye by their number, a great many about horoscopes.

Clearly, I was in the presence of a serious historian, perhaps even a professor of German history, now working in the Reich's Ministry for Education. The thought of that possibility instantly made me even more anxious and I feared my fraudulent 'expertise', as he called it in the letter, was about to be horribly exposed. But then he spoke, and I had something else to fret about.

'Well, you can do that tomorrow. It's as easy as boiling an egg.' He tugged the cuffs of his olive-green shirt, brushed each sleeve and straightened the chest strap of his leather cross belt.

'What is, sorry?'

'Joining the party, you numbskull! Just go to your local office and five minutes later you will be a fully-fledged National Socialist, how about that? With all of the benefits that brings, and none of the handicaps of not being. I'll make a note. Check you encounter no obstacles.'

'Oh good, thank you.'

He picked up his fountain pen, pulled off the lid and laid it with great precision to the right of a stack of papers directly before him. He looked at the lid for several moments, then straightened it and slid it a few inches over. Like his head, his hands were disproportionately small.

He looked up after a few moments and said, 'I like to keep a piece of paper to hand so that every time I have another good idea, I can write it straight down. Look, I've had four already today.' He held up the sheet of paper – I saw in his mesmerizingly jagged script the word 'sub-humans' in capital letters.

He took the pen in his right hand and pressed it to the thick paper with such force that his knuckles blanched, and I could hear the scrape of the nib – a sound that has the same effect on me as fingernails down a blackboard. He had written two lines when he pulled a ruler from a side drawer, turned it upside down and underscored the first line, then once more for emphasis, with the same meticulous precision of a draughtsman. He wrote his 'T's like daggers and I was able to work out that two of the words he underlined contained my name – a double dagger at the heart of Otto, and one to make sure I was done for at the end of Eckhart!

My eyes wandered over the picture of the Führer in his armour on the horse. Underneath there was a wooden plaque which read, in large black letters: *Oh Jove, let the Germans realise their own strength and they shall not be men but gods.*

'Hubert Lanzinger, Austrian,' he said, without looking up, still writing.

I swirled my fedora around over my index finger and said, 'Sorry, what?'

'From the Tyrol in fact, Lanzinger. Studied at the Academy of Fine Arts in Vienna.'

I shuffled my feet and looked down at my sorry brogues. 'I beg your pardon, sir. I'm not following you.'

It was several seconds later, still writing, when he continued: 'I knew it would win your approval – what with your fascination for the Teutonic Knights and Germany's glorious past. It is heartening to know that we, the Nordic people, played a full part in helping to crush the Cathars – I don't like heretics. Hundreds of knights from the North heeded the call and headed south to exterminate them. But why am I telling you? You know all that! In fact, I learned that from you. Ha! Lanzinger evokes that glorious epoch in our history quite marvellously, does he not?'

I stared at him blankly, spinning my fedora a little faster.

He looked up, pen hovering. 'The portrait, you silly blockhead! What on earth did you think I was talking about?'

'Oh, I see, I am so sorry. Yes, he looks terrific on a horse. I confess I was unaware the Führer is a keen horseman. Did he sit for it?'

I do this when my nerves are a-jitter – I burble. Lifting the pen and cap, one in each hand, so that they were horizontal at his eyeline, he drew the two pieces together, his eyes following them so that they became crossed. Wiping the pen on his thigh, as a scout might a knife, he inspected it again, laid it down, folded his arms and leant forward on his elbows, eyes sparkling, a smile tugging at both ends of his mouth.

'Herr Eckhart, are you stark raving mad?' I was about to vouch for my sanity when the phone rang, and instead I startled, quickly scratching my scalp to pretend I had an itch. He picked up the handset, nestled it between shoulder and ear, and began nodding his head. At the same time, with fastidious movements of his hands, he tidied the pile of papers, patting his palms against the four sides until they formed a perfect rectangle, then smoothed his hand over them towards his chest, as he might over a sleeping cat. When he was satisfied they were no longer dishevelled, he placed his fountain pen on top, aligning it so that it was exactly flush with the long side margins of the paper.

He listened to his caller for a minute or so, jabbing away, 'Ya… Uh-huh… ya…'. When he narrowed his eyes, raising the brows and shaking his head, I wondered whether there was more than a dash of Japanese blood in his veins.

The conversation, evidently, was not going well. The boyish face hardened into a grimace, the puckered lips suggesting he was about to lose his temper. And indeed, he did lose it, but in the strangest fashion – without raising his voice or cursing, the effect all the more menacing because he was so very mild-mannered.

Almost whispering, he leant into his desk so that his nose was no more than six inches from his desktop, and said:

'No, no Doctor. I said Angora rabbits and I mean Angora rabbits. I want wool. I will not tolerate fur. No other species will serve. I used to breed animals for a living, you know. I studied genetics and rearing. Believe me, it won't be long before you have enough wool to lay a blanket over all Germany. I should know... No, no, no, what do they say about rabbits and breeding? Exactly, Herr Doctor. And yes, you are being a nuisance. I am in an important meeting. Angora, angora, angora. Good day.'

Raising the handset over his shoulder he went to slam it down, but pulled up just short. Holding it with just thumb and forefinger, he dropped it gently into its cradle. He turned to me, clasping his fingers together as if in prayer, and rested his wrists against the desk, blinking and smiling at me beatifically. (He does have a very winning smile, and a lovely soothing voice.) His head fell slowly to one side and I found myself mirroring him so that we were looking at each other from a 45-degree angle.

He said: 'Homosexual.'

I said: 'I beg your pardon?'

He said: 'Homosexual.'

I said: 'Where? Me?'

He said: 'Him.' And jabbed at the telephone. 'The doctor.'

'Gosh, really? How can you tell?'

'Do you like women, Herr Eckhart?'

'Yes, very much. Or some of them at any rate. Not all of them. My mother can be – '

'I like women too. Bumped into my Marga coming through a revolving door in a hotel and tipped snow all over her when I took off my hat to apologise.'

A cackling laugh gave way to a long sigh and a wistful, faraway look. 'Looked as though she had walked straight out of an ancestral forest. She was even wearing fur. Eyes blue as an Alpine lake.'

'Gosh.'

'No, the era of the homosexual is over, Herr Eckhart. If I had my way, they'll all be drowned in a swamp. A very big, deep, mushy swamp, Herr Eckhart.'

'Gosh.'

He swung back into his seat and jabbed his finger at the phone again, bursting to speak but unable to get the words out.

Stabbing his finger still, and speaking in a high, strained voice as he might when passing a hard stool, he said: 'Him, that man, the Doctor, the head of an important Department of Science is...' And he leant forward conspiratorially. '... is a gigantic homosexual. I mean huge. Do you honestly expect me to believe, Herr Eckhart, that when that pansy needs a new research assistant, he will be choosing from the finest scientific minds in Germany to fill the void? Think about it. No, of course not. He will choose another homo. And these people can spot each other at a hundred paces.

Maybe more. Trust me. Homosexuality, Herr Eckhart, undermines the achievements of the state. Destroys its very foundations.'

'Gosh, I had never thought of it like that. Thank you.'

He nodded at me for several seconds and the thought crossed my mind that he was waiting for me to applaud him. Then he jerked his head upright and clapped his hands together like he was playing the cymbals.

'So, Herr Eckhart.'

I looked at him, eyes wide as dinner plates, leaning forward, elbows on my knees, our faces no more than a metre apart, holding my breath.

At length, he said: 'Herr Eckhart, I believe you and I are on the fast path to becoming very, very good friends.'

I thought that was quite a hasty rush to judgement considering that in the five minutes or so we had become acquainted I had said little more than *well, er, um, no* and *gosh*. But being a coward, I said in a gale of breath: 'I do so hope so!'

He shot to his feet with such speed that I flinched, and the legs of my chair scraped over the parquet floor.

'Follow me!' he said. 'I have a sight that is going to swell that little chest of yours with pride.'

In the far corner of the back wall there stood a coat-stand, from which there hung an assortment of military jackets, coats and headwear. Opting for the long leather coat, he folded it over an arm, then wriggled a peaked cap onto his head. He slid the coat-stand to one side to reveal a door, flush with the wall and the same colour. As he was reaching for the handle, he swung around with a look suggesting he was expecting to find me making rude signs behind his back. I recoiled a little. A smile wreathed his face and his eyes were ablaze. 'We are full of surprises here, Herr Eckhart. Come see.'

Seeing was difficult because it was very dark, and I hesitated before following him into the short windowless passageway. The door eased shut behind us with a click and the darkness became total. Panic swept over me such as I hadn't experienced since Mother locked me in the woodshed for stealing a marzipan pig when I was six. I groped for a wall switch and was about to cry out when I heard a door open and a light came on. He was standing at the far end with one foot in a birdcage elevator.

'Come! Come!' he said, beckoning me with outstretched arm. 'Quick, quick, you don't want me to be cut in half.'

I trotted in after him and he pulled the scissor gate across before punching Down in the brass button box. The elevator dropped at speed, and I felt that peculiar seesaw sensation in my stomach.

'Can you guess?' he said and shrugged on his double-breasted coat, fastening its three buttons in rapid order.

'Guess, sir?'

'What you are about to see?'

'No, I confess I can't.'

'How tall are you?'

The elevator not so much slowed to a halt as hit the bottom and bounced, and I grabbed the handrail to avoid squashing him into the corner of the small wooden car. It settled with a clunk and he took a side-step towards me so that our shoulders were touching.

Straightening my posture, I said: 'I haven't been measured since I was at school, but I believe I am about one metre seventy-five or six. Something like that, give or take.'

'Wonderful. And how far back can you trace your Aryan ancestry?'

'I'm sorry, my what?'

'Your Aryan ancestry – your Nordic roots, you great nincompoop?'

'My father is keen on genealogy and I believe he found records dating back to an Eckhart cordwainer in the 1600s.'

'Excellent, and your mother?'

Given her mood since my return I was tempted to say that in all likelihood she came from an uninterrupted line of swineherds, but my host didn't look in the mood for levity. He was standing right in front of me and staring deep into my eyes again as though looking for something he had lost. He was so close that the peak of his cap was almost touching the bridge of my nose and I could smell his lightly vinegared breath mingling with the sandalwood.

Squeezing back against the handrail, I saw through the diamond grille of the gates that we had arrived in some sort of maintenance or delivery area. A van pulled up sharply at the entrance to it, the back doors flew open and a man in overalls tumbled out of the back clutching his cap, followed by two men in suits and hats. One of them gave the man a shove in the back and I was so distracted by this spectacle I stopped thinking.

'You were saying, about your mother's antecedents?'

'My mother, yes sorry; her father owned a timber business, and so too his, and his father was just a plain woodsman, and the one before that, and his too I imagine because the family name is Holzfaller, and they have probably been felling trees in the Odenwald since the dinosaurs.'

'First-class, even better. Good, honest peasants, chopping wood, waining cord. If only all of us today were like the old German people with their lovely customs and wholesome attitudes to life. A yeoman on his own acre is the backbone and strength of the German character. Come on, let's step on it, I have early dinner before the opera. Furtwängler's conducting.'

He ripped open the gate and a huddle of soldiers tossed away their cigarettes and snapped to attention on seeing him emerge from the shadow. They Heil-Hitlered him, as if in a chorus line, and he threw out a lazy arm as if dismissing them. In the concourse to the rear of the building there was a small fleet of vans parked in a neat row facing the railings of the garden, drivers lounging against them, smoking and reading newspapers. Over in the far corner of the depot, the man in overalls took a kick up the backside and scrambled up a metal staircase.

I tripped after my man, following him through a door and down a long, steep flight of steps into the basement of the building, along yet another corridor, through a set of swing doors and into a large, brightly lit storage area full of boxes and pallets. He led me to the far corner where four pale tea crates had been arranged in a square, each of them imprinted in black Gothic lettering with the words *Department VIII* and below them, *Eckhart, O.*

The lid of one of the crates had been unsealed and he lifted it off.

'Here, you ready for this?'

I'd had quite enough starts and shocks for one day but none greater than the one occasioned by the sight that met me on stepping forward. It was so great that I stepped straight back and dropped my hat.

'I thought you'd be surprised.'

He reached in, took a copy and handed it to me. 'Go on, take it, you great fathead. It's yours. Your work!'

And it was. There it was on the cover – *Parzifal, the Cathars and the Search for The Holy Grail*! By Otto Eckhart! Me! I turned the book over and over and rifled my thumb over the pages. It had been exquisitely produced with the very highest quality materials – a burgundy, soft leather cover, my name and the title in gold blocking, a marbled interior, thick handmade paper and bright, perfectly clear illustrations. I tried to speak but I couldn't get a word out. The breath was stuck in my lungs, and I had to swallow several times before I was able to splutter my shock.

This curious little man in his oversized leather coat was still beaming at me. In hindsight, I am very pleased that I did not act on a powerful impulse to lunge and hug him. It was as beautiful a book as I had ever handled. All the anxiety that had been mounting towards full-blown panic since I arrived in that building was washed away in a surge of relief, elation and gratitude. It was a joy untempered by rational thought and I wanted to yell *'Yes!'* and throw my arms above my head. If you are an unpublished writer, you will understand my reaction. If you have been a failure in any field, a disappointment to yourself and others, you too will understand.

'There are five hundred of them, and I am sending one to every senior official in the Ministries of the Reich and the Schutzstaffel.' And he pointed to the oak leaf flashes on his collar. 'It will both inspire and educate them. I have sent one to the Führer himself, of course.'

'But…'

'Hold tight, keep your shirt on, man. There's more.' He took out an unsealed envelope from the inside pocket of his coat and handed it towards me, wafting it.

It was a regular letter envelope but fat, almost rigid.

'The publishers, Eher-Verlag, have been kind enough to agree to my request that you receive a fair and reasonable fee for your work, Herr Eckhart. I am sure you won't mind that I have given them the rights to produce a more commonplace edition for the German people.'

I took the envelope, weighing the heft of it in my palm, and lifted the seal flap, my hand now shaking a little. They were bank notes, blue ones, the 100 Reichsmarks bill, dozens of them, more money than I had ever seen, more than I had earned in my entire life.

'There are ten thousand Reichsmarks there, Herr Eckhart. Part payment for the work completed, part advance for your next assignment.'

Ten thousand Reichsmarks – that was about four times as much as Father earns in a year as a schoolteacher. I held the envelope in quivering hands, giddy and breathing fast.

He wrestled back the sleeve of his coat and consulted his rectangular watch, tapping its face.

'I will be at Wewelsburg Castle this weekend. You know Wewelsburg, of course. Take the train to Paderborn. You will be met at the station. Two o'clock on the nose. Then we'll go through the details of your assignment.'

He put out his hand and we shook, me saying – or rather stammering – 'Sir, I have been meaning to ask about my assignment. What manner of book do you have in mind?'

'Patience, boy, patience. I'll see you at Wewelsburg, come ready to travel.'

He consulted his watch again, turned on his heel

and, walking on, gave me a little wave over his shoulder.

I blurted, 'But, sir, one more thing, sorry!'

He spun around and turned his head to one side as if to say *make it good*.

'I am very sorry, but I'm embarrassed to confess that I don't even know your name, or your post, your institute. No one has told me, and you haven't...' My voice trailed off, and he looked down at his shiny boots, cupping his chin between thumb and forefinger. When he looked up his face was stern, but a boyish smile spread over his face. He walked back to me and put out his hand and we shook.

He said: 'Yes, forgive me, Herr Eckhart. I forget that you have been away, and you are right – I do like to keep myself deep in the background. I let Goering and Goebbels do all the grandstanding, the prancing about in the limelight. My name is Heinrich. Heinrich Himmler. Reichsführer-SS Heinrich Himmler.'

Letting go of my hand, he took a step back, clicked his heels and raised his arm, fully extending it this time so that it was like a trident. Still smiling, in a very quiet voice, almost inaudible, he said: 'Heil Hitler, Herr Eckhart.'

After a pause I raised my arm and said, 'Yes, heil Hitler, Herr Himmler.'

CHAPTER TWO

I made my way along Prinz-Albrecht-Strasse, past the Museum of Prehistory down towards the Potsdamer Platz, lighting one cigarette after another, laughing out loud one moment, throwing my head back and groaning the next, the money bulging inside my suit jacket, mind whirling, cursing the jam I was in – *Scheisse! Scheisse!* – and a few steps later, rejoicing in my great good fortune – *Oh mein Gott! Oh mein Gott!*

My encounter with that peculiar little man and the notion of working for him was pulling my emotions and thoughts in as many directions as the streams of Berliners heading home after work. It was plain child-like excitement, a joy spiced with a sense of mischief, like I had found the door to the candy shop wide open and robbed it and I was now running for home not quite knowing what to do with my haul of Peppermint Pillows and Mozart Balls.

I was so stupefied that, walking and heaving on my cigarette, hat down, I stepped straight out into the traffic on Saarland Strasse. I was that close to being smeared like a giant bug on the engine grille of a double-decker. The horn blared and I was yanked by the elbow back to the kerb and given a short, bracing appraisal of my character by my pop-eyed rescuer. 'Vacuous blockhead' indeed, but thank heavens she was right there.

Crowds of home-bound workers and shoppers filled the pavements, surging into the underground stations like flood water into drains. I needed to sit down and gather myself. Just as that thought came to me, as if a puppet-master was pulling my strings, I found myself tripping over Himmler's favourite shoeshine boy. He was kneeling down before a customer, at the top of the steps right outside the exit from the S-Bahn station, just as Himmler had said. The man, an officer of some description, boots like shards of black ice, sprung from the wooden throne. Spinning a coin into the air in the same motion, he tipped himself out of view into the underground before the boy had even caught his payment.

I settled into the leather seat, still warm, and said: 'Reichsführer-SS Heinrich Himmler recommended you to me.'

The boy was a sufferer of rickets, legs like recurve bows about to unleash. Poor lad may also have had scurvy by the look of his sunken eyes and inflamed gums. I gave him my best smile and touched the brim of my hat. Unimpressed or slow on the uptake, he just carried on dabbing his brush into the tin of polish, mouth hanging open. He knelt and looked at my shoes, his blackening brush hovering over them, and then back up to me with furrowed brow. He said: 'For sure? Herr Himmler?'

The polish was on in a few flicks of the wrist and

he soon had the cloth, clenched knuckle-white tight in his little fists, and was running it over the brogues, back and forth, back and forth, as though trying to rub out their very existence. By the time he was done I had shoes glossy enough to court-martial a Prussian general for slovenliness.

I rose from the throne and handed him a Reichsmark, ten times the rate advertised on the peeling board propped against the wall. Bending towards him so the next customer wouldn't hear, I said: 'Tell me about Herr Himmler. What kind of a man is he?'

Perhaps it was a mental condition brought on by his abysmal health, or acute shyness, or shock I had paid him so much, whatever, but after a few moments of silence, the boy began quivering like a whipped kitten. He just stood there shaking his head, lips fastened, limbs trembling.

I gave him a few moments then said: 'Never mind, never mind, just curious my friend, that's all.'

There were probably better-informed people in Berlin to pronounce upon the subject of Heinrich Himmler's character merits and demerits, it was true. But it is my experience that if you want an opinion on the affairs of state then seek out the barber, the cleaner or the barman, and he will get you far closer to the truth than the man burdened by superior education or a higher office in life.

But this lad was no more going to hold forth than swim to the moon, and I said: 'No matter, my friend. Here, take another and perhaps buy yourself some fruit. Mush it up if it hurts your gums.' I handed him another mark, my last, and made haste for the Anhalter, from where the last Frankfurt train of the day was ten minutes from pulling out.

I like long train journeys. They give me the perfect excuse to do nothing. I can read and daydream without self-reproach. I had a great deal to think over, and I needed to let the tumultuous events of the day settle into some sort of order. I dropped into a window seat with a view to the west, the train pulling out beneath a spectacular murmuration of starlings.

It may just have been the sheer relief of knowing I was leaving Berlin and heading home, but right at that moment, I confess that I was feeling staggeringly pleased with myself. I don't think I have ever held myself in such high regard. Perhaps it was the shoeshine boy, someone with genuine and grave problems, that cheered my outlook, made me understand how lucky I was. Optimism had put to flight the demons of doubt and I granted my imagination *carte blanche* to gorge itself.

I sat back, legs outstretched, shoes beaming back at me, hands clasped behind my head. I closed my eyes and the train began to jerk, rattle and snake its way through Schöneberg and Tempelhof. What a day, what a reversal of fortune! I arrive in Berlin, broke, aimless, unpublished and unsure of my future. I leave well-off, published, employed and flattered by one of the most powerful men in Europe. I had finally arrived. (Aged twenty nine, certainly, but may I refer you to the tale of the tortoise and the hare?)

The train chugged on, its hypnotic rhythm and a deep weariness combining to deliver me into those marchlands where thoughts and dreams meet and the mind doesn't care to distinguish between the two. I have an awful feeling that I may have been grinning as I dozed, the sudden elevation in my status and in my prospects filling my head with happy images, my vanity unleashed. I even pictured my statue in the market square in Michelstadt, the citizens laying wreaths and bouquets at its feet. A violent blast of the horn and I am back in the real world and we are hammering through a small station in the countryside. I brush down my thighs, smooth down my hair and straighten my back.

The train is going full pelt, fields of young crops and neat farmsteads flashing by, files of men from the Reich Labour Service, in their shapeless grey uniforms, still digging and hoeing in the last of the day's sun. More sober thoughts steal into my mind, pushing out the more fanciful ones, and soon they have taken full control of my imagination, mutating themselves into demons of doubt. I try not to worry, grasping the last flights of my fantasies, but they are like phantoms and they mock me and fade from view.

Soon I'm chewing at my thumbnail, scratching the back of my neck and spinning the fedora on my index finger. Fear creeps over me like a skin complaint, there is a dull ache in my chest, a hint of sweat, my arms folded now, legs crossed tight and I am hunched forward. What had I let myself in for?

We rattled over the bridge just below the ancient university town of Wittenburg, all the exhilaration I had felt earlier heading in the same direction as the great sinking sun, its deep orange answered in the rippling surface of the Elbe. By the time we screech and grind to a halt outside Jüterbog and wait for the farmer to clear his herd of renegade cows from the line, my misgivings have inflated into full-blown anxiety. The man opposite leans forward, taps me on the knee and asks if I need a doctor. I nod and smile and say I am suffering a little indigestion, nothing more. He doesn't look so great himself in his muddied grey uniform, with his pale face and baggy eyes. The insignia on his chest pocket tells me he is a member of the Reich Labour Service – or the 'Reich Slavery Service' as Father calls it. I thank him for his concern and return to my fretting.

Who am I kidding? What on earth have I got myself into?

• ◆ •

I was the only passenger on the branch line from Frankfurt to alight at Michelstadt. The steepled church, silhouetted under a near-full moon and a spread of stars, had long since rung its last bells of the day. I made my way up the hill, across the dry moat and through the ancient city walls, the timber-frame buildings enveloping me in the narrowing street.

The town was so still that, in the windless night,

smoke plumes from a dozen chimneys rose straight and solid as poles. The only noise was the leather of my soles slapping the cobblestones, every step lifting a little of the great burden of worries weighing on my mind. Weary flames wobbled beyond coloured windowpanes, and bats dived and wheeled beneath the slanting gables.

On cresting the hill and reaching the church in the market square, the rolling meadows and wooded hills east of the town lay bathed in moonshine, framed like a painting by the tunnel of houses and shops in the street ahead. I was almost home, and I sighed so loudly you might have heard me from the other end of the square.

By day, I'd take the paths through the woods, the shorter route, but never at night, and I headed towards the dusty track that rises and falls and winds through the pasture. I heard the hoot of an owl before the last townhouse was behind me, its plaintive calling hanging in the mist over the bowl of meadow into which I descended. The track twisted across the far slope up to the treeline, the owl still marking the rhythm of my march. The Odenwald comes to life at night and, in the utter stillness, I heard the red deer, wild boar and goats, and heaven knows what other creatures, rustling and scurrying, hunting and fleeing, playing out Nature's great game of survival.

The lane tracked the arc of the forest edge, the moon so bright I could see that my shiny shoes were caked in a fine pale dust, the lane appearing as though lit from below as it trailed downwards, over the stream and then up again to the house, curving through the herd of Simmentals, statuesque but bells still tinkling. As I climbed the gentle slope, I was surprised to see such a thick column of smoke rising from the chimney, and light coming from the row of four windows on the ground floor. This was exceptional for my parents. They rose at first light and were rarely awake beyond ten o'clock, let alone midnight.

I was just short of the post-and-rail fence ringing the garden and yard when I stopped in my tracks. An automobile, a Hanomag by the bulk and shape of it, was parked to the side of the house over towards the outbuildings. A private automobile was a rare sight at any time out here, and on the few occasions my parents did receive guests it was never during the week, and never so late. Passing through the gate, latching it quietly behind me so as not to rouse the animals, I paused and listened.

The voices, of which there were at least two, all male, were muffled by the heavy brick walls and timbers, but they were clearly raised and angry. I broke into a trot up the path and stopped just short of the long rectangle of light stretching out from the sitting room window. Father was standing before the fire, declaiming vehemently, his hands outstretched above his shoulders, his head bouncing with each thrust of his argument. I had never seen him so passionate, so furious. At school, the children's nickname for him was 'the church mouse', but there he was, as I had never seen him before, roaring.

I was mulling my options, unsure whether to interrupt or wait it out in the barn, when my father thrust out an arm, his finger pointing in my direction. He stepped from the hearth, ushering out his guests with sweeping movements of his arms, like he was splashing them with water. The outdoor light in the wooden porch sprung to life, the door swung open, and two men spilled over the threshold. One wore a double-breasted suit, the other the black uniform and swastika armband of which I had seen so many in Prinz-Albrecht-Strasse. For a few moments, all four of us stood frozen where we were, eyes darting between us.

The man in the suit, his mouth clamped in fury, punched his hat back into shape, yanked it onto his head. He turned to my father and snapped: 'Report to the Darmstadt office at nine in the morning, Herr Eckhart. I trust a good night's rest will clear your mind of its current confusion.'

Both men Heil-Hitlered him but he just bowed his head and said, his voice calm now, 'Good night, gentlemen.' The suit nodded at me and strode towards the Hanomag, the military character staring at me with a tough-guy face for a while longer before following on.

My father's face, stiff as a marble bust, relaxed into its customary repose. He said: 'Come on in, son. We need to talk.'

•◆•

I had intended to rise early and walk with Father to the

railway station but, wrestling myself from a tormented dream, I opened a pasty eye and was alarmed to see the bedside clock reading five past eleven. Father and I had burnt our way through at least half a dozen logs before climbing the stairs and it was half past three when my head finally found the pillow. I was so troubled by our talk that it took at least another hour before the fears and worries, blazing like a brushfire through my mind, were finally extinguished by a tiredness that would brook no further anguish.

I dressed and descended the creaking oak stairs into the kitchen and dining area. Logs crackled in the fireplace and a large pot steamed on the stove, the room thick with the aromas of bone stock and vegetables. Through the side window, I saw Mother leaning into the henhouse, pulling out eggs and placing them in the wicker basket hooked over her forearm. She closed the roof to the laying area and, tilting back her head, stood staring at the sky for several moments. She shook her head as if ridding it of unwanted thoughts, picked up a second basket, and strode down the yard out of view in the direction of the pig pens.

The homely scene was at odds with the agitated state of my mind and soul. I crossed the hall into the sitting room. A small trail of smoke rose from the embers of the previous night's fire and I threw on a handful of kindling and two small logs, the fire bursting back to life as though I had ordered it to stand to attention. I slid into the small leather armchair, foot over one knee, chin in my hand, looking at Father's empty seat opposite, retracing our conversation – or rather, my dumb comments and Father's neat summary of Germany's current mess – the time while I was away travelling and idling and only paying fleeting attention to events at home. Not really caring because I wasn't there.

He had delivered his exposition with schoolmasterly clarity and detachment. I had never seen my father, a mild man, roused to such indignation. At the start, I made a stupid point about Hitler and the Nationalist Socialists seeing off the Commies, building a bulwark against Stalin – and my father was off.

The Reichstag fire was just a plot, he said, so Hitler could seize his emergency powers, but it was the nationwide book-burning by the German Student Union that really got him going. So much that I had to pat the air in case he stirred Mother from her sleep.

'…Did you read of that in France? When students answered the call to action against "un-German spirit" and burned great pyres of "unsuitable" books right in the heart of Berlin, and in the Opernplatz no less, the very centre of our great culture? Students of all people – the stewards of our future! Otto, can you see yourself emptying the great libraries at Heidelberg, wheelbarrowing shelves of learned books and hurling all that knowledge onto a great bonfire?'

He was shaking his head, as though he was never going to be able to believe that it had happened.

'Have you heard them talk of *Gleichschaltung*?'

I confessed I hadn't.

'Don't be fooled by the innocence of the word. They have hijacked our language too,' he said, clenching his fists now. 'Its true meaning is something quite different. *Co-ordinating* the entire population means manipulating them with propaganda and cowing them with all manner of threats and punishments. *Co-ordinating* has meant the banning of all other political parties, disbanding the trade unions, shutting down the free press, attacking the Church, bullying and threatening every last institution and community of Germans that doesn't commit to its bogus vision and regressive dogma that would have us all believing in fairy tales and racing back into the mists of a Nordic past that never existed.'

I looked away at the reference to Nordic myths. He leant forward, smiling, and put his hand on my shoulder. 'Fairy tales are for children, Otto, not for grown men – and certainly not for responsible statesmen.'

I have thought about that moment many times since, felt the hand on my shoulder, seen the look in my father's eyes. It took me some time to see it for what it was – my father saying, in effect, 'Otto, it's time to grow up. It's time to be a man now.'

He leant forward to poke the fire, sighing, his eyes full and glistening in the light of the leaping flames. 'Hitler is a madman who will lead us to destruction, Goering a clown and a playground bully, but the ones to watch out for are those weasels Goebbels and Himmler.'

At the mention of the Reichsführer-SS, in whose

office I had been sitting just twelve hours earlier, I startled, actually sprung forward, and quickly changed the subject.

'So those men just now – who the hell were they?'

'The suit was Gestapo, the uniform an SS henchman, a rank-and-file moron. Ever since I ran down the Swastika flag outside the school on April 20, the Führer's birthday, we have become intimately acquainted.' He laughed through his nose at the prim euphemism.

'What do they want?'

'What they want is for me to sign up to the party, just like almost every other teacher in the land. I am the only teacher between here and Frankfurt without a membership number.'

'Why don't you just do it? Just pretend you're on board, then carry on as before. What's the worse they can do then?'

He breathed out hard and threw me a smile. 'I am a history teacher, Otto, and I seek out the truths of the past so that we might learn from our errors for a better future. The monsters and dragons and evil spirits you read about, those are just myths – symbols or metaphors at best – but the monsters I speak of come in human form. They are real, Otto, and they are rewriting history and forcing our schools to teach it, and the future they seek is a dark one, and it is doomed. I won't do it. I'd rather drown than lie to a room of young school children who know only what they are told to know.'

I could feel my mouth drying as the import of his words sank in. I had to clear my throat and when I spoke my voice was hoarse.

'And if you don't, Father? What then?'

'I guess I'll find out in the morning in Darmstadt!' He fell silent, the glow from the fire playing over his face.

We must have sat there for another ten minutes before he opened his eyes and levered himself out of the armchair. 'Come on, we must rest.'

Looking at his empty chair then in the bright light of late morning, I felt a seizure of emotion, thinking of him at the Gestapo office in Darmstadt, holding his ground, infuriating his inquisitors with his common sense and decency.

And in the light of all he said, what was I to do now? What of my assignment for Himmler? What about all that money? Before I could begin to answer those questions, I heard the back door shut and I went through to the kitchen. My mother is not often lost for words, but she didn't even turn around when I wished her good morning, just carried on transferring the eggs to the bowl on the dresser. I could tell that she had been crying and I went to her. She put down the basket, threw open her arms and pulled me towards her.

'Your father and his confounded scruples!' Her tears ran down my neck and she squeezed me so tight I thought I might suffocate. 'He's probably on his way to Dachau right this moment.'

It was me lost for words now at this rare display of raw emotion – love and fear and whatever else – so I just patted and squeezed her. 'I'm sorry Otto,' she said, releasing me from the clamp of her embrace. She walked over to the window and stared over the meadows towards Michelstadt, dabbing her nose with a pocket handkerchief.

'What will become of us? No income, unable to pay the rent, eat even! We'll be itinerants and then we'll be imprisoned too and we'll die behind barbed wire, with no-one but tramps and homosexuals and communists at our gravesides.'

The last comment made me laugh – it is sometimes difficult to tell whether my mother is being serious or humorous. I laid my hand on her shoulder before heading through to the sitting room, where I took a sheet of writing paper and an envelope from Father's desk and sat down to write to Himmler. My mind was made up. There was no question of me doing Himmler's bidding now. I wrote fast to catch the afternoon post so that the letter would be waiting for him at Wewelsburg Castle.

I wrote that my mother had fallen gravely ill, which wasn't a complete lie; she was sick with worry that was for sure. I expressed my deep regret at having to postpone my employment with his office. I promised that I would return his money at the first opportunity and awaited his instructions as to how I might arrange that. I apologised profusely for the unfortunate change in my circumstances, thanked him graciously for his kindness and faith in me, and wished him all the best in his patriotic endeavours. I licked the envelope and tapped it against the edge of the desk.

There, it was done. My adventure, my graduation to adulthood, was over before it had even started. Amen to my glorious new future; now for some piping hot soup. Mother and I sat down, and she ladled the steaming broth into our bowls while I carved the pumpernickel.

She said: 'He's stubborn as a mule that father of yours. It's going to be the ruin of him – and us. I wish he would just come to heel, and we can carry on as we always have, minding our own business, being good respectable Germans.'

'But it's admirable he's standing up for his beliefs, no? We should be proud of him.'

'Beliefs don't fill stomachs, Otto!' She was blowing on her spoon and her outburst sprayed soup in all directions. 'And what good are your principles if they're stuck behind a barbed wire fence digging holes? Anyhow – tell me about Berlin.'

I looked away, then down into the steam and dished in a few mouthfuls. 'Quite promising, actually. Funny little bureaucrat character, looks like a rodent, only with spectacles and a Charlie Chaplin moustache. Mad about his German history. And I mean *mad*.'

'Is he going to take you on?'

I was bursting to show off about the publication of my book, but the words reared to a halt in my throat. I didn't want to add to the anxiety in the house. I'd wait for the right moment and prepare my announcement after Himmler replied to my letter.

'Yes, he wants me to write a piece about myths and Aryans for some periodical, that sort of thing. It's quite the zeitgeist at the moment – or *volksgeist* maybe.'

'Oh, Otto! All that fuss and bother, crossing half the country just for a few paragraphs about aliens? It'll barely cover your railway fare.' Her spoon hovered before her lips, her puffy eyes fixed on mine. 'I hoped you might come home with a real job.'

'Mother, please don't start all that again. You know I'm trying. It's a start, a foot in the door. And it's Aryans, not aliens.'

'You need to find your purpose in life, Otto, and you need a good woman too. Most men are long married by your age. Your father and I were 22, and he'd been teaching for two years. I worry for you, Otto, I wonder, I mean you're not a… you know…' And she tilted her head, batted her eyelids, and made a little dancing motion in her seat.

I spat out my soup. 'Mother, what a thing to say! Even if I was homosexual, there would be nothing I can do about it, any more than I can help the colour of my hair or the size of my feet.'

'Germany is no place for sensitive men right now, Otto, that's all I'm saying. Heike told me after choir practice last week that her nephew is a ballet dancer and he said they're rounding up all the artistic types and taking them heaven knows where and making them wear pink triangles so that normal healthy men will know to keep their distance. They've lost half their troupe for *Cinderella*. Just be careful, Otto, that's all. You write about elves and wood fairies after all.'

'And dragons, Mother. Now that's enough – it's 1937, not 1837. And it's a company of a ballet dancers, not a troupe. Dancers come in troupes.'

'That's dangerous talk, Otto. It's precisely that sort of knowledge that could land you in hot water in these times. It's probably one of the sneaky questions they ask to catch you out.'

She dropped her spoon into her soup, looked over her shoulder at the clock above the stove and sprung to her feet, making her way back to the window.

'Where is that wretched father of yours? He could have walked on his head to Darmstadt and back by now.'

'I'm sure he's fine, Mother. He is a grown man and he can look after himself. I'll probably bump into him on the way into town.'

'Town?'

Tipping my bowl and scraping out the last spoonful of soup, I rose, gave her a kiss, and took my jacket from behind the door, pulling out my letter. 'Yes, I must send this. Catch the post before it's too late.'

'Good, get some colour in those cheeks. You read too many books, that's your trouble. Name me one healthy writer and I'll show you a dog laying a fire. You'll become a drunkard or a consumptive, just like the rest. And tell your father to hurry.'

I pulled open the door. 'The Führer is a writer and an artist – I bet you wouldn't say all those things to him. And he was a tramp.'

'Hope for you too then. Frankly, you would make a very poor Führer, Otto. I mean, look at your shoes.'

'They're my walking shoes, Mother. They're allowed a bit of dirt.'

'I very much doubt, Otto, you'll find any dirt on Herr Hitler's shoes.'

I pulled the door to and stopped, my hand still on the handle. Before me lay a prospect of the most extraordinary beauty, one I had looked upon a hundred thousand times, but offering itself to me right then as if it was my first encounter. Bright green meadows rippled with flowers under a mellow spring sun, shuffling cattle, heads down at the graze, bells chiming, swallows fresh back from Africa divebombing the stream, Freya and Mani tossing their manes whilst lapping the paddock, courting birds bursting from hedge and branch, the bees droning and mining the flowerheads, and the steeple on Michelstadt's hilltop presiding over the scene just as it had done for 500 years – all of it heedless of the troubles benighting the only creatures capable of its veneration. I have to say, right at that moment, with that timeless scene before me, it was very hard to picture the storm clouds that Father saw massing and rallying over the horizon.

God, I'm fickle. Is it just me whose mood can turn on a penny like that? All the worries in the world one moment, banished the very next step, carried away by nothing more staggering than a commonplace view of the countryside on a good clear day? The answer to that is yes, in all likelihood. In any event, it was with a light step and a light heart that I made my way through that railway poster of a scene and up towards the woods, thinking *everything was going to be just fine.* Nothing was going to change. Water will find its own level, the world will keep spinning, the sun shining, moon rising, tides ebbing and flowing.

And Mother could ascend to Heaven and still find something to fret and quarrel about. She'd probably step onto the cloud, run a finger over the gates and take St. Peter to task for filthy housekeeping. And Father, perhaps he should a read a few more happy-ending legends and a little less grim history, with all its strewn battlefields and baskets full of heads and carts with corpses. When have you ever closed a history book and thought 'Ah, that's better. Isn't mankind just terrific?' It is only in the imagination and in the natural world that we can be truly happy. If you don't like the real world, there are two very good ways of escaping from it – literature and nature. And if that Himmler functionary was the best the forces of darkness could put up to scare us, then the real world had very little to worry about. I descended towards the dark treeline, where the woods tumbled towards the stream as it bent around into the bottom, leaves stirring in the breeze, crows wheeling and cawing overhead. I trampled on my stunted shadow a final time and stepped into the trees, the warmth of the sun on my back gone in a stride.

The Odenwald is not one of those pitch-dark German pine forests we read about in unsettling fairy tales; there are clearings and streams open to the sky and, when the sun is directly overhead, pillars of light everywhere, as there were right then. But walking in from open fields, the eyes widen in the sudden dimness, the cool and the damp clamp the skin, the air goes still, and the further you walk the more you are aware you have entered a very different world to the one you have left behind.

I had trodden this path many times, but my feelings were little different to the ones I had experienced the first time that Mother allowed me to go to the market in Michelstadt unaccompanied. I was only eight or so, and I remember vividly the fear getting the better of me and me breaking into a run, the relief of emerging in the meadow on the other side. I was no longer terrified of course, but a residue of that fear, a mild apprehension about what lay out of sight, has never left me on entering a wood, every rustle like an anxiety that has sprung up from a dark recess of the mind.

This part of the woods is like a peninsula hanging from the main mass, and I had been walking no more than five minutes, with another five to the meadow below the town, when I became aware of movement on the path up ahead. Or rather I became aware of a sound because it came from the other side of the gentle slope I was climbing. It was an animal sound but not one I could identify, and it was muffled by the stream gurgling over the rocks. It was clear and curious enough to stop me in my stride and tilt my head, as all animals do when they sense danger, and stay completely motionless so as not to attract the attention of the predator. I was about to start walking again when it came once more – a lowing, a little like a calf in distress but not quite.

I stepped off the path and picked up an old branch, snapping it over my knee and keeping the heftier half of it. I am embarrassed to confess that my heart was beating as though I had just swum the Neckar against the flow. A wild boar is only a danger when it is wounded or feels threatened, but I was taking no chances after what happened to Holger, the butcher's son. The boar knocks you to the ground first, so hard it can dislocate a knee, then wheels back and sets to work on the most vulnerable parts of the body with its razor-sharp tusks. Holger missed an entire term of school after he disturbed a sow with her piglets and barely lived to tell of the attack. It is said that his genitals were shorn clean off – and it's a fact that he used to be a great one for the ladies but has never married or even dated a girl since.

I held the stick out to my right above my shoulder and crept towards the crest of the slope, the path on the other side lengthening towards me with every step. The lowing, or groaning, was mixed with a feeble whimpering. Whatever the species of creature to be found on the other side, it was clearly in considerable pain. I sprung onto a large rock in the middle of the stream so that I might be safe if it charged.

I teetered from side to side on the wet, rounded surface of the stone, almost sliding over into the water, but when I gained my balance and straightened up, I could see the source of the noise no more than 20 metres ahead of me. Slumped over the moss of a fallen tree, head and arms over the other side, lay a figure in a uniform of grey trousers and jacket, a leather bag at his feet, a bicycle lying in the middle of the path. I leapt onto the far bank, ran towards him and knelt down, placing my hand in the middle of his back.

The wind had been knocked out of me and all I could manage was 'Sir! Sir!' On the upper sleeve of his left arm, there was a flash with the symbol of a spade – the insignia of the Reich Labour Service, same as that worn by the exhausted man on the train. My first thought was that he had suffered a heart attack from the effort of cycling uphill over the rough ground of the woods.

Such was my shock, I can't recall exactly what I said but I burbled something along the lines of 'Sir, can you walk? What has happened? Where is your pain? My house is a short distance, we can call the doctor. Who is your next of kin? Are you having a seizure? Have you drunk too much beer? Who are you?' I was making little more sense than the stream burbling behind me.

The man tried to talk but there was barely breath in his body. I had no medical training and I was at a complete loss as to what to do. The bicycle! I would take it and race to fetch Doctor Steiner from Michelstadt. I explained my plan to the man, but he shook his head and, placing his hands on the log, tried to push himself up. The pain of this slight effort was so great he howled, and despite my efforts to lift him twice, he gave up and slumped forward again.

On the third attempt, I put my hands in his armpits again, and in one violent movement he threw himself back and, twisting and roaring, slumped with his back against the soft moss of the trunk. His head fell backwards as though he had no muscles in his neck or shoulders, his forage cap dropping behind him. His hair was matted with blood and his face was so swollen it was almost twice a normal size, his bloated eyes completely sealed like a badly beaten boxer's.

I knelt and placed my hand on his shoulder. His breathing was rapid and short. He took my other hand and clasped it, and tears spilled from his swollen eyelids, running down the weals of his almost inhuman face, his head rising and falling as though he were fighting the urge to sleep. He tried to speak but it was so faint, it was lost. I leant in close so that my ear was just inches from his mouth and then I understood.

'Otto, my dear boy, what is going to become of us?'

•◆•

No sound strains the nerves quite like the tick of a clock, telling you over and over that life is passing you by and, by its implacable logic, that you're a tick and a tock closer to being dead. A thousand ticks and tocks, you end up thinking what's the crazy point of it all, being marched towards your extinction, tormented most of the way by grief and worry and fear, your meaningless part in it all. Those were my thoughts at any rate, just sitting there, waiting.

It is just not true that Time stands still in a life-or-death crisis. You feel every measured step of its remorseless march, knowing that it can never be halted or reversed, that sooner or later you too will stumble and collapse on its wayside – and on Time will go and go, away into wherever, leaving a great long trail of us, each a small pile of bones, then dust, along its path with neither beginning nor end. Was Father's time come? It was of no concern to the clock, it just kept on, *tick, tock, tick, tock, tick… Don't know about you, but I'm fine thanks, not even breaking stride here. Tick tock, tick tock…*

Not one word had passed between us over the kitchen table since bumping and wheeling him home in the farm cart. Mother sat facing one way, cradling a cup and staring halfway towards the fire. I am not sure she took a single mouthful from it that entire time, just gazed vacantly into the middle distance. I sat half-facing the other way watching the pendulum back and forth, at intervals rising to throw a few more logs into the stove or the fire. The only other sounds were an occasional creak of a floorboard overhead, a pigeon cooing down the chimney, and from time to time, a rush of breath from Mother. Even the comic eruption of the cuckoo announcing that it was five, then six o'clock, failed to excite so much as a twitch.

Then we heard footsteps directly overhead, slow and sombre, a pause at the top of the staircase and a hesitant descent. He paused again before making his way to the foot and pushed open the door, Mother and I rising as he entered. I fancied I'd be able to know the prognosis by reading his face, but it was blank as an overcast sky.

Steiner swung his black leather bag onto the kitchen table, ran a hand through his thinning white hair and said: 'Watch him closely over the next twenty four hours. It'll take time, but he is going to recover.'

From the corner of my eye I saw Mother's shoulders collapse, and she let go a whimper. I dropped my head and blew out my cheeks. She stepped towards him and for a moment I thought she was going to launch herself and smother him in kisses with her sodden face.

Steiner forestalled that possibility, continuing: 'Three, perhaps four ribs have been broken or heavily bruised, his face is too swollen to say yet if he has any bones fractured there, or damage to the eyes. I have stitched his ear and scalp. And he will need to visit the dentist when he has recovered.'

Mother covered her face with her hands as if the wounds were her own and rolled her head from side to side.

The doctor went on in the same soft voice – did they learn that at medical college? 'Send for me at once if he coughs blood or his breathing becomes laboured and shallow. The chance of internal bleeding is small now – but be alert to it. Unless there is another emergency, I will come again this time tomorrow.'

I turned away and walked to the window, grinding a fist into my palm. Silhouetted against the falling sun, the church steeple rose from the peak of Michelstadt's half-shadowed hill like the spike of a Pickelhaube. What species of bastard but a madman or the devil himself has motive to beat an old man to within a few punches and kicks of his death? And not any old man either – a schoolteacher, steadfast neighbour and man of unfaltering charity, an exemplary German?

Steiner sat down at the table, took out a pad of paper from his bag and a pen from the inside pocket of his suit. He filled an entire page in rapid order, tore it out and handed it to Mother.

'Here – this says he must rest for six weeks. He is sedated now but he will need more around midnight. The instructions are up there. When the Labour Service thugs come, show them that note – and if they quarrel, send them straight to me.'

Mother said: 'But what if the Gestapo – '

'Send them too – I fix their families as well. I am quite sure my medical dictionary will show Herr Eckhart to be suffering a great many complications over the coming months.'

He glanced at my mother and smiled. She took her purse from the dresser and unclasped it, but Steiner held up his hand, looked at his watch and reached for his bag. 'I must get on.'

She thrust out some Reichsmarks, but the doctor waved her away and made for the door, shaking my hand as he passed. He climbed into his car and sped out of the gate, disappearing down into the valley, a cone of dust trailing behind him. When he re-emerged, he had shrunk to a beetle-sized spot crawling up the hill into Michelstadt and was swallowed by its ancient walls.

Mother was at the table now, elbows planted, fingers gripping her hair. I took the letter to Himmler from the pocket of my jacket hung behind the door. I held it before me in both hands, my mind torn in half. Father will not teach again unless he backs down – and he would sooner beg than yield. He will end up in a camp. I tapped the letter in the palm of my hand, Mother's anguish fretting the room, and stuffed it into my trouser pocket.

I brushed my hand over her shoulders as I passed and, heaving myself up by the handrail, took the stairs two at a time. I slid the travel case from beneath my bed, placed it on top and emptied my drawers and wardrobe of their summer clothing – linen suit and shirts, cotton trousers but also thick socks, walking boots and one thick pullover – who knows where *he* had in mind for me. The small case was so full I had to sit and bounce on the lid to snap the latches shut, then I knelt back down and lifted the Ottoman rug, reaching under for the envelope. Counting out three thousand Reichsmarks, I pocketed them, wedged the rest in my wallet and went down the landing to Father.

He lay propped up on a pile of pillows, his face still almost twice its normal size, unrecognisable, his head crowned with bandages, a trickle of dried blood running from the shaved area above his stitched ear. I leant forward and kissed his forehead, then whispered my promise in his good ear, tears falling on his bloated face.

I hurried downstairs, almost tumbling over my case – I didn't want to draw this out, nor do battle with Mother. She was now in the high-backed armchair by the kitchen fire, arms limp over the rests, feet on the tiled hearth. I placed the case by the front door, pulled on my trench coat and, taking out the letter to Himmler, went down on my knees at the fireplace.

I held the letter for several moments, its watermarks highlighted by the flames, my hand trembling a little from the emotion of the day. Or nerves maybe about what lay in store. I could sense every cell in my cowardly body militating against my decision – so I knew it must be right. I could dodge and duck and run away and disappoint people no longer.

I tossed the envelope onto the logs, the paper twisting and buckling like a living creature. The flames, reluctant at first, raced from all sides, closing in on my handwriting. The last words to go were *Reichsführer-SS*

Heinrich Himmler, and I smiled at that small pleasure, watching the charred wafers of the letter vanish into the throbbing heat.

Mother's head had fallen to one side, her mouth slightly open, the light of the flames leaping over a face still chiselled with fright. I stole past her into the sitting room, to Father's desk and, perching on the corner of the chair, wrote fast, keeping it vague. I sandwiched the wad of Reichsmarks between the folded note, then crept back into the kitchen and laid them on the side table by her book, *The Sign of the Four*, Sherlock Holmes staring out at me from under his deerstalker.

I wriggled my fedora onto my head, lifted the latch and eased open the door. I stood for a moment, travel case at my side, watching Mother's chest rise and fall, shadows from the fire bounding over the room. The familiar scene slowly vanished as I pulled the door to, inch by inch, ending with the merest click of the latch.

CHAPTER THREE

I checked into The Three Hares on Braunstrasse, Michelstadt's oldest hotel, so I might roll out of bed and down the hill onto the five forty-seven, barely having to open my eyes. It meant too that I had the evening to prepare for Himmler, going through my notes, refreshing my memory of a book I had written with neither love, nor care nor regard for the truth. And if Father was to deteriorate overnight, I'd soon hear about it from Berthold Voigt, the hotel's proprietor, swaying and mumbling behind the reception counter, writing my name at a slight diagonal in the guestbook.

No news of note inside a radius of ten miles failed to find Berthold's ears within an hour of its airing. For centuries, Michelstadt's official business was discussed upstairs in the Rathaus, perched just across the road on its heavy timber stilts, groaning under the weight of its colourful window boxes and the self-importance of the town councillors within.

If it was a proper debate you were after, or an insight into what was really going on in the town, you walked straight past the old townhouse and into the racket and smoke of the bar at The Three Hares. Here was the town's true parliament and Berthold was its president, his capacity for retaining local intelligence and opinion matched only by his capacity for holding his schnapps and Pils. So long as Berthold was alive, Michelstadt had no need of a local newspaper or telephone exchange.

A man no one in the town could remember ever seeing sober, he somehow remained a model of discretion if your news happened to be of a confidential nature.

'Berthold, I'd be grateful if you could keep my presence here tonight under your hat.'

'Normally, it's the police or a wife with our guests, but with you, I guess it's your mother.'

'Correct.'

Berthold gave me a theatrical wink and a knowing smile, just about discernible through the accordion of rosy fat bunching from the neck up.

Leaving him to wobble his way upstairs with my case, I went straight through to the dining room. I had eaten nothing but a bowl of broth all day, with all the drama, and my stomach had grown a voice in protest. Frau Voigt – Erma in a good mood, which was not today evidently – stabbed a menu at me, snapping questions about my father, fusillading schnapps-powered profanities about the Gestapo. She was apparently of a mind and mood to write to the Führer himself. 'That,' she assured me, 'would put a big fat snake in their pants.'

Throwing a look over her shoulder towards the bar area, she leant her massive breasts on my shoulder and whispered in my ear, 'If Uncle Adolf knew even half the crimes the police committed in his name these days, the poor man would have a coronary!'

She snatched the menu from my grasp and said: 'Right you are then, the liver dumpling soup with an herbal garnish to start, and the fillet of trout in almond sauce to follow. And I'll bring you a Pils, then some hock.' And she wobbled away, everything bouncing and jiggling like a strawberry blancmange in an earth tremor.

I don't like offal. Trout is fine, but I won't eat liver dumpling soup if it is my last chance of staying alive. Asparagus was what I craved, and the fields all about were bursting with row upon bushy row of the stuff at that time of year. Everyone else in the room seemed to be enjoying a plate of succulent white stalks wrapped in ham and swamped in Hollandaise sauce. Why not me too? I guess she just thought 'The last of the liver dumplings are about to go off, oh look there's little Otto Eckhart, I'll lump them on him.'

When she came back with my stein of Pils, I gathered myself and said: 'Frau Voigt, you will forgive me for saying so, no offence to your dumplings, but I want the asparagus to start.'

She could not have looked more astounded had I just announced that all my life I had been tormented by erotic dreams about her.

'Is that so, Herr Eckhart?' She slapped down the Pils hard enough for the foam to spill over the rim, and waddled back towards the kitchen, throwing open its saloon doors with such force that they sprung straight back.

She bellowed: 'Kaiser Eckhart has changed his mind! He wants the asparagus.'

Her sing-song falsetto was so piercing that a hush fell over the tables and stilled the chatter in the bar beyond the stone arch. Heads turned from their beers, eyes squinting through the cloud of tobacco smoke. One man, bent over a table in the near corner, held his gaze on me a while longer, drawing on his cigarette, then cocked his head and touched the brim of his hat. He was familiar, but the light in the bar was low and I could put no name to him. I acknowledged his greeting with a smile and reached for my Pils, figuring he was most likely a teacher at Father's school or some other acquaintance of my parents.

Throughout dinner, I caught him glancing up at me from the tight huddle around his table so often that it became unsettling. Had I been a woman I would have assumed he was making eyes at me, entertaining impure thoughts about what he'd like to do to me after his beers. I ate my food far quicker than I would have liked and when I had scooped in the last mouthful of chocolate marble cake, I smeared the napkin across my face and, dropping it into my chair, made haste for the reception area.

A sharp 'Herr Eckhart!' brought me up and I turned to see the man beckoning me over to the table. I stepped down through the arch and, my eyes adjusting to the dimmer light, a jolt of recognition made me slow my pace as I neared the table.

'What a shame we didn't have a chance to be introduced properly the other night. Your father was in something of a rush to be rid of me. Otto, isn't it?'

Detective Inspector Muller.

I nodded, but barely. His three friends took me in, stony-faced beneath their hats, hunched over their steins, smoke curling from fists.

'I would offer you my hand but as you can see… ' And he lifted his right hand from beneath the table to reveal a fat fist of bandage. 'A hazard of my occupation, you will understand.'

He held it there for a good few seconds, looking straight into my eyes, a mocking smile beneath a bulbous nose in a farmyard face.

I said: 'Guess you get some tough customers.'

'Not so much tough as stubborn and stupid these days, I'd say.' The smile widened and the pig nostrils flared a little. 'But we get there in the end, one way or another. Don't we, boys?' He turned to the table and raised his beer, and the others made a half-hearted effort with theirs, more interested in their cigarettes.

The rage rising through my body was constricting my lungs and fogging my head, and I could find no words to reply.

'Anyhow, forgive me, Otto – may I call you Otto? – how is that father of yours? Word is he suffered a nasty fall. I did warn him to be careful in those woods, but he just won't listen to reason that one, will he?'

I kept staring at him, breathing through my nose, chest working like bellows in quick time, incapable of speech, decision or movement. In the wild, an animal that doesn't want to be eaten or attacked will look away from a predator in submission and I can only assume that Muller read my frozen pose and glare as a challenge, the animal in him being dominant over the human part.

He rose to his feet and leant into me, the brim of his hat touching my forehead. I can still smell the cheap smoke and the beer on his breath, see the old meat stuck in his incisors and the sheaves of bristle hanging from his great nostrils. I cannot say whether it was fear or fury, but I stood where I was, not so much as a blink on my face, my only movement that of my racing heart. I was aware of the din in the bar falling to a murmur and then to a hush. I felt a hand clamping my upper arm and Berthold was saying: 'Otto, come, come, I cannot wait till Christmas for you to settle the bill.'

Berthold pulled me up the step and away through silent restaurant tables, my eyes still locked on Detective Inspector Muller over my shoulder, and his on mine. In the hotel lobby, Berthold was half-panicking, half-laughing. 'Otto, Otto, what on earth are you doing? You know who that it is, don't you?'

In between breaths, I said: 'I know exactly who that is.'

And I made my way up to my room.

I mentioned earlier that I had a plan, but that's not quite true. If I wanted to sound like a man of purpose and action, I could take all the events that follow from this point in the story and have you believe that they were part of a cleverly calculated scheme. If I did have anything I might describe as a plan at this stage, it was a mighty fuzzy one. A powerful urge to do something, anything – that was the extent of my strategy; just take my seat at the table and see what cards I was dealt. Inaction was a strategy that hadn't exactly been working out so well for me over the years.

So I set off for Wewelsburg Castle and, after three station changes, by the late afternoon I was standing under a grey sky outside a small, undistinguished railway station, looking at my watch every minute or so, wondering if – hoping that – Reichsführer-SS Heinrich Himmler had already forgotten about me, preoccupied as he should have been with more pressing matters of state.

In amongst the ordinary scenes you might expect to encounter outside a provincial station – a porter helping an elderly lady with her luggage, the blast of a steam-powered whistle – two happenings stood out from the rest. Right next to me outside the station entrance, a short-cropped youth in a storm-trooper uniform unfurled a poster from the fat roll under his arm, took a brush from his bucket and pasted the poster to the board under the sign reading *Paderborn Hauptbahnhof*.

I had not been back in the country long enough to regard these sights as unremarkable and I watched him intently.

When he was done slapping on the adhesive, he took a step back and smiled at it, brush dripping into the bucket, tilting his head from side to side. Like he had done the artwork himself. You know the poster. It's the one showing an eagle sitting on a swastika and looking over its shoulder, all of it coloured red, grey and black. Behind the suspicious raptor, on guard for threats, is a crowd of men, women and children, all smiling, all giving the arm salute. The only closely drawn adult is a figure down at the front who looks not unlike the Führer, complete with Chaplin moustache – the message being, that Adolf is just a regular Hermann like the rest of us. At the top of the poster, in jagged Gothic script, there is a direct command to the reader: *Germany wake up!* The artwork is good, the message simple, the image arresting; you had to admit it.

The youth sensed me staring, turned his head and, working a ball of chewing gum around his open mouth, popped his eyebrows and kept them there. He may just as well have said, 'Yes, goofball?' I looked away, down to the roadside, and there lay another novel spectacle – a woman in round, horn-rimmed sunglasses pulling up at the wheel of an enormous curvaceous black Mercedes, its roof rolled right back and its coachwork so polished you could read a book in its reflection.

She was wearing a purple beret, with a purple silk

scarf tucked into a black silver-buttoned tunic, cigarette smoke curling from her hand hanging over the door, a camera around her neck. She gave me a shy smile and shook a little wave. I returned both gestures, then did that awkward thing with my face, my eyes going left and right and my lips puckering with compressed air – being unaccustomed to beautiful women in luxury touring cars trying to get my attention. When I dared look back at her, she shot her hand up and beckoned me over, her smile bordering on a laugh. I bent down to pick up my case, glanced up at the poster thug, and raised my eyebrows at him, holding them there for a moment before touching the brim of my hat and striding down to the Mercedes.

'Come on, hop in. You don't want to cross the boss today. He's in a murderous mood. Put your case on the luggage deck – actually just throw it on the rear seat.'

I walked around to the other side, running my hand over the giant headlamps and down the sweeping curve of the fender, the baritone engine rumbling under the hood. I placed the case in the back, careful not to scrape any of the polished wood or red brushed leather upholstery and levered myself up the running board onto the sofa seat in the front. The woman, smiling through her cigarette, offered me a gloved hand.

'Beauty, isn't she?'

She certainly was. And the car. The workmanship of the walnut-cased dashboard, the whole interior exquisite, as modern and sophisticated as anything I had ever seen. Were it a hotel, it would have been the Ritz or the Adlon.

She pulled out the silver-plated ashtray, ground out her butt and said: 'We can top 150 kilometres if you like. There's a long straight below Wewelsburg. You feel as if it's going to take to the air when you cross the bridge, get that lovely warm feeling in the pit of the stomach. She's got eight cylinders – eight! – and, with the supercharger – see that exhaust tube on the right of the hood – it gives you 200 horsepower. Your regular Hanomag, like that one there, has got about 20.'

'I'm not sure if Herr Himmler will be too impressed if I turn up like Manfred von Brauchitsch crossing the line at Monaco. Will he?'

'It's okay, he won't see us.' She cupped a hand over the quartz dash clock, the sun having broken cover. 'Too busy reading his horoscope and trying to contact Heinrich the Fowler through his mystic in the castle crypt. Besides we'll be under an avenue of trees.'

'Is it yours?'

'Don't be daft. You can buy castles for less. Goering and Heydrich each got one because the Führer has one, so Himmler felt he had to get one as well. They're like kids. But Heini gets sweaty if you go over sixty. Pathetic really. You don't recognise me, do you?'

'I confess I don't. Forgive me.'

She took off her sunglasses and beret, reached behind to pull out a tortoiseshell hair clasp and shook out a heap of glossy black hair.

'Ingrid! Remember? Sorry, I wasn't overly friendly to you in Prinz-Albrecht-Strasse. He'd been at me all day about one thing or another. "Take this down... get me a coffee... get Bormann on the phone, get me Todt... send this to Rust, send this to Josef... where are my opera tickets and tell Marga I won't be home tonight... book me a table for two in the Kaiserhof... have you arranged the decorators for Gmund?... have you bought Gudrun's birthday presents yet, the stilts and the turtle?... go and get me some liver salts..."'

'His secretary – of course! You look so – '

'So normal? Yes, one's humanity is extinguished by lunchtime in that place. It's like a dungeon. In fact, it is a dungeon, or part of it.' Her laugh was a nervous one.

'Well, I wouldn't say normal but...'

I almost said 'beautiful' but pulled up just in time and she came to the rescue, re-arranging her hair and hat and sliding her sunglasses back on.

'Wewelsburg's a madhouse too – it's like Camelot without the fun, full of fantasists and mediums. And Weisthor, ugh, wait till you meet him. Thinks he's a warlock who has cousins living in Atlantis. I'm serious. Calls himself an "Irminist ancestral-clairvoyant", whatever that means. Thinks he can talk to the dead. But at least he won't put his hand up your skirt when he's rolling drunk. Which he will be. Here, take this.'

She looped the leather strap over her head and handed me the camera.

'It's the latest Leica – the IIIa. My father is on the

design team at Wetzlar so I get all the latest models and lenses. Don't be fooled by the compact size. It's probably the best camera of its sort in the world. I'll show you later, now hold tight!'

I wedged the camera between my legs, she rammed the car into gear, and we surged forward. I grabbed the door handle with one hand, my hat with the other, and planted my feet in the carpeted footwell, pinning myself into the seat.

Ingrid swung the giant vehicle out onto Bahnhofstrasse, slicing between two buses heading in opposite directions, then spun the wheel hard left, and I toppled into her then back against my door as she righted it. We shot towards a brewery van, the deliveryman flattening himself against his barrels and she shouted over the roar of engine and air: 'You might want to take off that hat!'

The speedometer was nudging 100kmh when we burst into open country; none of the postcard beauty of the Odenwald but a gentle, honest landscape, lightly rolling hills, patchwork fields, small dairy farms and old stone houses, neat pockets of woodland – all passing in a smear of colours like a movie reel set on fast time. The road was straight and, virtually free of traffic, and the breath rushed from me in relief that, even if we were to die, we would take no one else with us. Ingrid poked me in the arm and shouted over the blasting air:

'It's armour-plated and the windscreen's bullet-proof. Isn't that great? She weighs three tons. That's why the engine's almost seven point seven litres.'

I have nothing to contribute to a conversation about automobiles so I nodded, smiled back and turned to my window, wondering why this woman, on the personal staff of Heinrich Himmler, 'the devil's spawn' according to Father, was being so friendly and open. Was it a trap? Was she playing with me, drawing me into her confidence to draw me out as another enemy of the state?

We pulled into a winding country lane and she was forced to cut her speed right back; the engine dropped to the gentlest purr. No harm in asking. What else did I have to lose?

'Ingrid, may I be frank? If you have so low an opinion of Herr Himmler, why do you work for him?'

Her face clouded and I said: 'Forgive me. That is none of my business. It's just the last week has been a little confusing.' I put my elbow on the armrest in the door and looked out over a pasture bathed in sunshine, a small herd of white Charolais swishing tails on the banks of the stream. She laid a hand on my arm.

'Otto, I know all about you and all about your family. I have seen the files on your father.'

She pulled the car over at the entrance to a track leading down to a timber farmhouse in the bend of a stream.

'Files? What files? Files about what?'

'Otto, you and your family need to steel yourselves. We all do. Soon there will be files on virtually every house, every family. I was given yours for your visit to Berlin. Why do I work for him? Probably the same reason you're here today – the money and the fear. Defy them and you may as well start walking to Dachau or Oranienburg now. I started in the Civil Service ten years ago, during the Weimar, and now I'm trapped.'

She let out a long sigh, tapping out a couple of Guldenrings, offering one to me and pulling the other out with her teeth. I cupped my lighter and she leaned towards me, took a heavy draw and blew the smoke back over her head.

'If I could get out I would. And if you could, you should. We all should.' She took another heavy draw and added: 'But it's too late. They talk of restoring glory – but you wait. Trust me, I hear everything. All the plans. It's going to make the last war look like a boating picnic on the Wannsee.'

I cupped my cigarette against the breeze and pulled hard on it. 'So, what does he have in mind for me? Have you heard?'

She shrugged her shoulders. 'Find Atlantis, prove Jesus was a German, breed hens with teeth... God, who knows? Something to do with antiquity, myths I suppose.'

'How do I play it?'

'You are dealing with a man who reads his horoscope before he has even brushed his teeth, a man who believes that somewhere up there in the Arctic is a place called Thule, an Aryan civilisation living in the centre of the earth, founded by Nordic pagans fleeing Christian persecution in medieval times. No joke. I mean – he seems completely normal but he's completely mad.'

'So, I just go along with it, nod and smile?'

'This is a guy who will believe anything if it plays into his master race fantasies. My advice? Be like him, like them, be ruthless, be cunning, spin lies. Beat them at their own game. But be honest, be yourself, and you'll lose. Adapt to survive. For now, yes, just keep nodding and smiling.'

She patted me on the arm, adding; 'And you have a very cute smile. Use it. I think he likes you. Now strap yourself in.'

I looked around for some manner of safety harness but could see nothing, and she leant right across me, wafting lavender, her hair brushing my face. She yanked out leather straps from under the sides of the seat and buckled them over my midriff, pulling so tight it pinched the skin through my pullover.

'Heini insisted on Daimler-Benz putting them in. He calls it his "seat girdle".'

'What about yours? I asked.

She shot me a look of mischief, cigarette hanging from her mouth, slammed her foot flat to the boards and three tons of automobile erupted out of the gravel track, jamming me hard against my seat. A kilometre of narrow lane lay ahead of us, twisting gently uphill towards a long avenue of trees, and she took the bends like a slalom skier through the poles, both of us rolling from side to side. Turning into the straight, she worked through the gears, twisted the dial on the Blaupunkt.

Strauss's 'Frühling' rushed into the surging air, so loud it was as if the entire Berlin Philharmonic had been dropped into the back.

Up ahead, the Renaissance castle, a mere pinprick on the horizon moments ago, rose from the valley, skirted by thick woodland on the slopes below, heavy grey walls and slate-tiled roofs between three towers, two of them cupola-capped, the north-pointing one crenelated and twice the girth.

The castle, pinned to the rock by a tube of sunlight, disappeared, the Grosser accelerating into a tunnel of trees – limes I think, but hard to tell – the sun flicking through the trunks, speedometer nudging one thirty. She braked hard and I lurched forward, my head close to the dash, hers to the steering wheel. She brought the speed right down to about thirty. A vehicle was heading towards us, flashing in and out of the light through the trees. The two cars slowed as they converged. Ingrid said 'Scheisse' and spun off the radio.

The driver had a long horse face, SS officer cap pulled down tight, a hunting dog at his side, their long noses high in the air. She offered the man a timid wave and after a squint of his narrow eyes he returned it with a slow nod and tilt of the head, sticking his hand out of the window and waving it up and down with exaggerated slowness, like he was calming an unruly schoolroom. He drove away, his eyes fixed on me till his face was gone.

'Who was that?'

She turned and raised her eyebrows at me. 'The Blond Beast, aka Reinhard Heydrich, head of the SD counter-intelligence unit, quite possibly the most unpleasant man ever born to a German mother, the next Führer they say, God help us. Avoid at all costs.'

'Is there anyone pleasant in the National Socialist Party?'

'Don't be daft,' she said, then after a pause: 'Actually, his little brother Heinz is okay. I had to look after him in Berlin last week. We fed the squirrels in the Tiergarten and he gave all his change to a tramp. But he's in the SS now.'

We crossed a stone bridge over a swollen brown river, swung left and wound our way up the hill, the great grey walls of the SS fortress looming ever larger on our right. Into the village clustered around its higher walls, crows wheeling over the northern tower, we pulled up at a round stone sentry box next to a guardhouse buttressed by heaps of stone and tiles and sundry building materials. A trooper in steel helmet and long grey coat raised the barrier and we proceeded along a narrow viaduct that bent around over a moat. Below, files of men in Labour Corps uniforms shovelled the bottom and heaved their barrows of earth up steep ramparts.

Edging the giant automobile between a high, narrow arch we entered a three-sided cobbled courtyard, deep and sunless, tiny for such a monumental structure. She brought the car to a gentle halt beneath a wall lantern, cut the engine, and the sudden thick silence was broken only by water dripping from an overflow pipe onto the hood. We looked at each other, raising our brows and, peeling off her gloves, she said: 'Come on, strong hearts. Play the game.'

The crash of the car doors rolled around damp stone walls rising so high they left only a small triangle of sky above. I took my bag from the back and squeezed the rear door shut, pushing it in with my knee so it made no more than a faint click. Six ordinary house doors lined the two longer walls like rows of terraced houses, an impression compounded by the sight of fingers tugging at a drawn curtain on the third floor.

I followed Ingrid towards heavy wooden doors squeezed into the angle where the longer walls pincered the larger north tower like tongs. An ornate pediment sat over the door, but the three windows in a column, perpendicular above it, were offset as if the upper floors had somehow been rotated to the left by about a metre, the asymmetry disconcerting. Or maybe it was just my nerves. I took a deep breath through my nose, my heart battering my ribs, and pushed the hat down on my head. Ingrid was reaching for the handle when one leaf of the doors jerked open. A guardsman stepped backward, chin up, and we walked into a large circular room, dark on our side but light on the other, where eight tall, recessed windows sat between pillars.

Our heels clicked on the highly polished marble, the noise lingering in the domed roof, my eyes adjusting to the weird light. The room was empty but for the dark silhouette of a small thin statue right in the centre. It stood on a dark-green sun inlaid in the floor, its spider-leg rays forming a 12-armed swastika zigzagging into an outer circle to form a sort of wheel. Ingrid was looking at the figure too, her hands clasped before her.

I laid down my bag and, squinting and leaning into the gloom, shuffled a couple of steps forward. As I did, the arms of the statue shot outwards and it came towards me, heels erupting like gunfire over the marble. I sprung back. Himmler slapped his hands on my upper arms, nodding his shiny bank clerk's face, eyes ablaze behind the pince-nez.

I waited for him to speak but nothing came, just lots of nodding and eye-smiling, and I began to go through my awkward-moments routine with my eyes and lips, like a schoolboy asked to come sit on a stranger's knee, not entirely sure about the correct protocol.

'Welcome to Wewelsburg, centre of a new universe, Otto, built precisely on a north-south axis so that this very tower where we stand now points to Thule in the frozen north, ancestral homeland of the Aryan people.'

He pulled his hands away as if I was suddenly scalding to the touch and reached into the pocket of his leather overcoat. Taking out a round metal case, silver lightning flashes of the SS insignia on its black lid, placed it in his palm and held it out to me, his eyelids shuttering.

'Well, go on. It won't bite you. It is going to protect you in your quest.'

I turned it over in my fingers and, clasping the lid by

its rim, wriggled it from the bottom half. It was a ring.

'It's stainless steel.'

'My, well, thank you. That's very – '

'So that it won't rust. It will live on forever, untarnished. If you were ever to fall in the cause it will be buried with all the other honour rings of German heroes. In a sealed vault, right here, a Valhalla for the SS. Isn't that a thought?'

'It is.'

'Weisthor designed it. Look at the detail. Have you ever seen anything so beautiful?'

I raised the ring to my face but was unable to see the finer detail in the poor light, just a Death's Head skull and crossbones at the top of it.

'Come into the light then, you big muttonhead.' And he took me by the elbow, led me over the inlaid sun into a block of bright light. He leant into me, cupping his warm, soft hands beneath mine, and I clamped my mouth and nose against an appalling cocktail of smells, a mixture of sandalwood shaving balm, gum rot and the vinegary residue of his lunch. It was so repulsive I gagged and put a fist to my nose.

He pulled away, 'Are you quite alright, Eckhart?'

I begged his pardon, mumbling about poor quality railway food and a hereditary gastric condition, and we continued the intimate inspection of his gift.

'Masterpiece, eh? Look at the runes among the oak leaves. That's the Sig rune either side of the skull, the sun rune representing our energy.'

'Heavens.'

'That one there. Oh, give it here.' And he snatched it from my fingers. 'That one there, the hexagon, is the Hagal. It encloses you in the universe and then you can control the universe. Clever, eh? But what am I saying? You know that of course.'

'Of course.'

'And this little fellow needs no introduction – the Hakenkreuz, the Indian swastika.'

'Very good.'

'And these ones underneath are... the wolf hook, I think. Or the bear. I'll check with Weisthor. And look on the inside.'

He handed it back to me, grinning at me like I was opening a birthday present, his face back to a forearm's length from mine, eyes afire. I turned it in my fingers, reading the engraving, written in a tight florid script, holding my breath, gulping down another wretch and I stepped away deeper into the light, pretending to get a closer look. But I could already see what it said: *Otto Eckhart. 13.5.37*, the date.

He took me again by the shoulders and closing his eyes, like a priest giving his blessing, said: 'Welcome Otto. Welcome to Germany's new knightly order, an aristocracy born of pure German blood, raised on pure German soil, a new elite for a new world order. Here, give it to me and give me your hand.'

I hesitated and he snapped, 'Come on, come on, I'm not asking you to marry me.'

I handed him the ring with my right hand and slowly raised my left.

'Not that one, you halfwit.' He seized my right hand and thrust the ring onto my fourth finger. He took a step back into the light, a dark silhouette now, and threw his arms open, cleared his throat of thick catarrh, the swallow audible, and for a moment I feared he was going to sing some sort of incantation.

Then he strode back into me. I clamped my nose. He whispered, 'Otto Eckhart, I offer you this ring as a public sign of your love and fidelity to the Fatherland. Your honour means your loyalty.'

We shook hands, and he consulted his watch, rolling his head. 'Right, time to put the shoulder back to the wheel of fortune. Ingrid, why don't you give our new knight a tour of the castle then show him to his room. We reconvene here at seven.'

'Very good, sir.'

Himmler disappeared into a passageway beneath the stairwell, his footsteps fading. After a short while, a door shut.

We exchanged tense smiles.

'What the hell was – '

She put a finger to her lips.

CHAPTER FOUR

Ingrid knocked lightly, the door swung open and we were back in the circular hall. I picked up my case.

'Right, brace yourself, Otto.'

We made our way up the stone steps of the corkscrew stairwell, the case clattering and scraping against the wall. On the third floor, Ingrid thumbed down the latch of a dark-stained oak door and pushed it open with her shoulder. I followed in her trail of lavender down a corridor so broad you might ride a horse along it, and so long, it was like looking into a telescope the wrong way, the exit at the far end no more than a rabbit hole in the gloom.

The passageway was lit by dim, half-moon wall lights fixed between an assortment of medieval paraphernalia, most of it looking fresh off a factory production line. There were crossed swords, heraldic shields, flags and pennants, battle axes and halberds, surcoats and tabards, drinking horns, maces and flails, gaudy reproductions of Nordic myths and legends – you know the ones, giant warriors in horned, iron-mask helmets and bearskins on the prow of a long boat, flaxen-haired, massive-chested maidens in sunlit glades, roiling oceans and raging fires, howling ogres and wizards with staffs and white beards to the waist.

The heavy oak doors to the guest rooms had each been given a name: *Henry the Lion, Widukind, King Arthur, Aryan, Westphalia, The Running of the Seasons, Runes, Teutonic Knights, The Emperor, Fridericus, Tolle Christian, Deutsche Sprache* and, curiously, *Christopher Columbus*. We were halfway down, silent on the heavy carpet, when we reached *Henry I, Slayer of the Slav*, and Ingrid turned, stabbed a finger at the door and grimaced, leaning towards me, 'That's his room – he is the reincarnation after all. You're right next door, I'm afraid.'

We stopped outside *Grail*, and Ingrid eased open the door, slowly revealing a square room of white walls and oak panelling, furnished with solid wooden furniture: a wardrobe, desk and chair, chest of drawers, mantel clock, half-length mirror, hand basin, a porcelain ewer. She pulled the door fully open and I had one foot in when I reared back.

On the single bed, a black uniform with silver collar flashes had been laid out like a dead man – peaked cap at the top, black leather boots at the bottom, riding breeches and tunic with red swastika armband, the sleeves folded over the chest in the repose of an effigy carved into a cathedral tomb. A dagger where the hands would be, lay over the chest, the blade pointing to a skull under the cap, the cap resting on a pillow featuring the red cross of the Knights Templar.

It was some time before I could drag my eyes away and look at Ingrid, her cornflower blue eyes holding mine, her face frozen in a tense smile.

'I'm sorry – I was overruled. Weisthor's sense of humour – he's envious, you know, worried you might usurp him in the affections of his master.'

'Who on earth is this Weisthor?'

'Himmler's pet wizard – a sort of mystic. But really just a loathsome drunk and a crank, and in and out of asylums. Heini loves him, swallows all his garbage about ancestral clairvoyance. But don't worry about that' – wafting a hand at the SS uniform – 'you'll only have to wear it when you're here or at a function.'

'But I'm not in the Schutzstaffel!'

She scratched at her jet-black hair like she had been bitten. 'I have news for you, SS Hauptsturmführer Otto Eckhart.'

'What?'

'Yes, he's bent the rules to make you an honorary member, give you a bit of authority as you go about your business.'

She spoke the whole sentence like one word as if trying to get rid of the news as fast as possible.

I stared. 'But – '

'His rules, so he makes them up as he likes. He's already ditched the blond-haired, blue-eyed, and height requirements. I guess after looking in the mirror.'

'But how will I pass selection? Look at me. I pull muscles drawing curtains.'

'Relax, relax. I made sure you won't have to do any of the warrior training. He agreed that you might struggle to balance a pinless grenade on your helmet.'

I dropped my case, walked to the bed and lifted the skull, weighing it in my hand, staring into the cavities of its eye sockets, then slid it face first over the chest of drawers into the corner of the wall.

When I turned back, Ingrid was crouching at the open window, snapping pictures.

'New hobby?'

'No, not at all. I love it. I'd go professional if I could afford to take the risk.'

'Landscapes? Portraits?'

'Anything that catches my eye. My father is sending me Leica's new long-distance lens.'

'Great, you can take a shot of me fleeing over the horizon from here.'

She smiled, making her way to the door. 'See you on parade at seven. Don't forget, it's fancy dress.'

I picked up the long, black-handled dagger, pulled it from its scabbard, and ran the blade over my thumb. It was sharp enough to shave with, its point fine enough to spear a pea, a Gothic inscription down one side reading 'My Honour is my Loyalty'. I thrust it into the scabbard, tossed it back and with both arms swept the entire uniform to the floor at the foot of the bed, the boots and belt buckle clattering over the floorboards. I lay down, hands beneath my head on the Knights Templar pillow, and kicked the air.

I thought of home and Father propped on his pillows, squirming at the thought of him seeing his only child in full SS regalia. I pictured the sleepy little farmhouse, smoke curling from the chimneys, hens fretting about the yard, Mother hanging the washing in a stiff breeze from the valley. I longed to be back there, and cursed the rush of blood that had come in answer to some inner calling to which I could give no name or grant no sense. What on earth was I doing? A muttonhead, a klutz, a fathead, a halfwit, all the insults he had rained down on me with his putrid breath. Yes, he was right about that much.

•◆•

My eyes opened to a paler light and I leapt off the bed. The wooden mantel clock read not quite six forty, and I dropped my shoulders, shaking the circulation back into my hands. The room was stifling, the radiator raging hot, and I levered open the window and leant my elbows on the sill, looking down on a cluster of red roof tiles, burning orange now in the falling light. Some children played chase amongst the gravestones in the overgrowth around the Gothic church, the spire casting a shadow almost twice its length over the village. The reciting tones of a Gregorian chant drifted on the light wind.

It was a mild day, the heating on full tilt presumably to counter the dampness of the old castle's stone. Half a dozen other windows along the wing had been pushed open, including Himmler's next door. A pair of hands shook out a small rug from a window on the first floor, strains of Schubert's *Der Lindenbaum* rose and fell from another, and a playful exchange – all giggles and titters – was taking place close by.

A man in SS uniform – or dark grey at least – was working his way up the cobbles from the heart of the village, weaving an unsteady path between the doorways and hanging baskets on each side. He had reached a lamp post where the street opened out into the market square and leant a hand against it, head bowed. His SS tunic – I could tell now by the flashes on the collar – was unbuttoned at the top and half a shirt was hanging out. I watched him run his other hand through a shock of unkempt grey hair and push himself off for a final effort.

Two sentries at the barrier were also watching his uncertain progress and just as the man lurched towards the barrier, my attention was distracted first by a soprano giggle, then a man's voice, in a *basso profundo* groan: 'Oh, my darling honeycomb turtle dove!' The voice held the last note for several seconds, as if in an opera, then it gave way to a long moaning sigh. There followed an extended and violent coughing fit and what sounded like a battery of back-slapping. I found myself looking to the left, at Himmler's window, and when I saw a pair of bare hairy arms appear on the windowsill and the coughing continued, I ducked back into the room.

I may have been out of practice, but I was not a complete stranger to the world of love, and not so unworldly as to fail to recognise a performance of its expression when I heard one. And unless Reichsführer Himmler and his wife were acting out some sort of amateur dramatic performance – well, trust me, if they were acting, he had most certainly answered the wrong calling in life.

'My darling honeycomb turtle dove!' I mean, please Reichsführer. I shook the images from my mind and turned to my own bed.

I stripped down to my underwear and began to transform myself into a junior officer of the Schutzstaffel. I pulled on the trousers and undershirt, snapping the braces over my shoulders, yanked on the shiny riding boots, worked my way up the silver buttons of the tunic to the neck choker, and tightened the leather belt around my waist. Adjusting the swastika armband, I crowned myself with the Death's Head visor cap, brushed myself down and swivelled on my heels to face the half-length mirror.

My God, what a clown. I did not need to look in the mirror to know that the uniform was at least one size too large for me, designed no doubt with a Nordic demi-god in mind. The sight staring back at me was so utterly ludicrous I began to laugh. I looked like a child trying out his papa's clothes. The cap half-covered my eyes, the tunic was so long it was almost an overcoat, the shoulders drooping over my upper arms, and the top of the boots covered my knees. I took off the tunic, put my thickest shirt and pullover underneath and tried again. Still laughable but better, and it would have to do. If I was to put on more layers, I'd be boiled alive.

The cap was more problematic. I couldn't present myself with it over my face, like a vaudeville act, or tip it back as a bus conductor might at the end of a hard day. I rooted around in my suitcase and pulled out two pairs of underpants, wedging them inside the cap, and turned back to the mirror. It was almost a perfect fit. I almost looked the part. I clicked my heels together and stuck my nose in the air, twisting left and right to assess my profile in the reflection.

A confession – it felt good, really good, especially when I took a few steps back from the mirror and my face disappeared under the shadow of the visor. I was no longer Otto Eckhart. I might have been anyone. I understood it instantly, one of those epiphany moments you get – the attraction of submerging one's identity in a corporate mass, one little part of a large whole, the self no longer important, not having to think for oneself, just wait for an order. *Hey you, storm that machine gun nest! (Yes, sir!)… You, kick the shit out of that communist! (Yes, sir!) You – marry that woman and have four blond children! (Yes, sir!)… You, go die for the Fatherland! (Yes, sir!)…*

I took the dagger from the bed and stood stock-still before the mirror. Suddenly, I ripped the blade from the scabbard, throwing my legs and arms out to the side into a fighting crouch. Then Father came into my head and the spell was broken and, ashamed, as if he were watching me, I slid the blade back, lobbed it onto my open suitcase and headed out into the corridor. Idiot.

I was pulling the door to when I heard Himmler's open. His wife darted out, throwing half-looks each way, and I froze. She was closing the door with almost theatrical care. I clutched the door handle, not daring to move, to make eye contact. She scuttled away towards the stairwell, skipping every other stride to hasten her retreat.

·◆·

We were whispering.

'You didn't tell me Himmler's wife was here.'

'Marga? She's not. That's his mistress, Hedwig. Were you audience to one of their hideous performances? Or his, rather. She's probably too busy trying not to breathe or kiss him.'

'Himmler – a lover? You're kidding.'

'Another secretary – chief secretary now of course. Cold as ice.'

'So how does that sit with impassioned calls for a return to traditional values, to old-fashioned German purity and decency?'

'Oh, they're all hypocrites. All of them – maybe not the Führer himself. Anyhow, nice figure but quite plain, isn't she? You'd think if you were going to be unfaithful, you'd go for the beauty, get your money's worth.'

'Is it public knowledge?'

'God, no! He'd be mortified. He has appearances to maintain. No, for Heaven's sake, don't let on to anyone. He'll have you in stripy pyjamas before the day's out.

Did she see you?'

'No, I'm pretty sure she didn't. We certainly didn't lock eyes.'

'Good. That would be complicated for you.'

Ingrid was looking me up and down and she took a step forward, straightened my collar and pressed down my cap so it sat a bit tighter over the eyes. The sound of slamming doors and rapidly approaching footsteps from the adjoining wing – a barrage of steel heels – made us stand to attention, my hands behind my back, Ingrid's cradled at the front.

Himmler swept into the General's Hall, heading a train of slate grey and pitch-black cloth, fairly senior SS personnel most of them, judging by the medals, ribbon bars and extravagant insignia, but then came a handful of double-breasted suits and some outdoors tweed too. He came to a halt on the dark-green sun and turned to face us, Ingrid taking a few backward steps into the shadow of the doorway, his entourage forming up behind him in a loose semi-circle fanning out from the rim of the wheel, two or three of them exchanging looks as though they had better places to be, and better ways to be spending their time. An elf of a man with pointy ears and darting eyes yawned, looked at his watch and swept back his collar-length silvery blond hair.

The uniforms sat on the officers perfectly, tailored and fitted to precise measurements, as easy on them as their own skin. The heat rose to my cheeks, even more conscious now of my small frame inside the bulk of clothes, the unnatural breadth of my shoulders, my face like that of a child under the king-size cap, underpants pressed to my scalp, boots like waders – a variety act parody of the men facing me.

Himmler half-turned to the group and said: 'Gentlemen, this is the brilliant young scholar I've been telling you about, whose great work now adorns your bookshelves. Otto Eckhart – SS Hauptsturmführer Eckhart I should say.'

Himmler paused. Was I to salute? Bid them good day? I met the problem half-way, scratching my temple with my elbow stuck out, muttering thanks. One or two nodded and flashed me a half-smile, a few others ran their eyes up and down me, the rest staring straight ahead, playing with their rings or looking up into the vaulted ceiling. He held out an arm, turning towards the semi-circle, and I stepped forward, like I had been called to the front of the class to explain myself, sweat clinging to my neck and back. He cleared his throat, the noise of it ugly enough to make the yawning elf screw up his face.

'Everyone in this room, Otto – except Ingrid that is…' And he gave her a bow, and Ingrid returned a slightly sarcastic smile. '…gathered at Wewelsburg for our annual conference, is either a founder or senior member of the Ahnenerbe. The Ahnenerbe, Otto, is the Reich's historical research unit, Germany's best kept secret and perhaps the most powerful weapon in our formidable arsenal.

'You will not have heard of our organisation, Otto. The Führer himself is barely aware of our existence. For the time being, we leave him to front the great challenges of our immediate future, until we are ready to present him with the fruits of our scientific labour – new proof of our ancestors' pre-eminence. At the Ahnenerbe, we have assembled some of Germany's greatest minds' – and he swept an arm along the semi-circle – 'to investigate our heritage as rigorously as never before, in order to show that it is our past that justifies our present and future, so that there can be no quarrel over our coming role in the world.'

The little yawner covered his mouth and turned away, Himmler pausing and giving him a look. When he continued, he turned up the volume and the pitch, and it grew in passion with every phrase. It was as if he was addressing an enormous outdoor rally, a crowd as far as he could see.

'We shall explode the myths and lies of the past, and sweep away centuries of bogus scholarship. Thus, we shall prove the truth! Through our scientific endeavour, we shall demonstrate that the mastery of our noble race stretches back to the very dawn of time.'

A film of sweat had gathered on his brow, glistening in the last rays of the day's sun, a light shower of spittle carried on every breath. Some stared at him with blank faces, others chewed their lips or looked at their shoes.

'SS Hauptsturmführer Otto Eckhart, please, come, let me introduce you to fellow adventurers on the hunt, like you, for the truth of the past.' And he gestured for me to follow him to one end of the crescent of uniforms, where the elf swallowed a yawn and met me with a look of insolent amusement and an outstretched hand. His thick greying moustache and sparkling eyes put me in mind of Albert Einstein.

Himmler said, 'Herman Wirth – a Dutchman, but we can forgive him that. That and his profligacy and his little eccentricities. No one knows more about our ancestors in Atlantis than Herman, and he's as German as a Dutchman could possibly be. We may have disagreed over his interpretation of Christianity in terms of early Nordic monotheism – and the odd accounting anomaly – but he will do very well, I'm sure, in his new non-executive role as Honorary President of the Ahnenerbe.'

Wirth's watery smile could not have disappeared faster, but Himmler had moved on to the next in line, a dark-haired character with a serious faraway face.

'Walther Wurst – Hermann's successor as active President of our bureau, one of our finest Indo-European scholars and Vedicists. Walther is a marvellous administrator, actually gets things done. And to hear him read aloud his ancient Sanskrit scriptures is something to behold – trust me, you will leave your body and be transported to another world and time.'

Wurst said something, but so softly I had no idea what, and we moved on down the line. I shook hands with the castle librarian ('Any book or paper you need, just ask Hans Peter'), then quickly on to an archaeologist specialising in Teutonic battlefield sites, then an authority on divination and dowsing rods. Next up, an anatomist with a hideously disfigured face specialising in the human nervous system, then a philologist, anthropologist and eugenicist from the University of Berlin ('His students call him the "Race Pope", Otto')... an explorer heading to the Bolivian Andes in search of Aryan palaces and temples... a zoologist... a professor of Finnish folklore, magical spells and wizards... an agriculturist specialising in animal breeding (current project – a giant cow you can ride, work, eat and wear)... the head of the Berlin School of Acoustics ('Music, I need not tell you, Otto, is a manifestation of race not culture')... another Dutchman, with a baby face and protruding ears, currently unearthing the origins of the Aryan race at a Cro-Magnon site in Bavaria... an Icelandic grammarian... the curator of the castle's private museum, tall as the pillar he stood before and, last in line, a racial diagnostician recently returned from Tibet, where he and his team had taken the cranial measurements of over 300 locals ('Heads insufficiently long for the purposes of our theories but some promising leads in the symbolism').

We returned to the centre of the sun and Himmler held out his arms, inviting me to be impressed by the assemblage. I was so hot beneath all my layers that the sweat was running down my backbone and streaming from my armpits. I muttered, 'What an honour,

Reichsführer, to meet so many fine minds in one room.'

He clapped his hands, exclaiming, 'Fine minds indeed, Otto, united in a fine cause! Together we shall turn the past into a weapon more powerful than a corps of Panzers. Gentlemen, thank you for your time. We shall see you in the dining hall for drinks very shortly. First, I have a surprise for our eager young Eckhart down in the crypt.'

Putting his arm in mine, he led me with measured steps in a sort of parade-ground slow march to the top of a broad twisting stairwell, faint candlelight from below flickering over its walls. He stopped and said: 'Now, Otto, the man you are about to meet is a bit of a character, an exotic fruit. Not everyone's favourite I should tell you – Reinhard can't stand the sight of him, especially when he's having a trance – but not everyone can recognise genius when it stands shining before them. Some can read the aura, others cannot. Whatever they tell you, I can vouch that this man is a soothsayer of the highest order, an outstanding clairvoyant, but a man of earthly gifts too. It was him, not me, who chose this castle as our spiritual centre; him, not me, who has overseen its renovation; him, not me, who designed our Death's Head ring and cap badge – and he's the perfect wizard when it comes to runic symbols, probably peerless in Germany. Literally a wizard, an Irminist warlock who can trace his ancestry all the way back to Thor himself.'

He released his arm and turned to face me, eyes afire

again, repeating: 'Thor, Otto. Thor. Isn't that just the most extraordinary thing?'

'Thor? Certainly it is, sir, but Thor, is he not, just a – '

'Please don't interrupt when I am talking, Otto. And yes, Thor, son of Odin. Thor is more than a myth, you know – our ancestors didn't just make him up, you of all scholars should know that – and we shall prove that too. We shall prove everything that needs to be proved, Otto. With rigorous scientific enquiry. Why else do you think I have assembled over 150 of the greatest scholars and scientists in Germany?'

He stepped towards me, taking my upper arms, leaning right into me, looking far into my eyes, and I clamped my mouth and plugged my nose from the inside.

'Otto, you should know better than anyone, there's been a great deal of claptrap written and spoken in the past – about our past. That's why we're all here. To re-write history. Correctly this time. Re-orientate our destiny, reconnect with our ancestors, put us back on the path intended for us. And it doesn't get much more impressive than Thor. Imagine that at the top of your family tree.'

I was overcome by an intense urge to scratch my scalp, and I went to take the cap from my head – and thus release myself from his iron grip and rancid breath – when I remembered it was full of underpants. So I stepped away and pretended to sneeze.

'Gosh, related to Thor? That is something else, Reichsführer. I can't wait to make his – '

'And not just Thor, Otto. He is a direct descendant of Arminius too.'

It was a relief to hear that there was flesh and blood in the lineage of Himmler's warlock and, compensating for my earlier scepticism, win back some credibility, I blurted, 'The tribal chief who slaughtered three Roman legions at the Battle of Teutoburg Forest in AD 9?'

Himmler smiled and bowed his head. '*Rem acu tetigisti*, Otto. I could stand here all day listing the great Germans of yore from whom this very special man is descended, and to whom he speaks on a regular basis, as easy as you and I make telephone calls.'

'Speaks to them?'

'Yes, that's his great gift. He's an ancestral clairvoyant for heaven's sake. That's what they do, these people. In fact, he is on good terms with more people on that side of the grave than this.'

'Come on, come and meet him.' And he started down the steps, disappearing around the first bend, his voice growing fainter but echoing. 'He will prove invaluable to you.'

I reached under my hat and underpants, scratching furiously, and hurried after him, a hand running over the flickering shadows on the wall, the fresh leather soles of my oversized riding boots slipping on the worn stone. 'My task? Yes, I've been meaning to ask – '

The stairwell was shaped like a tornado, narrowing the further we descended and, watching my feet all the way down so as not to fall, I reared up sharply at the bottom and only just avoided barging into the Reichsführer. He had his hands on his head which he was shaking from side to side and mumbling, 'No, no, no, no, no!'

Blocked by the narrow arch in which we stood, I crouched and peered under his armpit but all I could see was a series of pedestals arranged equally around the crude stone of the rotunda wall, candles on wall holders above them, some building materials and tools, and a circle sunk in the middle of the room like an ornamental pond.

Himmler stepped aside, still shaking his head, to reveal the source of his consternation. A man in a grey uniform was lying on a low stone altar, his face pointed up to the swastika laid into roof of the vault, a long mane of salt-and-pepper hair spread behind him, an arm dangling to the floor, his finger in the trigger guard of a revolver.

I stammered: 'Is he – is he dead?'

'No, no. Weisthor is never dead. Our wizard has just had a little too much potion once again.'

He strode with purpose across the room, arms swinging as though there was a brass band playing. I followed him around the sunken circle, venturing, 'He's probably drained, spiritually.'

We stopped and turned to look down into the circle, empty but for a small metal pipe poking up at the centre of it.

He said: 'And what you are looking at here, Otto, is the Eternal Flame.'

I squinted and leant forward but could not see so much as a flicker of fire emanating from the pipe.

'We have a few problems with the gas supply presently. Wretched peasant in the moat sliced through the supply pipe on Tuesday and we can't get a gas engineer in until next week. Then it will burn forever again.'

'That is good news, sir. Eternity would like to get on with it, I'd imagine.'

'Exactly so, Otto.'

We stepped up to the altar and I recognised the prostrate figure as the man I had seen staggering through the village. A large wet patch covered his groin. Himmler removed the revolver from the curled finger and handed it to me, then placed one hand on the man's shoulder, one on his hip, and rolled him off as if he were no more than a sack of barley. It was a drop of less than a metre, but it was still lucky the drunk wizard landed on his side and not his face, a low moan confirming there was still some life in there. He pushed himself up on one hand, head wobbling, eyes seeking focus, then collapsed back to the floor.

Himmler leant over the altar, barking, 'Karl Maria Weisthor – you are a disgrace to your ancestors.' And then to me, softly, 'He's a very impassioned character, Karl – brilliant men often drink too much in order to douse the creative fury of their minds. Tomorrow, you shall meet the real Weisthor, mind as clear as a crystal ball. After his breakfast Pils to clear away the fog.'

'Excellent, sir, I am very much looking forward to

that. What is he doing with this?' I held up the gun.

'Oh that? Nothing, it's of no concern. Karl carries a loaded revolver wherever he goes, even to his bath. Trusts no one but me, and least of all Frenchmen – so watch he doesn't get too trigger-happy over there. It's an old family feud – something to do with the Gallic chieftain Vercingetorix and one of his ancestors.'

'I beg your pardon, sir – France? With Weisthor?'

A noise, somewhere between a howl of pain and an attempt at song, rose up from the wizard and we put our hands on the altar and leant over. His head was lolling from side to side and he was mumbling as if in conversation.

Himmler flashed me a look and said, 'I think he must have made ancestral contact.'

I heard myself saying, 'Perhaps he's being admonished by Thor?' and quickly turned to Himmler with my earnest face to show I was not being impertinent.

'Yes, perhaps. In fact, that's almost certainly what's happening. He's let down the family line by drinking too much and he's being castigated by his elders.'

Adjusting my cap, struggling to contain a mounting hysteria, I said, 'So, Reichsführer, you want me to conduct some further research in France? In partnership with Weisthor? That's fine of course but I find that two –'

He cut a hand through the air and stepped towards me, his breath leading the way. 'Research? Research! No, no, no, no, no Otto! We'll leave the research to the researchers. No, Eckhart – what I am talking about might just turn out to be one of the most important missions yet undertaken by the Third Reich.'

'Really?'

'I am talking about an historic enterprise that will have you feted through all Germany and beyond. There will be bronze statues of you, mark my words.'

He craned in even closer so that we were almost kissing now, my face puce with the effort of not breathing. Whispering, he confided, 'Top secret, this – just you, me and the team itself. But we are currently running a project that will prove, once and for all, that Jesus was an Aryan, and not just some dirty Arab as the traditional teaching has it.'

I was looking at him wide-eyed and red-faced, cheeks about to burst.

'I can see your excitement, Eckhart. So, we prove Jesus was a German, to all intents and purposes, and you come back with the Holy Grail!'

I could hold on no longer and in an almighty gale of breath, I bellowed: 'Holy Grail?'

'I thought you'd be excited, but calm down, you great mooncalf. There's still some way to go. You're halfway there for sure, as you say in the book, but you have to close in on the prize now. And fast. I need that Grail, Eckhart, and I need it fast.'

And he looked at his rectangular watch as though he were talking about a deadline of minutes.

'But, the Holy Grail, sir. I can't just –'

'And right here…' – and he swept his hand along the

length of the altar stone – 'Right here, Eckhart. This is where the Holy Grail will sit, guarded by the light of the Eternal Flame. Forever, Otto.'

'Once they have fixed the gas.'

'Well, obviously, you clot-head.'

CHAPTER FIVE

So, I get a pat on the back and a ruffle of my hair – *he actually ruffled my hair* – and I'm told to pop out and fetch the Holy Grail, like it was his favourite pastry or a novelty tobacco pipe.

'Off you go, bring me back the Holy Grail, there's a good fellow, just shop around, make a few enquiries, it'll turn up. Aha, there we go, found it! Up there on the top shelf in Monsieur Bibelot's curio shop amongst all those other holy relics. "Excellent, thank you, it's a little chipped around the rim and it could do with a scrub, get those wine stains off, but I guess it'll do, thanks, I'll take it. Here, I'm in a good mood today, I'll give you 50 francs for it. Oh look, and there's the Messiah's burial shroud – I'll give you 100 for the two of them…'

The Holy Grail! There's good reason why it has become a byword for seeking the impossible. Had he asked me to nip out on my unicorn and bag a rainbow for him, I'd have been feeling a little more confident in my task. Truth is, the Grail probably doesn't even exist, and if it does, it's most likely going to be ten feet under a barber shop in the suburbs of Jerusalem.

And what is the Holy Grail anyhow? No one knows.

The commonly held view is that it's the chalice from the Last Supper, others say a bowl, a dish, a plate, a cauldron, a stone. Some say it's just an abstract notion, a figure of speech denoting the spiritual quest in us all. But let's just say it is something you can hold, the chalice Jesus lifted at the Last Supper saying to the disciples, *'Take this all of you and drink from it. For this is the chalice of my blood, the blood of a new and everlasting covenant…'*

Fine, but after the Gospels recorded that moment, there followed about twelve hundred years of silence on the subject. The first mention of the Holy Grail is to be found in an unfinished twelfth-century Romance poem, *Perceval*, by Chrétien de Troyes, a troubadour – yes, a troubadour, the next rank up from jester and one down from Groom of the Stool. A troubadour was a wandering lyric poet whose sole role in life was to invent – *invent* – tales of courtly love to entertain idle noblewomen with little to do but stare out of an embrasure, waiting to see out the next siege, plague or famine, dreaming of a gallant knight galloping up their drawbridge.

The German version of the Grail story is, *Parzival*, by Wolfram von Eschenbach – you know it, of course. What German over the age of four doesn't? It is woven into our identity, as German as sausage and beer and Christmas, up there in epic poetry's highest gallery with Dante's *Inferno*, Gottfried's *Tristan und Isolde* and Milton's *Paradise Lost*. I know the great epic poems of ancient Germany better than I know myself – *The Song of the*

Nibelungs, Parzival, Hildebrand, Kudrun … name one, and I'll recite you stanza after stanza. The Odenwald is rich in Teutonic lore and I was breastfed on its legends. And look where that led me – straight out of dreamland and into the nightmare of the real world, but a 'real' world turning out to be even more phantasmagorical.

I took refuge in myths and legends as a means of escape from the responsibilities of adulthood. But this Himmler character truly believes these fairy tales to be worthy of serious scholastic enquiry, not for artistic or cultural ends, but political and racial ones. You should have heard him and Weisthor over breakfast the morning I left Wewelsburg. I left that table, my head spinning from the madness of his vision.

The man dreams of building an Aryan empire stretching all the way from the Arctic Circle to the Levant, its legitimacy drawing heavily on the nonsense of the Nordic myths. He's deadly serious about it. Heading back up to my room to pack my case, I was quite convinced that, were someone calling himself a professor to walk into his office later that morning and tell him he had compelling evidence Hansel and Gretel were pure-blood Aryans, and that the witch in the woods was a Slav or a Jew, by lunch the Reichsführer-SS would have dispatched an archaeological expedition to find the site of the old woman's cake-and-candy house.

Here's a bit of advice for you, no charge levied. If you want people to take you seriously as a scholar, just litter your text with footnote symbols – asterisks, dagger symbols, roman numerals and so on – and fill the bottom of each page with tiny print and abbreviations like *Ibid, op.cit, ff, unpub., passim*... You'll be amazed by the transformation of your reputation. Stick at it and you'll end up a professor at a university. Me, that's what I did. Look at me now – a great scholar apparently. And neck-deep in the sauerkraut.

I only have myself to blame. I leapt on the wagon, playing up the Nordic connection to the Christ story in my stupid book, massaging the bruised patriotic ego a little, spinning a few more yarns into the myth. Not for a moment could I have foreseen anyone was going to take me seriously, least of all a man of such immense power and influence.

The publishers of course saw my shoddy 'scholarship' for the balderdash that it is – but this Himmler character, I mean, heavens, what a doughnut. *Parzival* may be a medieval literary masterpiece, but what it most certainly is not is a document of incontestable forensic evidence on which to base a detective investigation into the current location of an indeterminate, probably non-existent holy relic.

So, you see my trouble? It was only a matter of time before I was to be exposed as a charlatan, a chancer making sensationalist claims to grab a quick Reichsmark and make a small splash, playing into the zeitgeist lust for Nordic mythology, talking up the manifest destiny of a nation. And when Himmler wises up to me, or one of his cronies takes him to one side, then I'm in big trouble

– hauled back to Prinz-Albrecht-Strasse probably, and jack-booted out of the back of a van – and then where? And what of Mother and Father?

These were my gloomy thoughts as France sped by my soot-caked window. I longed once again for the comfort of home, Father healthy again, marking his schoolbooks at the fireside, Mother rolling the pastry at the kitchen table, sighing and barking at me for my idleness, Germany a normal country once more.

My mind kept wandering back to the final breakfast at Wewelsburg, my last chance to have engineered an escape from this mad escapade. And I blew it. Why? Same old story. Because I lacked courage – the courage to challenge him and his pet warlock over their ridiculous vision for Germany based on all that twisted and bogus history. I just sat nodding as they held forth. And my God, did they hold forth – on the new religion supplanting Christianity in the soul of Germany, the Führer as the true Messiah, Jewry the true Devil, *Mein Kampf* the true Bible, the new rituals of solstice celebrations for Christian feast days, patriotic gatherings for church services, a new doctrine of unthinking obedience, self-sacrifice and veneration of the Führer, the supremacy of German blood and soil, yeomen in lederhosen hoeing their plots, women in Heidi dirndls pumping out ranks of blue-eyed beauties – 'like a string of good German sausages', Weisthor interjected, twice repeating his choice of phrase, the image somehow repellent as we spooned and dunked our eggs.

I am not a devout man, but as a walking companion, I'm going for Jesus Christ over Thor every time. And you could see their difficulty in squaring Jesus and Adolf, Christians and National Socialists. Not obvious bedfellows. The Jews as the chosen people for Heaven's sake! And not the German tribes? What *was* He thinking? Why go for rock and desert and not lovely fresh woodland and meadows? Why brown skin and brown eyes over pure white and blue, black hair over blond? He, the Creator, must have just closed his eyes, spun the globe, counted to five and thrust down his finger. Judaea it is! Imbecile!

On and on they garbled and raved and waxed about the coming Nordic Empire. And there's me, pathetic, nodding away, chuckling nervously, mumbling my approval, 'Absolutely... excellent idea... he'll make a marvellous Messiah... incredible it's taken so long... The Jews, huh!'

The two men were focused intently on slicing the heads off a fresh round of eggs – one because he was so fastidious, the other because he was still drunk – when I saw a glimmer of an opening to wriggle out of my quest, or at least raise some doubts about it in their minds, get them wondering if it was such a great idea after all. I gathered myself, cleared my throat and leant forward. Being the coward, I made my stand on intellectual grounds, not moral ones, and I squeaked: 'Very inspiring, fantastic, so true, but, but – and I am just covering our backs here – if we despise Christianity and Judaism so deeply, will people not see it as a little strange that we should be so eager to co-opt the holy relics of these fatuous religions and hold them aloft as trophies for our great country? I mean, who cares about the Holy Grail, when, as you put it so well, the only true Messiah is the Führer, not a mere itinerant carpenter of Judaean provenance?' Ugh! I squirm when I recall hearing myself. Pathetic!

Slicing a rectangle of toast with slow precision, dipping it into the yolk, his mouth open waiting to receive it, Himmler stared at me as though I had just confessed I was the Chief Rabbi of Jerusalem and had to rush off to a bar mitzvah with my communist Mongol girlfriend.

He laid down the toast, placed his elbows on the table, his chin on his hands and – almost pausing between each word, as though I were a foreigner asking directions – said, 'Otto, you great cretin, have you not listened to a single word I have said to you over the last few days? Was Jesus a Jew, Otto? No, he was not. What was he, Otto? He was an Aryan of Amorite-Germanic extraction. An Aryan. *Ergo…*' – and he rapped a fist of knuckles on the top of his head – '*ergo*, Otto, the Holy Grail is not a Christian relic but a Nordic one. If you remain confused, may I suggest that the next time you visit a library you seek out some images of him from the Early Byzantine period. Do they paint him as a semi-negroid? No, they do not, Otto. He is an Aryan as plain as the day is long.'

'Well, yes, but by then the Church had…'

He held up his hand and, his voice quickening and rising, eyes misting behind the half-moons, continued: 'Must I remind you that the great scholars of the new Reich are out there right now, busy proving that we – we, the Teutonic tribes of prehistory – did sweep into the East and establish ourselves as the ruling class until some sort of catastrophe – a flood or famine perhaps, I don't know. Does it matter? What does it matter? – led to our decline and the rise of the sub-humans, the Jews, the Slavs, the French and so on… And you still cling to the myths and lies spun to you by the corrupt Church of Rome? No, Otto, of course you do not.'

He folded the long slice of eggy toast into his mouth and worked it around his cheeks as a squirrel might go to work on a large acorn. When you play someone inferior at tennis, your level tends to drop to theirs. I was now flailing to fire back any sort of rejoinder at all. I stammered like a fool, caught between speaking frankly and exciting the temper of my host and benefactor. Weisthor, draining his Pils and burping into his napkin, brought our conversational rally to a close. Leaning forward, he whispered, 'Otto, you have taken a bit of an intellectual drubbing, haven't you? Put simply, what Heinrich is saying is that the Holy Grail is an electrifying pan-psychic symbol of the hegemony of the Aryan race. Let's leave it that, shall we? And go and find it.'

Himmler stabbed a freshly dripping slice of toast at me and said: 'Precisely!'

The one high note to be struck over our eggs was Weisthor's announcement, on lurching to his feet, that he would be unable to join me in the foothills of the Pyrenees for at least several weeks. He had, he sighed, to finish his planning document for a project involving the construction of a 20-kilometre-deep elevator shaft down into the kingdom of Agarthi. In Hungary or the Himalayas. He wasn't sure about the best route in, and it was this detail he needed to nail down in consultation with the Ahnenerbe's geological department. Himmler agreed that this should be his priority. If I needed any guidance in locating the Grail while in Languedoc, I was to cable the Ahnenerbe's Berlin headquarters and Karl Maria would make the appropriate ancestral enquiries from there.

I was in a state of some agitation, reflecting on the madness of my new employers, for the greater part of my journey south from Paris Montparnasse. Seated in the front carriage for seven hours, the monotonous roar and chug of the engine, the shrill blasts of the whistle, the screeching of the brakes, the smoke and steam battering my window, the furious intent of the train to get to Toulouse – all of it compounding my disquiet about the vague and impossible task – and dangerous one – that lay before me.

But from the moment I crossed platforms and boarded the branch line train to the medieval town of Foix, my mood began to transform. The four-carriage train weaved its way at a leisurely pace through the lightly rolling plains of the Ariège, the villages and towns growing fewer and further between the closer we headed towards the Pyrenees. The unsettling thoughts of Berlin, Wewelsburg, Himmler and Weisthor – the new Germany! – began receding deeper into the backcountry of my mind with every little station stop.

Brushing the banks of the picturesque river, we puffed through endless fields of young wheat and sunflowers, orchards of plum and apple, groves of walnut and chestnut, all bathed in the sweetest May sunshine. Then on we went into a new landscape, the foothills of the Pyrenees, spliced with wooded gorges, the great peaks beyond still crowned with snow, my spirits rising by the kilometre.

It was of course only an illusion. The distance from my troubles was only geographical, but it was an illusion I was only too happy to indulge. Stepping out of the station at Foix, I breathed air so fresh I could taste. Gazing up at the magnificent little castle on its rock with its flowing skirt of red roofs, all my troubles melted away as fast as the cascades of thawing snow spilling down the escarpment beyond. This place lifts my spirits quicker than a double espresso or a shot of pastis.

Foix was the end of the railway line, but where I was heading, the old Cathar village of Montségur, feels more like the end of the world, an impression reinforced by the fact that the road up from the plains comes to an abrupt halt there. If you want to proceed further south, up into the Pyrenees and across to Spain or the Principality of Andorra, you must do so either on foot or horseback. Either that, which I don't recommend you try, or you head back ten kilometres to the main road and then go east or west for some distance, before you will find a stretch of asphalt that probes a little deeper into the mountains. The main crossing routes are found in the low foothills along the coast at either end of the range.

My taxicab twisted and crawled its way up the switchbacks through steepening wooded hillsides, the evergreens happily rubbing shoulders with the ash, beech and chestnut – the middling elevation of these foothills welcoming the leaf-bearers too. From the turning at the hamlet of Montferrier, for the entire route to Montségur you will see no dwelling other than the occasional stone shelter for the goatherd and the hunter. Otherwise, it's just the woodland and the meadows carpeted with flowers, the odd herd of cattle, golden eagles and griffon vultures soaring and scanning high above, all with the optical illusion that the Pyrenees are rising higher and higher the closer you advance along the narrow unwalled track.

There was good reason why the Cathar dissidents of the thirteenth century chose Montségur as the location to make their last stand against the Pope's crusader army. An army had to get there first, then once they had witnessed the impregnability of the tiny castle, they'd have to go away and come up with a clever way of bringing up the cannons and all the other impedimenta necessary for a year or so of sieging. Seven hundred years on it was toiling enough getting there in a self-propelled vehicle powered by an internal combustion engine on a tar-and-chip road, albeit a crude one. Heaving a thousand tons of iron and provisions over that terrain will have made for extremely thirsty work. They must have really wanted to exterminate those Cathars – half a million of them all told, the bloodiest organised slaughter of a single group of people Europe has ever known.

Not that the hairpin bends and the plunging drops to our right appeared to concern my driver, Raymond, his elbow on the open window, face shrouded in the thick blue smoke from the Gitanes wedged in his teeth. He spent much of our journey twisted around to share his colourful opinions on the progress of the civil war raging on the other side of the mountains. At every bend, I had to bite my lip not to yell, 'Eyes on what little road there is, *s'il vous plaît mon ami*!'

But that was the lesser source of my discomfort, compared to my German-ness, sitting there so Teutonically on his back seat. It was evidently a cargo he would prefer to have left unshipped at Foix. By the time – three Gitanes later – we had negotiated the final rising bend and came upon the castle of Montségur, I had drunk deep from the well of his wisdom on the subject of Germany's national characteristics.

A town called Guernica in the Basque country had been laid to waste by Luftwaffe bombers just a few weeks earlier. I had known nothing of this at the time, the atrocity not being suitable propaganda material back home, I supposed; on cresting the last hill, I was apologising as though I had dropped the bombs with my own hands. I had no way of verifying his claims but he – a half-Basque – was so passionate in his account of the slaughter, I felt ashamed. Ashamed too that I was now a junior officer in my country's military, happily putting its name to atrocities in wars of no real concern to them. I suppose I did have Spanish and Basque blood on my hands.

When I asked him to be dropped below the path up to the castle, a mere pinhead on its steepling outcrop, he swamped me with apologies of his own, insisting he had meant no offence to me directly. Once you got to know one, he promised me, there was great merit to be found in the character of the German – a reassurance he qualified with quite a long list of counterweighing imperfections, such that he came full circle and ended up lathering me with apologies all over again. Indeed, the cycle of insult and contrition might well have gone on forever, me standing at his window, nodding and frowning, holding out my francs, on and on until my hair went grey and I dropped dead of malnutrition.

I offered my own reassurances that no offence had been taken, that I was keen to walk down to the village for the air and the view, and that he might well be onto something about the lust for blood buried in the soul 'not of the commerce-minded German, but of the war-mongering Prussian.' Big mistake. Raymond had some strong views on the Franco-Prussian War of 1870 too, and several minutes into his disquisition, sensing he was not anticipating another fare that day, I dropped my money and a good tip into his lap, bade him good day and a pleasant journey back to Foix and mind those bends, *au revoir, a bientot!*

He shouted after me, 'Hey, Hermann, what are you planning to do in Montségur then?'

Over my shoulder, I told him the truth. 'Find the Holy Grail! What else?'

Raymond threw back his head and roared, the pale green Renault Monasix rocking on its suspension under the force of his mirth. I could still hear howls of weeping laughter on the wind as he made a three-point turn in the gravel and disappeared back down his side of the hill. Fair enough.

•◆•

When I had last been in Montségur, the snow lay half a metre deep and the tiled roofs of Montségur's dwellings and farm buildings, packed tight as stones on a beach, were lost under a blanket of white. From where I set off now, back in January the only indications of a human settlement below had come from the wood smoke rising from the chimneys, the occasional peel of the three bells in the gable of the little Romanesque church and the incessant tamp of the blacksmith's hammer. The village's one rubber-wheeled tractor had become the sole way in or out, the steep icy road too treacherous even for hobnailed boots and winter horseshoes.

How different it was now. The verges of the road swayed with angelica and cornflowers, afternoon sun beat down on the cattle in the meadow below the village, icy water trickled through mossy rocks, and the songs of courting birds streamed from quivering undergrowth. It was every bit as beautiful as any scene to be found in the Odenwald or the lower Alps – and that's perhaps why I had felt so at home here. That and the warmth of most of its inhabitants and, of course, my fascination with the story of the Cathars, whose extinction was sealed right here when two hundred of them, to save the others, offered themselves up and were burnt on a giant funeral pyre just outside the village, in the field right below me to my right, bringing to an end a century of persecution by the Church.

Oral tradition, myth, legend, nonsense – call it what you will – but they still tell you stories down here about the siege of 1244 as though they themselves had witnessed the events at first hand. I have spent entire evenings in the bar, staggering away to bed with the impression that it was only the previous week the siege had been brought to its bloody end. But the one story no one will be drawn on is the one in which I now had the greatest interest – the Holy Grail.

In my research I had found several references in near-enough contemporary accounts alleging that on the night before the Montségur surrender, four knights smuggled out the Holy Grail and other relics, scaling down the steepest side of the outcrop under the cover of darkness. According to whichever account you read, the treasures were then taken over the mountains to Montserrat Abbey near Barcelona or the Templar town of Tomar in Portugal, perhaps even ferried over the water to Glastonbury in England. Everyone has their own version of events.

Many claim the relics never left Languedoc at all and remain hidden nearby, possibly in one of the many huge cave networks in which the Cathars sought shelter from their persecutors. And it is the locals' uncharacteristic silence on the subject that has made me wonder whether, just possibly, there might be some truth in it. Anyhow, if ever it is sensible to set out on a hunt for the Holy Grail, which of course it is not, Montségur was no bad place for me to while away a few months. And hope that Heinrich Himmler was going to forget all about me.

Halfway down the coil of switchbacks, I could see a few villagers, matchstick figures beetling about amongst the narrow, cobbled streets and alleys. It was still so steep that I had an almost bird's-eye view and when I turned around, the little castle up on its eyrie was lost to view. The road continues into the village, the switchback snaking into three short stretches through the houses, stopping at the gate into the meadow, a wide glaciated scoop of grassland reaching out towards Spain, twisting around corners through dizzying cliffs and slopes.

Unlike Raymond, or Himmler for that matter, I

won't make sweeping comments about races of people or even the inhabitants of one small village. It is all very well to say 'Oh, the Norwegian is a dependable fellow... the Hindoo is a man of peace... the Jew is so astute with his money...' but there is a second side to every coin. So, the man telling you that the Norwegian is reliability itself, is just as likely to say, 'The Irishman is a fiendish crook... the Englishman a pompous bore... the Frenchman an insufferable hypocrite.' And you hear people all the while making these dreadful denunciations and mindless estimations of entire races – millions of people, dismissed or endorsed with a couple of adjectives.

No, I won't do that, and I was reminded of the folly of such an attitude to life as the road flattened out a little and I found myself back on the cobbles of Montségur. For in that village, there are many wonderful, friendly, generous, resourceful and intelligent people, but there also as many bores, curmudgeons, adulterers, bullies, misers and misanthropes. If I am unable to generalise about the people of a tiny village – where you would imagine the remoteness of the location would create a greater uniformity of behavioural characteristics – how can Raymond disparage an entire nation of people made up of so many independent states and cities, faiths and race communities? How can Himmler say that all Slavs are sub-human?

I was barely one foot inside the village when perfect proof of my diversity argument came bounding up the cobbles. At first, from its luxuriant coat and lolloping gait, I thought it was one of Montségur's many dogs that run wild through the alleys and lanes. It was only when he threw his arms in the air and shouted 'Otto!' that I realised it was Poilu, the village werewolf.

I am not kidding. I cannot for the life of me remember the proper medical term for his complaint, but Poilu suffered – if that's the correct term – from a congenital condition commonly known as 'werewolf syndrome.' He was covered in a coat of shiny brown hair from head to foot, including the face. It should really be called 'primate syndrome' because if Poilu were to strip naked and sit up a tree in the monkey house peeling a banana, no visitor to the zoo would bat an eyelid. The more astute observer might stop and remark about the peculiarly striking similarities between that species of hominid and that of *homo sapiens*, wondering why no one before Charles Darwin had made the obvious connection. But even a pre-eminent zoologist would likely walk on to the reptiles' house none the wiser that it was a human being squatting on that branch enjoying the banana.

During my long stay in Montségur, I was never able to establish whether it was a village yarn or a matter of truth that, moments after Poilu's birth, his father ran from the family guesthouse, pursued by his naked, bleeding wife, and dropped the boy into the communal well next to the church square. Poilu, so the story goes, plunged 40 feet, plopping straight into the half-submerged bucket. (His father having assumed that his wife had suffered a mental disturbance and indulged in non-marital relations with some form of beast. How else, he later pleaded, might one explain the emergence from her loins of a creature covered in fur?)

The mother, Beatrice, highly distraught, cranked the bucket back to the surface, turned Poilu upside down and slapped the water from his lungs. She sat straight down on a bench in the shade of the plane trees and applied him to her breast, triggering uproar amongst the old men enjoying a late afternoon game of pétanque. They laugh about it now, but I understand that at the time, the incident was regarded as the most dramatic event to occur in the village since Simon de Montfort rode in to exterminate the last of the Cathars seven hundred years earlier.

It took an eminent doctor from the Society of Medicine in Paris to confirm that Poilu was indeed a human being, one of no more than a few dozen on the entire planet to be born with 'werewolf syndrome.' His father, another Raymond – most of the men in this region are called Raymond – was delighted to learn he had fathered such a rare and exotic creature. The froideur of the other villagers took a while longer to thaw, but once Poilu had learned to smile and laugh and walk, all the time showing no special love for fruit or climbing trees, his popularity soared.

He was christened Bertrand, but everyone knew him from the day of his birth as Poilu, which means 'hairy' in French. It was also a term of endearment for French infantrymen of the Great War, because they often sported shaggy beards – and there was an element of that same endearment for Poilu's spirit too. At sixteen now, an awkward age for many, he remains the most likeable and engaging of children and, though I would never dare say it in earshot of the inhabitants, he is also, by some distance, the most intelligent creature in the village, possibly in all Languedoc.

I only mistook him for a dog because, it being warm, he was wearing nothing but shorts and slipper-shoes made of dark canvas and flat roped soles. He was also a long way off when I spotted him and, in his excitement, he was leaning well forward as he ran up the hill, arms lolloping before him.

It was an easy mistake to make and I was by no means the first to do so. Poilu has suffered a great many misunderstandings over the years, especially with hunters when he's been out foraging for mushrooms or just larking about in the woods. He has been fired at several times, once receiving a full blast of shot to his backside – it took the dentist three hours to remove all the pellets, his father plying him with Armagnac to dull the pain.

And, proving the problem, he did leap up at me as though he were a long-lost dog and me its master. Had he been born with a tail – and that may well have been a close shave – it would have been wagging furiously.

He buried his furry face under my armpit, and I sat down my suitcase to give him a tight hug.

He said: 'I have been waiting in the square for you all day.'

'You have? But I might have been years.'

'There is a telegram waiting for you.'

'What? Already?'

'Yes, from Germany.'

I groaned, suspecting bad or irritating news. Heini asking if I had found the Holy Grail yet probably. Or Mother reminding me to wear a hat in the sun.

'I put it up in your room. Mother made it up after I told her you were coming. She's made a pig trotter casserole too, to celebrate your return. Tomorrow, we're having whole veal head.'

'Oh… Good.' I might have said it more convincingly, but over the previous months I had tried to forget the French custom of eating any creature from land, sea and air from its nose to its tail. If it has a pulse, the French will cook it, any of it.

'I like it when you come. We eat so much better.' He put his hand in mine and we walked down towards the little church square, winding between the piles of dung, me wondering quite what on earth the Trencavel family ate when I wasn't there, a few villagers smiling and waving from behind their garden walls as we passed.

'So, how have you been, Poilu? Have you been studying hard?'

'Can we speak in German?'

'Certainly.'

And so he did, like a native – born in about 1600, all his languages being learned from old books.

'Well, I am very happy, thank you for asking. They've released me from that boring school for the rest of the year.'

'No! Why ever? You are the best pupil.'

'Exactly. It's because I have finished all this year's work and next.'

'So, what do you do with your time now?'

'A great deal more than I used to. I have translated Ovid's *Metamorphoses* into French. I tried to turn it into German for you, but there were too many classical allusions and I got bored. So, I'm doing Horace's Odes for you instead. The rest of the time, it's easy.'

'The rest of the time? Men have spent their entire lives translating Ovid, barely having time to eat or wash. *Metamorphoses* has 12,000 lines – of poetry!'

'Yeah, yeah. So the rest of the time I'm the *bon a tout faire* for the village. I do everything. Milk cows, deliver the post, help in the bakery, look after the honeybees, wash the old people. And Father Pietro let me serve mass last week when he had a really bad hangover. I am always doing something.'

'You served mass? Good heavens. And how was your ministry received by the congregation?'

'They didn't notice. Madame Marty is blind and hard of hearing, Madame Dondaine is yet to emerge from her winter madness – she bit me when I was forcing in the Eucharist.'

Poilu showed me his hand as proof but, owing to the fur, I could see no wound.

'The Church is still a danger to the people of Montségur, I see!'

'Not really. It's more of a village hall these days. The table-tennis table is in there all year round now. Father wants to convert it into a winter sty for his Gascons. Or a boxing ring. Father Pietro wouldn't notice or care. He spends most of his time at the bar, or down the well.'

'The well – still?'

'Yes, more and more in fact. He says if he doesn't maintain it, it will collapse, and the spring will ruin the foundations of all the buildings downhill from it. But I think he has a longing to be in Hell.'

You can hold your breath at the edge of Montségur and reach the church square at its heart – and the well – without the need of a second breath. Over 200 people live there but it is one of the quirks of mountain life – perhaps of human nature – that in spite of the great space available, the inhabitants choose to live piled on top of one another. That is the case almost literally in Montségur where four rows of houses hug the tight twists of the lanes down the steep hill to the meadow. If you stood outside a house on the top row you could throw a stone and hit a man standing in his garden on the bottom row.

That's exactly what happened when Poilu's father Raymond fell out with the blacksmith, Fournier. On Poilu's first birthday, Fournier had forged a portable iron cage and left it outside the Trencavels, together with a basket of fruit, a straw bed and a small drinking trough. For weeks afterwards, the blacksmith was subjected to a hail of stones from the top of the village. The stones clattered onto the corrugated iron roof of his smithy throughout the day, the blacksmith responding to Raymond by making monkey noises, jumping up and down and scratching his armpits. After a lucky shot struck him on the skull one morning, Monsieur Fournier took to wearing his Adrian helmet from the Great War whenever he ventured outside his home or smithy. It wasn't until the Paris doctor produced the certificate confirming Poilu as *homo sapiens* that the two men were able to bury their feud and pick up their long friendship over a bottle of pastis.

I exhaled, loud enough for Poilu to throw me a look. The Ariège may be one of the most rustic and least wealthy regions of France but, with such an abundance of nature about them, the inhabitants live well and, with time on their hands, they have been able to construct very charming dwellings in which, during the hottest months, they sit and wait for their vines, fruit trees and fields to ripen. The Trencavels are one of the wealthier families – Raymond holding down half a dozen occupations – and the family home consists of three storeys, with sky-blue shutters for the eight windows and a pergola for shading running the length of the house draped in vines now just coming into bloom. Between the ground-floor windows, sits a two-leaf door of pale green that tends to be left open in the warmer months, day and night, with the result that humans and animals come and go as they please.

As I reached the top of the steep steps from the lane, Raymond was standing in that doorway, arms outstretched, a giant smile splitting his enormous beard, swallows shooting back and forth over his shoulders. He threw off his huge straw hat, strode across the gravel terrace, hens erupting over the flowerpots to avoid the tramp of his great knee-length boots. Still holding my suitcase, fedora still on my head, I found myself heading skywards at great speed. I was being lifted by the armpits, so high I could see into my room on the first floor. When he brought me back to face level, he beamed at me like I was his grandchild, kissed me four times on the cheeks, threw out his arms again, and I crashed back to earth with a thud and a stumble.

'Otto, you're back! If we do go to war again, it will be terrible to have to bayonet you. I may even lock you in the byre until hostilities are over.'

'Why, thank you, Raymond! It's a great pleasure to see you too, and I do so hope it doesn't come to bayonets or byres while I'm here.'

'Come in and see Beatrice.' And he slapped me on the back with such force that I flew into the house as if I had been running to greet her.

The house opens straight into the living area, and Madame Trencavel was in the kitchen half to the left over a steaming cauldron on the iron stove, an array of copper utensils hanging above her head. She was holding a pig trotter on a ladle, sipping the sauce from it, her head rocking from side to side, 'Cette Chanson est Pour Vous' crackling at full volume on the wind-up gramophone.

I dropped my suitcase and walked over, she dropped the trotter back into the cauldron with a splash and, wiping her fingers on the apron over her black twilled dress, she turned and gave me a greeting only slightly less enthusiastic than her husband's. Fortunately, she is a little shorter than me, with a delicate figure, and there was no chance of me cracking my head on the heavy-beamed ceiling. Instead, she squeezed me until my eyes almost popped into the trotter casserole (they'd still get eaten), only stopping when the needle scraped over the record and Raymond boomed, 'If I have to listen to that buttock-oyster Jean Sablon one more time, I think I am going to break that record over my knee!'

Beatrice shrugged her shoulders and, whipping out her dishcloth, snapped it at him and bit back, 'Well, if you want to buy me a new one, please do! Now, Otto, you must be exhausted. You are to sit down there, drink Kir and eat salted almonds, and tell me why Germany wants to go to war with us again.'

I was tired, it was true, and I settled into the deep leather armchair by the window, with its view over the rooftops down into the valley washed in gold with the last of the day's sun. Beatrice laid down my glass and bowl of almonds on the shelf next to me, I crossed my ankles and placed my shoes on the footrest and let out a long sigh. To be a thousand miles from Heinrich Himmler in any direction from Berlin can only be a relief, but to be back in the company of the Trencavels, the beauty of the Pyrenees laid out before me… Well, it had been some time since I had felt so unburdened of worries. In fact, not since my last visit here had I felt that almost physical sensation of happiness.

I began to doze off, twice jerking myself awake, and seeing my tiredness, Beatrice had the good grace to go back to her trotters and postpone my news about life in Germany under the National Socialists. She was laying down my third Kir, this time with a bowl of olives, garlic cloves and chilli flakes, when she yelped as if she had stood on a nail.

'My God! Your telegram! Poilu!'

Poilu came scampering in through the back door, wearing a beekeeper's netted pith helmet.

'Poilu, go and fetch Otto's telegram. My apologies, I completely forgot.'

I sat up and levered myself onto my feet. So had I, my mind deliberately burying all thoughts of Germany, no doubt.

Poilu shot down the stairs and handed me a little brown envelope stamped twice in blue with the word 'Urgent'. My stomach twisted, and I presumed the worst about Father. I tore at the envelope, fear physically yanking at my heart. Unfolding the letter,

I was relieved then instantly alarmed to see in the heading that the origin of the communication was Mitte district, Berlin. It was from Ingrid:

Himmler knows you know. On guard!

CHAPTER SIX

I set off down the hill to the post office, swallowing burps and rubbing the life back into my eyes. An uncomfortable night wrestling with Ingrid's warning – Himmler knows I know what for God's sake? – had not been helped by a belly full of goose liver paté, pig trotter casserole (two trotters each), Rogallais cheese, a cherry clafoutis, the better part of a carafe of coarse red wine, and two Armagnacs. On a Monday.

Madame Dondaine was engaged in lively conversation with herself on a bench in the recess of the high stone wall. I slowed up, weighing whether to interrupt and wish her good morning, when Poilu came haring around the bend, scattering sparrows. He waved an envelope at me and shouted: 'Another one, Otto! Just through on the wires.'

God, who now? Or what? I ran a thumbnail under the flap, asking, 'Do you sleep in that beekeeper's helmet, Poilu?'

'Only when I forget to take it off.'

I pulled out the message from the little brown envelope and unfolded it. This one was from Berlin too, but the address of origin was 8, Prinz-Albrecht-Strasse, the sender 'HH'. I groaned loud enough for Poilu to look up from the caterpillar he was picking up with a stick. It read: *You saw nothing, you say nothing. Honour means blind loyalty. Dishonour the end.*

I stared at the slip of paper, Poilu staring up at me. What on earth was he on about? Saw what? His leading sorcerer Weisthor being insensibly drunk? His plinth for the Holy Grail in the crypt and the ridiculous Eternal Flame that had gone out owing to a problem with the gas supply? We walked on, around the bend into the bottom of the village – and I pulled up sharply. What an idiot. I wriggled out the shiver running down my back. Hedwig! Of course. She *had* seen me in the corridor at Wewelsburg then.

So, he knew I knew his dirty secret, one with potential to wreck the reputation of the chief of German police, make a mockery of his campaign for a return to wholesome German living, destroy his career and leave his grand ambitions for a Teutonic Empire in ruins. I chuckled – but the laugh was gone as quick as it came, in a blink and cough, banished by a wave of nausea and a surge of fears that made me even more lightheaded and unsteady.

'Do you want to come and see my new beehives? I built them myself.'

'Not now, Poilu, not now. Later, I promise. I must go to the post office. Come on.'

'You look like a corpse.'

149

'Not all knowledge is good, Poilu. Sometimes it can be deadly. And your father pours a brave wine.'

'Deadly? Like Hegel. Or Kant.'

'No, I mean fatal to its possessor. Not mind-numbing.'

The post office doubled as a bistro and it was busy as usual but quiet, the air heavy with smoke and strong coffee, the locals buried in newspapers, *Paris-Soir* and *La Dépêche du Midi* mainly, all carrying grim headlines about the war in Spain. Fournier, the blacksmith, had the paper spread out over the greasy leather apron canvassing his vast belly.

I squeezed past his table, raising my eyebrows by way of *bonjour*. He folded the paper and turned it towards me. The lead story concerned the siege of Madrid, but Fournier poked the headline of a side column: *German Warships Shell Almeria, Many Dead*. I shook my head, saying 'C'est terrible, c'est dégueulasse. Je suis désolé.' It was, I was. What business of ours was Spain's civil war?

He glared and mumbled, 'You'll be coming for France next – again.' I repeated my distress at the news, put my hand on his shoulder and made my way to the post office counter. Ordinarily, I'd receive hearty greetings in the café, sometimes even a kiss or an embrace, but not this morning. Another bad day to be a German – and thank God no one knew I was now a Hauptsturmführer in the SS. One or two half-looked up, no nod or smile, just a blank face, and sheepishly I wove through the silent smoky tables, Poilu following like a faithful dog.

I quickly filled out two telegraph forms at the counter,

handed them to Madame Califano and received a curt, formal, 'Je vous remercie, Monsieur Eckhart.' To Himmler I wrote: *No idea what you are talking about! Loyalty absolute.* To Ingrid: *Thanks. Keep me posted.* Madame Califano typed in the messages in a blur of fingers, counted the words and said: 'Trente-deux francs et quatre-vingts centimes, Monsieur Eckhart.'

'Really? That seems a bit steep.'

She shrugged and dropped the change into my hand, a cigarette hanging from her mouth, and I hurried back out into the lane. Had it been a barrage of flowers the Germans had let loose over Almeria, Madame Califano would have talked to me just the same. It was not on account of her charm and social graces that she had risen to the position of Chief Postmistress in Montségur. His face creased in apology, Poilu said, 'French people prefer smallpox to Germans these days, I'm afraid. I still like you though.'

I thanked him, patting him on the shoulder, and spilled out my predicament. (I was careful not to pat Poilu too often and never on the head.) Dear Poilu was never going to turn his back on me, even if the Luftwaffe chose to bomb Montségur itself. It was a sad truth of my life that this teenage medical curiosity from a remote mountain village was probably my best friend in the world, possibly ever. Now I realised he might even be able to help. And I did need help. I had to start taking action. I needed to stop being so passive and feeble, be more assertive, stop allowing other people to determine my fate and walk all over me, stop waiting for the next bad thing to happen and then moan and get knock-kneed over it. I needed to grow up, and fast. Bad things were brewing. Poilu was more resourceful, bolder and more determined than me – and he was half my age and, to all appearances, half orangutan.

'So you see, I need to move quickly, Poilu. The whole Grail thing is absurd to you and I, but not to Himmler and his gang, and I have to show I'm on the trail of it, feed them some evidence I'm onto something, win back some favour, buy some time to think of an escape route, a solution. These people are pitiless. They wouldn't hesitate to…'

'There's an obvious place to start.'

'Father Pietro?'

Poilu nodded. 'They say he knows more about the Grail legend than any living person.'

'I know – a former curator in the Vatican's Holy Relics collection. But he wasn't much help when I was writing my book, was he? He avoided me like the Spanish Inquisition. A turbulent priest, that Father Pietro, spooked. And he wakes up drunk.'

'You are right, but you need some leads; he needs pastis and cigarettes. Answer: get him drunk, buy him some smokes. No harm in trying. He let me say Mass for six Gauloises. He's going to be in one of two places. This way!'

We set off at a canter up a steep straight alley, a shortcut through the switchbacks to the top of the village, ducking our heads beneath the laundry hanging from first floor windows. Heart pounding, lungs heaving, cursing and vowing to quit smoking, when I finally trailed and wheezed into the church square, Poilu was leaning over the ancient stone well under its little bandstand canopy. A rope ladder fixed to the railings behind ran down into the darkness.

He shouted: 'Father Pietro!' The words echoed and faded to nothing. 'It's Poilu, Father!' Turning to me, he added: 'He falls asleep on the ledge down there sometimes but that's usually after a day in the bar. Come on, this way.'

'What about the church?'

Poilu threw me a look. 'The last place I'd look.'

Another alley, cobbles cushioned by damp moss, led along the upper terrace of the village to a smaller square where the tabac, the bar, the boulangerie and the butcher's each claimed one of the four sides. We stopped in the shadow of the fountain, a surprisingly ornate affair for a small village, four gargoyles at the top of a column spewing spring water into a wedding cake of basins, the bottom one ringed in colourful flower boxes. The shuttered doors of the bar had been folded back against the walls and two weather-beaten old farmers sat playing chess over Kirs under a tricolore awning.

'Look, there he is, having his breakfast.' He nodded towards the bar and, finding his wristwatch in the fur of his wrist, said, 'I'm late for Monsieur Califano's weekly wash. I must hurry. Good luck.'

Father Pietro sat at the counter, fist under his chin, eyes as milky as the glass of pastis into which he was pouring water from a small carafe. He was perched on a stool at the corner and, without acknowledging him, I took the one on the other side of the right angle, my back to the square. Michel, the proprietor, sidled down the bar polishing a glass with his apron. He raised his eyebrows by way of taking my order, none too friendly. He too must have heard that I had issued the commands to bombard Almeria and raze Guernica.

'Café serré et—' And I waggled a finger at the priest's pastis, half trying to stir the gloomy man's attention.

'For you or for him?'

'Me.'

The priest drained his glass, slid from his stool and looked at me warily from under his shaggy salt-and-pepper eyebrows. Tough to gauge the age of a drunk, but I figured he was younger than he looked, maybe forty-five. And he looked a little older since I last saw him.

'Good morning, Father.'

'Is it?' He made for the door.

I tossed a full packet of Gauloises onto the counter and they slid towards his empty glass. 'Are you sure I can't get you a drink?'

He looked back at his seat, waved me away with a backward swipe and walked out. I jumped off my stool and followed him into the square, shouting after him: 'Please, Father, I'm in trouble. I need your help.'

He stopped but didn't turn around, then continued to shuffle past the fountain, head down. I turned to Michel, held up a spread hand to indicate I'd be back in five minutes and trotted up to Father Pietro.

He was waiting for me. Much can be lost in translation when an Italian with a heavy Sicilian accent talks to a German, even in perfect French, but there could be little doubting his meaning, just from the tone and stress alone. 'If it's help with your fool's errand you want, forget it and fuck off.'

'Father, I don't believe in holy relics any more than I believe in miracles.'

'Then why are you following me? What do you need of me?'

Walking side-on to him, scissoring my legs back and forth, I explained the crazy task I had been assigned, my fear of Himmler, his lunatic plans, my worry for my parents, the urgency to come up with something credible to protect me from the Nazis. We had reached the far end of the square by the time I had finished rushing out the abridged version of my story. He sat down on the wall of the well, staring past me up at the gabled belfry of the church, mid-morning sun shafting between the trinity of bells.

'That's all I ask, Father. I tell Himmler that I have hired you, a former curator of the Holy Relics Collection in Rome, such a great authority, to guide my search – he'll lap that up like a dachshund. I'll send him periodic reports, photographs, testimonies, create the impression I'm getting closer, string it out, hope he forgets about me... Feed me whatever moonshine you like. He won't be able to resist that. He'll believe anything that plays to his vanity. Himmler – the man who led the hunt for the Holy Grail! And brought it back to its rightful home – Germany!'

Father Pietro snorted a sarcastic laugh, rubbed his palms up and down his face and blew out his cheeks.

He looked down at his worn leather sandals – I'm pretty sure to hide some brimming tears because he was croaking a little when he spoke. Maybe it was just the hangover.

'I guess we now have something in common then.'

'We do?'

'Yes, we do. I know what it is to be chased, harried, bullied and threatened too.'

'You do?'

'Yes, by an organisation every bit as ruthless as your National Socialists.'

'You mean Mussolini and his fascists?'

'No.'

'The Mafia then?'

'No.'

'The Communists?'

'No.'

'The French legal system, the authorities here?'

'No.'

I shook my head. 'Okay, I give up.'

'Who has persecuted more people in the history of

European civilisation, prosecuted more wars than any other ruling body, dynasty or government?'

'Ah! The Roman Catholic Church?'

'Correct.'

'But why you? You're a priest, one of their own?'

'In title only. I lost my faith years ago – no secret there. But *they* really didn't like that. Imagine, a man working at the heart of the mysteries of the Holy Roman Church amongst all those relics – and he loses his faith. It was heresy for them. I might just as well have jumped on the altar in St Peter's and bared my arse at Papa Pius himself.'

I sat down next to him, hands on the wall. Not looking straight at him, figuring he might feel less threatened and talk more.

'What happened? Was it overnight – a reverse epiphany – the collapse of your belief?'

'I was raised in a devout family, I knew nothing else, never questioned it. The relics were my fascination – a physical, real link to Christ and the disciples, the saints, to God himself! The thrill that you could touch a garment worn by St Peter, see the finger that Doubting St Thomas stuck in the wound of the Risen Lord … But in the end, it was the relics themselves that killed the mystery for me. They shook my faith, made me think about it all a little deeper.'

He looked away, exhaling hard and scratching the side of his scalp.

'So, what changed?'

Genuinely curious now, not just seeking favour, seeing the padre in a new light and warming to him, him opening up. I had known him for many years, prompting and probing him for knowledge, to get at his story, and now finally, he was giving himself up.

'The rapture, the mystery – it soon goes. Soon goes when you're on the inside, see the goatshit for what it is. Believe me. Take the Holy Foreskin. This is no joke. I have seen four Holy Foreskins, all their owners claiming the little prepuce they bring in a jar of pickle belonged to the Messiah.'

I cut off my nervous laugh and apologised.

'No, you're right to laugh. Guy must have had a lot of penises because when I left – exiled in disgrace – we had seventeen claims on our books for the Holy Foreskin. Like one of the Three Wise Men corked it in a ceramic jar at the stable in Bethlehem, labelled it "Messiah – Foreskin 25/12/0".'

Father Pietro picked up some gravel and tipped it back and forth between his hands, then tossed it behind him into the well.

'It's a big top circus,' he continued. 'Relics are the window display to draw in the customers. It's a giant con, a hoax. The Church is keen to push the myths. It's all part of the mass hypnosis, holding onto the power.'

'So, how did it end there for you, over in Rome?'

'Long story. There was a big criminal investigation at the Vatican, all *sub rosa* of course, all hushed up. I don't really want to go into it again but, in short, there was a heist in the Relics collection – a whole lot of stuff was taken. They pointed the finger at me because I was suspect by then, everyone knew my faith had collapsed. They claimed it must have been an inside job, and that I had the best motive – I was going to defrock myself and sell it all on the black market to my hairy criminal friends in Sicily. You know, they assume, Sicily *ergo* gangster. So, I spend six months in a monastic cell – a prison cell really, solitary confinement. The only person I see is my interrogator from the Vatican's *Corpo della Gendarmeria* and – '

Father Pietro paused, heavy emotion bearing down on him, running his fingers over his head like he was washing his hair.

' – well, let's just say, they must have really wanted to get back what had been taken.'

We sat in silence for a while, watching the house martins swooping in and out of the mud nests under the eaves of the church roof.

'Why here? Montségur?'

He turned towards me and held out his hands as if to say, *think about it*. I saw he had no fingernails on either hand.

'You're the scholar – work it out. We're in the last stronghold of the heretic Cathars. It's a penance – their idea of a joke and a threat all at once.'

'They want to remind you they will go to all lengths to besiege you?'

'Correct. That they can crush me, just as they crushed

half a million other non-believers. So here I am for the rest of my life, imprisoned, a penniless broken drunk, living off the kindness of others. A kind of Purgatory, neither here nor there, neither Heaven nor Hell, no going forward, no going back.'

'Why don't you just leave? Start a new life?'

He paused, then turned, waited till I looked him in his watery eyes and said, 'Yeah, nice idea but...'

'But what? Why not? Just get up and go.'

'My friend, you should know the answer to that. Sure, I could go on the run, maybe to Mongolia or Tahiti, but they'd still hunt me down. And if I were to run, it would prove my guilt. I'm trapped.'

I looked away sharply as though I had been flicked. Lost in his story, I had forgotten my own situation vis-à-vis being trapped by my predicament. He put his arm over my shoulder and said:

'Come on, your pastis will be getting warm and your coffee cold. Let's make a plan. Let's take on Hitler and the Pope. You and me.' It was the first time I had heard him laugh.

•◆•

I hadn't received a telegram for almost a week and I was starting to believe I was out of the woods – or I had mapped a route out at least – when Poilu came panting up the steep steps to the sun-bathed terrace outside the Trencavel home, clutching one of those small brown envelopes. Since my return Poilu had learned that telegrams tended to portend trouble for me these days, and his fuzzy face was set hard, his lips puckered. I placed my pen and daily dispatch for Himmler in my lap and took the message from his outstretched hand, emitting a low groan.

My trousers were rolled up to the knee, my blistered feet luxuriating in a half-barrel of warm water and Epsom salts, insisted upon by Beatrice ('The best thing to come out of England, Otto!'). I turned the envelope over in my fingers, tore at the corner of the fold, then leant over and placed it under my glass of rosé on the upturned flowerpot.

'You not going to open it?'

'I want five more minutes of happiness, Poilu. Father Pietro has run me ragged again. Don't be fooled by the pastis and the Gauloises. That man has got some stamina.'

'Did you go back to Rennes-le-Chateau?'

'No, Lombrives today – where the Cathars used to hide, the largest cave network in France, some say Europe. I'm going for Europe because there is not a muscle in my body that is not crying out in protest.'

'Did you know the Cathedral Cave alone is bigger than Notre Dame?'

'And to get to it you have to crouch like the Hunchback for about five kilometres.'

'You've given up cigarettes – you should be normal again by now.'

'There is nothing normal about a day out with Father Pietro – for the body or the mind.'

'But think of all the good you are doing for him – no one has seen him so happy and full of purpose. Michel says he's down to one bottle of pastis a day and one packet of smokes – and he's started talking to people.'

I rocked back on my chair, looking up at the clusters of tiny grapes hanging from the pergola like so many stalactites. 'Well, I am glad some good is coming from this farcical escapade. Okay, right.'

I swung forward, took the telegram and a deep breath, and ran my finger under the flap. It was from Michelstadt. I read it three times to take in its full import, then put it back in the envelope. I sat back, my mind plunged into dark thought, then stood up in the barrel and turned my head and hands to the sky.

'Zum Teufel! Scheisse! Sturer alter Ochse!' Loud enough for a pair of collared doves to erupt from the pergola foliage.

Poilu took a step back, hunched his shoulders a little, and piped: 'Reichsführer-SS Heinrich Himmler?'

'The Führer, yes. But worse. Führer Eva Clara Eckhart – my mother.' I looked at my watch, adding, 'When does the post office shut, Poilu?'

He glanced over his shoulder at the clock under the church belfry. 'Seven minutes.'

'Grab me a towel.'

Madame Califano was turning the key in the lock when Poilu and I burst into the bottom lane from the steep alley. She was bent forward, her vast breasts, the size of a collier's mooring buoys, fighting the gravitational pull

162

of the earth. Or maybe it was the other way around, the earth's core straining on a tangent towards Montségur.

I said, 'I need to send an urgent telegram, Madame Califano. It's – '

With some effort, she straightened her back and through the cigarette clenched in her yellow teeth, she coughed: 'I'm shut.'

'… to my mother. It's of the utmost importance. I beg you.'

She let the smoke curl over her face a while, then turned back the key, pushed open the door and waddled back to the counter through the upturned chairs. I scrawled out my message while Madame Califano rolled and drummed her fingers like a vexed piano tuner, a thrill mingling with my alarm. In a few moments, the words I wrote would be flying across half a continent and, in about fifteen, Dieter the telegram boy would be on his bicycle, his feet a blur on the pedals, racing through the meadows up to the old farmhouse, my mother opening the door, wiping her hands on her apron, Father buried in a book behind her. A sadness washed over me, picturing him there, scarred and defiant.

Madame Califano put the message down and pointed to a word and said, 'Spell it out please. Your handwriting is worse than my cat's. And I don't speak German.' She thrust me a look with a bayonet on it, adding, 'Yet.'

'D-a-n-g-e-r.' She typed as I spoke.

'And that.'

163

'P-i-g-h-e-a-d-e-d. I am not sure of the exact equivalent in French, Madame Califano, but you know, stubborn, obdurate… like a mule or an old goat – or a big lazy ox.' It was my turn to throw a look, and she responded with the briefest flash of teeth from the topmost corner of her mouth, possibly a smile.

She pressed a few more keys and switches. 'Alright, all done. It's gone,' she said, her head bouncing in time with her breasts as she counted the letters with a dancing finger.

'Vingt-sept.'

I handed her thirty and said, 'Keep the change. I am very grateful to you.'

We walked back up to the top of the village along the twisting main street, the gradient gentler on my stiff limbs than the steep alley, Poilu leaving me alone in my thoughts until we rounded the final bend.

He said, 'If it's private don't worry, but if it helps, do share what's distressing you.'

'My father is a stubborn old bastard – that's what. And now he's in double danger – through no fault of his own, an accident of birth.' I leant up against the wall. 'God, I want a cigarette.'

'What good is that going to do him?'

'Do you know what *mischling* means, Otto?'

He put his furry hand on his furry chin and furrowed his furry brow.

'Yes, literally it means a mixling – a half-breed, a mongrel, a hybrid.'

'Full marks.'

'A little like me, I suppose – wolf-boy.' He laughed at his joke and I put my arm over his shoulder.

'Well, in Germany today, Poilu, it's no fun to be a *mischling*. It's not like here. The authorities, Himmler's bunch, have discovered my father's mother was a Jew from Silesia – a Slav. That wasn't a problem for Germany when my father was fighting the Slavs on the Eastern Front.'

'I don't understand the logic of that.'

'And by reason of my grandfather falling in love with my grandmother, my father is now an undesirable, *Untermensch*, a passive enemy of the state. That makes me a mini-*mischling*, not tarred but tainted with the same brush. Does that make any sense to you?'

'None whatsoever.'

'And the fact he's a devout Christian, a great patriot with an Iron Cross to his name and an outstanding teacher is entirely immaterial.'

'How can he help where his grandmother was born? And what does it matter if she was Jew, Christian or Muslim? They're all Abrahamic religions that claim descent from the Judaism of the earliest Israelites.'

'Quite, Poilu. The next rally at Nuremberg – I'll get Himmler to put that in.'

I turned around, leant my head against the wall and stared down at my oversized espadrilles, leant to me by Raymond. 'Oh my father, Poilu! The main problem is that he is still refusing the demand made on all teachers to join the party. Now they've found out about his grandmother – a Jew in name only and, as you say, so the hell what anyway? – he's in even more trouble.'

Poilu said, 'Hmm,' and we tramped up the steps to the terrace. Halfway up, I found myself looking at two stylish green-and-white saddle shoes beneath a shapely pair of ankles – and calves fit for a mannequin. Above, there hung a pleated emerald-green dress with a tie belt around an hour-glass figure. Above that a V-neck collar, a necklace of black stones and, by the time I took the last step and reached the terrace, the broadest smile of the whitest teeth. I was looking at Ingrid. She had her Leica to her eye, and she clicked.

'Well, don't just go red and stand there. Do I get a hug?'

I'd been thinking about Ingrid a great deal over the last two weeks, but it was only now, with her right before me in all her remarkable beauty, that it struck home I was hopelessly in love with her. It had been so long since my last love that I had forgotten how to identify the emotions I had been feeling since laying eyes on her at Paderborn station. Either that, or Ingrid being so far up nature's chain of hierarchy from me, I had buried the acknowledgement of the truth in the deepest burrow of my mind. And it was the truth. I had a whole world of troubles on my mind – Himmler, the Holy Grail, Germany's grotesque transformation, the great conflict all say is inevitable, my father trying to get himself jailed – but it was Ingrid who occupied my thoughts more than the rest combined.

I stepped forward into her embrace, squeezing her hard and drawing in a deep draught of her lavender scent. Madame Trencavel appeared in the doorway with a smile the width of her face, giving me a double thumbs-up signal behind her back, then shot back into the shadows as we disengaged.

I had told Ingrid all about Poilu in my letters and, avoiding the mistake made by so many, she knew not to jump onto a chair or pat him or order him to sit. She was grace itself, extending her hand and beaming, 'You must be Poilu. Otto says you are the cleverest boy in all France.'

It was difficult to know if Poilu was blushing behind his shiny coat, but he looked down and shuffled his feet, whimpering, 'Let me get you a glass of wine' and scampered into the kitchen, pursued by a pair of swallows.

I was suffering paralysis of the tongue, a condition that had afflicted me since childhood whenever I suspected my feelings were laid bare for all to see. I managed to get out, 'But, but – '

'But – what am I doing here? Well, I'm on leave, Otto, and I can go where I like. Germany is still a free country – for a few of us at least. And after all your descriptions of the life and landscape here, I thought why not?'

'Does *he* know you're here?'

'Of course not. I told him I was going swimming and hiking in the Bavarian lakes. He thought that very patriotic.'

There was a hint of forced jollity in her voice, and my face must have darkened because hers did too. She stepped towards me and put her hand on my arm.

'And we need to talk about your father. And you.'

Poilu emerged with two glasses of wine, laid them on the wrought-iron bistro table under the vines and retreated indoors. We sat down.

'I know. My mother has been in touch. He's a *mischling*.'

'I found his files. It's not hopeless. But he must join the party – and, should he do so, there is a good chance they would bury the inconvenience of his antecedents. You need to persuade him. A man of his influence and standing in Michelstadt – it doesn't look good for the party if he defies them.'

'I know, I know. But he is a man of cast-iron principle and he's frightened of no-one. How he had a son like me is a mystery.'

She slapped me on the knee and said, 'Don't be silly. Everyone's a coward, including your father. Fear is a natural animal reaction; courage is a decision. You're stronger than you know, Otto. If you don't want to be a coward, you just have to decide not to be one.'

Beatrice emerged from the house bearing olives and salted almonds and laid them down on the table.

She said, 'Otto, the other room is booked – another

German came to see the castle! Germans, Germans, Germans... That's all we get these days. Do you not have any castles of your own?'

'Did he leave a name?' Ingrid flashed me a worried look as she asked.

'I didn't catch it – he was speaking in medieval French from a station in Paris and I couldn't hear him well above the whistles and hubbub. Said he was *en route* to Spain. On business. He's arriving on the last train so you'll meet him over breakfast. Anyhow, I have changed the bed and put Ingrid in your room. You can have Poilu's bed and he can curl up on the floor.'

Ingrid thanked her and asked if she could help in the kitchen.

'Not unless you want to make the *Gribiche* sauce for the *andouillette*. Otto, why don't you take Ingrid up to the castle? It will be a spectacular sunset.' She looked down towards the church clock, adding, 'We will eat at nine, you have plenty of time. Raymond has invited half the bar.'

I lifted a blistered foot onto my knee and grimaced.

'I'll soak some bandage in apple cider vinegar, then you should put on some thick socks and you'll be just fine, Otto.'

She darted back into the house and Ingrid and I exchanged smiles, her whispering, 'What's *andouillette*?'

'France's revenge. Sausage, but not as you know it – boiled pig's intestines wrapped in more pig intestine. The colon, if we're unlucky. Don't let the smell of urine put you off.'

'Did I tell you I converted to vegetarianism?'

'They hang people for less in France. Just hold your nose and wash it down with the red wine. Then wash that down with the Armagnac. Then you'll be happy to eat your own foot.'

A walk was my very last wish at that moment – but I would have walked up Mont Blanc barefoot to be with her. *Le Pog*, the local name for the little mountain, is shaped like a slender Christmas tree, the castle the decoration on top. I had walked it every day since giving up the cigarettes but, bathed in the dying sun, it had never looked so majestic, and the higher we climbed, the higher my spirits rose, Ingrid's shapely ankles and calves leading the way. Such is the effort on the lungs, we walked in silence for the most part, pausing occasionally to take in the rising splendour of the scene, exchanging smiles and platitudes.

There was not a whisper of wind, even at the top, and the walls outside the postern gate were warm against our backs when we emerged from the castle and sat down, still panting. I unstrapped the knapsack and uncorked the wine and we threw back the first one like water. The village, down to our left, had become a single-roofed dwelling from that height, and *Le Prat des Cremats* – The Field of the Burned – where the last Cathars perished, no more than an emerald-green handkerchief. We could barely have been further from the troubles of the world – and yet.

Right before us – beyond the long, jagged spine

of the Pyrenees, Spaniards busy cutting each other's throats, ideologies clashing like thunderclaps, rolling and reverberating through every European home. Behind us – vengeful Germany running its blade over the whetstone again, unfolding its maps, gathering its men from the fields and factories.

I asked Ingrid about developments back home and she said, 'Must we? Can't we just enjoy this and forget that?'

She said it sharply but hung a smile on the end, and we lost ourselves in small talk and jokes about our boss, the great Lothario with his 'beanpole bunny-rabbit', the Nordic god-warrior in his pince-nez, our mood rising, the wine dropping. Then Ingrid laid her hand on mine and squeezed it.

'I am so happy to be here, Otto, and out of Berlin. I wish I didn't have to go back. I wish we could spend the summer here.'

We!

The touch of her warm skin acted like a surge of electrical current, and I lit up with feelings of the heart and stirrings of the body I hadn't experienced for years, feelings that exhilarated and startled me in equal measure and left me at a loss for words again. She squeezed my hand once more and I felt stupid and unmanly for being incapable of saying something chivalrous or affectionate. I found myself looking at her beautiful profile – even her nose had beauty! – my mouth open, but all the words sent forth by my feelings crowded and choked in my throat. I looked away, reached for the bottle and poured us the last of it.

After a time, gathering myself and making that effort obvious by clearing my throat like there was a fly down there, I ventured, 'May I ask you a question?'

'Certainly – so long as it's not political.'

'No, it's just, I suppose I'm at a loss to understand why you – why you have shown even the slightest interest in me, let alone gone to the lengths you have for me and my family. Why so kind to me?'

She swung her head and, almost admonishing, snapped, 'Don't be a fool, Otto. Because I like you. You are gentle and thoughtful and clever. Will that do?'

I thought for a while, still none the wiser or more convinced, then continued, 'But you must have half the men in Berlin fighting for your... your companionship, your hand? And yet here you are with me.'

'Now you're straying back into politics, but I'll let you off this once. Truth is, I am not remotely interested in what admirers I may have these days. Fire-breathing blockheads in uniforms most of them. They take me for cocktails and dinner and tell me how to strip and reassemble a Mauser, how I might kill an attack dog were I to find myself unarmed and on the run – one places one's fist down in its throat I am advised – how the reoccupation of the Rhineland is just the first step, yawn, yawn. Then they are astounded and affronted that I am insufficiently aroused to go to bed with them.'

'I can't even strip a bed.'

'See, you make me laugh. You have the innocence of the old Germany they all claim to crave. Long may you never be able to strip a Mauser. Your artlessness is refreshing, Otto.'

'Artless – why, thank you! Did you ever work in the Foreign Ministry? You mean naïve and gullible.' Then, not thinking, I blurted, 'But what about raising a family? Most people by our age are settled now. Do you not worry that you might miss out?'

She didn't reply and I turned to her. Her head was down, and she was running a finger around the rim of her glass so that it sung.

I mumbled, 'I am sorry, Ingrid. That was a question too far. I shouldn't have –'

'My fiancée died in '32, Otto.'

'Oh God. I didn't – '

'It's alright. I'd tell you soon enough anyhow. He was a reporter with the *Berliner Morgenpost*. There was a violent clash between Communists and Rohm's stormtroopers. He went to the help of a wounded Commie. He was dragging him to get medical help, the stormtroopers assumed he was also a Commie and – and they kicked him and the Commie to death. I haven't been too much interested in romance since then.'

I wanted to put my arm around her, but it was awkward propped against the wall as we were, and I scratched my ear instead. I felt an urgency to say something loving and comforting, but that was awkward too, restrained by my bridled character as I was. I muttered something conciliatory and agreeable, then started fussing about with the glasses and packing up the knapsack, hating myself for my lack of heart.

We got to our feet using our backs on the wall to lever ourselves up. She stumbled on a loose rock, tilting towards me, and we thrust out our arms, catching each other by the elbows, our faces no more than an inch or two apart. It was long enough anyhow for us to look into each other's eyes for a significant duration of time – I felt the warmth of three of her breaths on my face. In a good story, I would have then put my arms on her hips and we would have leant into each other, slow and hesitant, our lips coming to the touch and, bathed in the copper glow of the sinking sun, the world stretched out before us in all its natural loveliness and its infinity of possibilities, we would have kissed until the sun slipped over the mountains, then walked hand in hand to the village bathed in the glow of the rising moon...

But.

But of course I spasmed with awkwardness and shyness, let go of her and pulled up the cuff of my shirt and clasped my Omega, frowning as if it had bitten me.

'Eight-fifteen. I suppose we should make our way down. Nothing worse than cold pig's intestine.'

Ingrid shrugged her shoulders. 'Yes, I suppose you're right. Apart from warm pig's intestine.'

We could hear the din before we had closed the gate into the field at the mountain's foot. We rounded the bend and saw a knot of people gathered outside the Trencavels', spilling out from beneath the pergola towards the walls of the terrace.

'Oh God, Raymond has got his squeezebox out.'

'Is he learning it?'

'No, he's been playing it for thirty years. That's as good as it gets.'

'Criminalising the accordion – now that *would* be grounds to invade. What are they celebrating?'

'Nothing.'

Beatrice waved to us as we came down the lane into the village, then stuck her fingers in her ears and made a gargoyle face. Father Pietro, sitting on the terrace wall, raised his Gauloises in our direction as we came up the steps. Raymond laid down his accordion on the table, prompting a cheer from his guests, and he lurched towards Ingrid with open arms and an almost indecent grin. Beatrice motioned to Poilu and, needing no further instructions, he seized the accordion and darted into the house. Beatrice held out a lacquered tray and we took two long glasses of dark sparkling liquid. Father Pietro held up his empty glass and Beatrice exclaimed: 'But I have only just filled it!'

I leant towards Ingrid. 'Hope you have a hard head. Meet the *Pompier* – sparkling wine, Pernod and blackcurrant. Two or three of these and you'll think *andouillette* has come from God's own dining table.'

We touched glasses and our eyes met again. Surely, she couldn't have feelings for *me*?

•◆•

I was half-dreaming the mountain-top kiss I might have had, remembering her warm breath on my face, the silk of her skin – I think I was smiling – when I felt sharp metal boring into my forehead. My eyes sprung open, my line of sight floating upwards. The barrel of a Luger, rough, yellow-stained fingers on the grip, a man in a slate grey double-breasted suit with thick chalk stripes, the shoulders almost twice the width of the tapered waist. I could see only the mouth beneath the Trilby brim turned down at the front.

'Sleeping with dogs, eh?' The hoarse whisper was familiar, but I could not place it. He rammed the muzzle harder. The skin broke and a tear of blood ran into my eye socket. My mouth was dry and sticky from the cocktails and the crude wine and now the fear. I couldn't swallow. A cigarette hung from the corner of his lips, the smoke rolling beneath the brim. I felt Poilu's warm coat against my feet. He must have climbed up in the night. The room was hot and stuffy, and I was lying naked but for my underpants.

'So the father's a traitor, an enemy of the state. And a *mischling* too it turns out. No surprises there, eh?'

Poilu stirred at my feet, twisting himself around. 'And his son fucks dogs. Or a baboon or whatever the fuck that is.'

He threw a half-glance towards the foot of the bed and I saw the big pig nostrils.

Muller.

'Take a sub-human out of his mud hovel, put him in

a nice house, give him a nice suit, he still fucks dogs.'

Shutters clattered against the outer wall from the room below. Ingrid! I lurched forward onto my elbows. A calamity if Muller finds her here, if Beatrice has given away her name. He pushed my head back down into the pillow with the muzzle and blood pooled into my eye. Ingrid! My heart jolted again as the memory erupted in the fog of hangover. My drunken pass outside her bedroom, taking her by the waist and lunging, mouth open like Dracula. No! The recollection was worse than waking to a gun at my head.

What was it she said? 'I think the Pompiers are doing the talking, Otto.'

And what did I say? '*In vino veritas*, O Ingrida!' God, what a cretin. Then a whole bunch of other love quotes in Latin. A part of me willed Muller to squeeze the trigger.

I asked: 'What are you doing here, Muller? Have you tired of beating up old men?'

'Ooh… Is little Otto growing some big testicles like his Papa?'

I had to get her out of the house.

'Your boss asked me to pay you a courtesy call on my way to visit our colleagues in Spain.'

Muller thrust down his free hand and yanked me up by my throat. Poilu sprung like a cat from the end of the bed, knocking off Muller's hat. He locked an arm tight around his neck, growling into his ear. Muller yelped – he actually yelped. Poilu levered his forearm tighter, tilting Muller backwards. The policeman's eyes bulged, and his roll-fat cheeks crimsoned, his hand with the Luger flailing around as he tried to balance himself. Poilu bent the inspector's huge frame towards the floor, the cigarette falling from his mouth. Muller raised his gun at me and tried to speak but Poilu's choke hold was so strong, he could only manage a gargling sound. I leapt to my feet and held up my hand.

'Poilu – enough.'

Poilu dropped his feet to the floor and stood back, eyeballing Muller. Muller turned the gun in his direction, loosening his tie, gasping for breath.

'Freak fucking beast, are you?'

'Werewolf.' He said it with a smile. 'It's true. I've got a certificate from Paris.'

Muller stiffened his arm so that the Luger was pointing at Poilu's heart. The cigarette still burning on the oak floorboards.

I stepped forward, holding up a hand and said, 'I wouldn't do that if I were you, Muller.'

'Yeah, why not? I'll have you framed for *un crime passionnel*.'

His finger tightened on the trigger.

'Kill him, and you'll be six feet under before the sun is over the mountains. Like you, they don't bother with the courts here.'

Muller turned back to Poilu, grinding out his cigarette. 'Get out of here you fucking abomination.'

I nodded to Poilu. 'It's okay, Poilu. Inspector Muller and I need to talk.'

Poilu circled Muller, keeping his eyes on him, showing some teeth, Muller turning too, keeping the Luger on him. Poilu reached for the door handle and Muller said, 'Not a word down there. Or you'll have to find a new lover.'

Poilu eased open the door. In the gap, I saw Ingrid emerge on the stairs, just her head and shoulders, visible to me but not to Muller. She looked up and I shook my head and waved her away.

'Hey Poilu,' I said. 'Don't forget to take that lady tourist up to the castle. You're late already.'

Poilu tilted his head and looked at me with a quizzical expression before understanding dawned across his face.

'You better hurry. You know how cross she can get.'

'Oh yeah.'

Muller said, 'Good idea, good riddance. And make sure she puts you on a fucking chain. Farmer doesn't want you breakfasting on his cattle.'

Poilu pulled the door to and Muller waggled the Luger at me. 'Get dressed. You and me are going for a walk and a talk. Be quick. General Franco's people are waiting for me.'

CHAPTER SEVEN

I looked at my watch. Ingrid looked at hers. The church bell struck a quarter past the hour. I looked at my watch again, Ingrid at hers. We exhaled through our noses in chorus, hands in our laps, watching the sparrows peck the gravel. The atmosphere between us was intensified by Raymond's monotonous chiselling of stone in the yard at the rear.

I put a fist to my mouth and cleared my throat. 'Do you know why birds eat grit, Ingrid?'

'No, Otto. I don't know why birds eat grit.'

'Look, don't worry, Ingrid. Fournier will be here in a moment. I'm afraid you can't just hail a cab in Montségur. They've only got one automobile.'

The tone was all wrong, a little as my mother spoke to me as a child when I was impatient for pudding. Ingrid snapped back, still looking straight ahead, 'I must not miss that train. If I'm a day late for the office, he'll start making enquiries.'

'You have plenty of time – a whole two hours before it departs.'

Another pause and then I leant forward, elbows on

my knees. 'May I ask — is that truly what is worrying you?'

She flashed me a look, not her sweetest. There had been a great deal of tension between us since the night before, coming down from the castle in silence. I was at a loss as to its cause. We had been getting along so well together all week. Now she seemed close to anger, to tears even.

It was not my blundering pass on our first night — she had waved that away as a 'commonplace consequence of excessive liquor, a daily occurrence in Berlin'. And once Inspector Muller was away to his Falangist friends over the border, none the wiser of her presence here, his hoodlum threats to me a fading rant now, we had had a wonderful week, as happy as any I had had. Or so I thought. We could not have rubbed along any better had we been a husband and wife of forty years. Following my juvenile indiscretion, I had behaved with perfect manners, the very model of gentlemanly detachment.

Then last night, back up at the castle again, a bottle of wine in the setting sun and then the lunar eclipse — I placed not so much as a little finger on her, let alone lunged at her with my mouth wide as a basking shark, dribbling Latin in elegiac couplets. If anything, I had been rather distant and mature, a model of ice-cool decorum. It was her playing the flirt, all fetching smiles, lingering looks and little touches. It was obvious she was trying to flatter me, make me feel good about myself after my embarrassment, and I pretended not to notice. For once, I had played my role perfectly.

'You were telling me why birds eat grit, Otto.'

'Do you really want to know? I think you're just humouring me again.'

'Again? But please, it's been bothering me for years. Birds, grit.'

'Very well. In short, the little stones act as teeth. Birds don't have teeth. Evolution has designed them to be as light as possible for flight. So that's also why the male has neither penis nor testicles – both sexes have what's known as a cloaca, a posterior opening, the end for all its internal systems including the digestive, the excretory and the reproductive.'

I shot a look at Ingrid. Was that a smile of derision or amusement creeping from the corner of her mouth?

'Please, Otto, go on. I find avian biology quite enthralling.'

'You sure? Fine. So the evolutionary demand for lightness is also why the female produces an egg in just 24 hours, why birds don't urinate; why weigh yourself down with a sack of the stuff when you can squirt it out as part of your stool? That's why the bones are hollow, and the feathers are waterproof. So instead of masticating food in a mouth with a heavy set of enamels, the grit does the milling in their stomach. It's brilliant.'

I watched Ingrid's eyebrows rise slowly up to her hairline and stop there. 'Fascinating. I shall reflect on little else on my return journey to Berlin.'

We reverted to hand-clasping and inspecting our watches. A light breeze stirred the vines above our heads, the sparrows chirped and pecked, and Raymond tapped away at his stone.

'Did you know that if our eyes were in the same proportion to our heads as those of birds, they would be the size of tea saucers. And that if – '

'Oh please, Otto.'

We looked at our watches in unison and then in opposite directions, her to the west, me to the east.

I had never previously felt anything but a slight deflation of the spirits laying eyes on Maurice Califano, the most corpulent and gloomy of the Chief Postmistress's four sons – some achievement in that household – but I positively lit up when his saturnine face, complete with downturned mouth, appeared at the foot of the broad stone steps up to the terrace.

'Good morning, Maurice! I forgot it was a delivery day.' Shooting to my feet, I exclaimed it as though announcing the cessation of hostilities on the Western Front. My bonhomie died somewhere on the steps, Maurice staring at me from under the peak of his kepi as he might look upon a wall or an ocean after a sleepless night. He burrowed into his postbag and, reaching up the steps, handed me two letters.

He said: 'Letters.'

'Yes, thank you, Maurice. I wasn't expecting you to hand me a fillet of trout.' My laugh tumbled down the steps, falling flat somewhere near his feet. He trudged away up the hill.

The quality of the stationery was reflected in the first letter's weight and, with a low sigh, I saw that the postmark denoted Berlin as the origin. The stamps were a new issue, featuring Hitler's head and nothing else. King now, eh? Even Stalin had resisted that flight of conceit. The second letter was lighter, and I recognised my father's neat hand at once and my shoulders slumped again.

Ingrid said, 'Let me know if I can help, won't you?' I nodded my thanks, her face expressing genuine concern once more, then she quickly turned away, adding in a more official voice: 'Send any telegrams and letters to my apartment from now on. Just to be safe.'

I wanted to tear open the letters, especially my father's reply to my plea to 'let common sense prevail' – my mood could hardly have been grimmer anyhow. But the sound of an engine turning over, or trying to, rose from the foot of the village. Wearily, Ingrid pushed herself to her feet – perhaps she was suffering another Trencavel hangover – and reached for her worn leather valise. Poilu shot from the doorway as if he had been crouched there like a sprinter. He took the case from her and Beatrice followed him out onto the terrace, summoning her husband with a train-whistle shriek. I tapped the envelopes in my palm, furrows deepening in my brow, and slapped them down on the table.

Ingrid worked her way down the line of Trencavels, enveloped in tight embraces and a birdsong of warm words. She turned to me, sucking in her nostrils a little, laid her hand on my wrist and craned into me as if bracing herself for a kiss from a bearded aunt. I tried to give her a full hug, but she stiffened and I had to make do with a pat on the back and the merest brush of the lips on both cheeks.

Fournier, blacksmith and village cab driver, pulled up below the terrace.

Again, her expression spoke of a warmth greater than that conveyed in her words and bearing. 'Thank you, Otto, for being so cordial. It has been very pleasant to get away from Berlin for a few days.'

Cordial? Pleasant?

'Ingrid – '

'Oh, a Peugeot 201 – a 1929 model by the look of it.'

'Ingrid – '

I took her case from Poilu and followed her down the steps. Fournier opened the passenger door and ushered her in with an extravagant bow and waft of the arm. I placed the valise on the back seat and quickly shut the door.

'Ingrid!' I almost shouted it but reined myself in and leant on the open window, speaking in German now. 'Ingrid – what is it? I know I can be maddening but we have had such a – '

She turned her head, the face more sad than angry

now, and she gave me a half-smile, put her hand on top of mine. I wanted to pull her from the car and squeeze her until she popped.

'Nothing, Otto, nothing. You have been a lovely companion and I place great value on our friendship as you well know. It's just – '

'Just what, Ingrid? I have apologised for my silly drunken behaviour on Monday, and we've had the happiest of times. Haven't we? I have tried to behave courteously and, well, I'm confused. I can't do anything right it seems.'

Fournier climbed into the driver's seat, his belly wedging against the steering wheel.

'That's just it, I suppose. Confused. You too? One moment you lunge at me, swearing undying love in Greek lyric poetry – '

'Latin.'

'And then –'

'Then, what?'

'Then, the other extreme. Last night, up at the castle… I mean, it was so beautiful and, as you say, we had had such a happy week and then, well… I am very fond of you, Otto, but I wonder whether you and I…'

'Wonder what? What did I do?'

Fournier put the car into gear and said: 'Right! Onwards, to Foix!'

She squeezed my hand and said: 'Have the courage to be yourself, Otto. You might surprise yourself.'

Fournier released the brake, the Peugeot coughed

and jumped away. I was left standing in a cloud of exhaust fumes, slowly raising my hand, muttering in my head 'Be myself? But I am myself. Who else might I be?' I watched the car climb the hill, the silhouette of her beret against the white of the windshield. The car slid around the bend.

I turned and the three Trencavels stopped waving and looked down at me with communal sympathy. I trudged back up the steps, head down, and found myself in Beatrice's embrace. She pulled back gently and held me by the elbows.

She said, 'No woman loves a man who loves himself but, Otto, she can do no more than merely like a man who doesn't like himself. Honestly, Otto, I have never met a man of such fine looks and physique and brains as you and blessed with so many gifts, and yet who thinks so little of himself. That lovely woman was there for the taking and you bottled out. You must learn to like and respect yourself, Otto. Otherwise you will never find love!'

What had begun in a consoling and encouraging voice ended in this harsh admonishment, and when she was done she slapped my folded arms and spun on her heel. Like I had let her down too, perhaps all womanhood. I stood motionless on the top step, thoughts spinning like balls in a tombola.

I snatched the letters from the table, marched into the house, and pulled my linen jacket from the hook behind the door. Poilu retreated across the flagstones, sliding on his beekeeper's helmet. Filling two canteens of water from the pitcher on the kitchen table, I dropped them into my canvas knapsack, yanking the straps tight. Beatrice announced we would eat at nine, her voice quiet, a hint of quavering.

I wriggled the fedora onto my head, instructed her not to wait on my account, that I may be some time, and strode from the house, down the steps and up the hill towards the gate for the path up to the castle. The late afternoon heat was topping out and I had barely reached the undergrowth and stunted trees skirting the lower slopes when I took off my coat and slung it over my shoulder. Propelled by inchoate rage, taunted by self-doubt, I did not pause once to take a rest or enjoy the beauty of the panorama as the sun slid towards the mountains. By the time I arrived at the top, the linen shirt clung to my torso as though I had walked straight from a lake. My imagination was exhausted from playing out a thousand scenarios with Ingrid, and the two letters hung on my back like canisters of poison gas bursting for release.

I walked through the arch of the old gatehouse and into the bailey, leaping across the fallen stonework and through the opening on the northern side, where the shadow lay at its deepest and the breeze at its freshest. I gathered my breath, half a boot over the precipice that dropped straight down for almost a hundred metres. I looked out over the wooded hills rolling down to the plain, the red roofs of Lavelanet, ten kilometres distant, running like a contaminated river in the cleft between the last of the slopes. If I had had my binoculars, I might have watched Ingrid's train snaking its way up to Toulouse. But to hell with that. I had blown it. It was over. If my love for Ingrid was a train, then I had boarded at Foix and alighted at Saint Jean de Verges – the next stop – travelling third class. *Cordial*!

I drained half a canteen of water, sat down against the battlements and took out the letters from the knapsack. I held them out, one in each hand, weighing in my mind which of the two might carry the graver news. I opted to read Himmler first – his never brought glad tidings and songs of joy – keeping alive the unlikely hope my father had written to announce a change of heart.

There were two letters inside the Berlin envelope: one short, barely half a page, typed and official, the other two-paged, dense and written in his hideous jagged scrawl in which all the letters look like the SS insignia – a whole page of lightning flashes with furious underlining.

In his earlier written correspondence, the Reichsführer-SS had afforded me the common courtesy of opening his letter *Dear Otto*. But the official letter began plain *Eckhart*, not even a *Herr* preceding it, just my family name, like I was a delinquent schoolboy staring out of the window, him throwing the blackboard duster at me. I still have the letters, so I am able to reproduce them here in full.

The official one ran:

BERLIN SW 11
Prinz-Albrecht-Strasse, 8
Eckhart,
Your letter of 25 July, 1937, is acknowledged. Latest request for patience denied.

9th Party Congress begins Nuremburg Sept 6. Holy Grail delivered to P-A-S, 8 no later than Aug 31. Immaculate condition essential. Time short. Spear of Destiny acceptable alternative.

Delivery to include explanatory notes of relic's Nordic provenance/Messiah's Aryan heredity. Revelation of past Jewish complicity/theft of relic welcomed.

Heil Hitler!
Reichsführer-SS H. HIMMLER

Incredibly, the typewriter on which the letter had been produced had a key for 'SS'. In the handwritten letter, I only had to look at the script to picture him seething at his desk, pince-nez steamed, the zig-zagging hand pressed so hard into the thick paper, the nib had punctured it in places. He wrote as most people scrub out. This time there was no greeting at all – not even a plain *'Eckhart'*! He could not bring himself to acknowledge my existence by granting me my name. I was now just the case number that sat in the top corner of the official letter. Why he had chosen to add a separate note was obvious – he wanted no official record of what he had to say to me. I barely needed to read on to measure the depth of the hole in which I now languished.

August 2

Hard to describe where my disappointment begins or ends! I have placed my personal and official trust in you, I have broken with protocol to make you an officer in the elite Schutzstaffel, I have published your book, I have arranged a handsome payment and I have assigned you a noble and historic task on behalf of the Fatherland.

And how do you and your family return my munificence and benevolence? With <u>dishonour, betrayal and treachery</u>!!

1. When my office contacted Inspector Muller of the Darmstadt Gestapo to request your family files, I was appalled to learn of your father's case. He is one of very few teachers left in the country not to follow their conscience and join the party! It was your patriotic duty to inform me your father is a political reactionary, a threat to state security, an <u>enemy of the Reich</u>.

2. It came as no surprise to learn your father is also a <u>mischling</u>, contaminated with Jewish blood. The Jews are our misfortune and your father is most certainly yours.

3. In spite of the generous resources at your disposal, after two months you have failed to bring me the Holy Grail. I grant you that Weisthor's indisposition has not helped your quest – he is still in a spa clinic in the Tyrol recovering *from nervous exhaustion – but still, you have been assuring me over and over you are 'hot on the trail' and 'close to a breakthrough'. Yet, what have you produced? <u>Nothing!</u> I suspect you have been leading me <u>into the woods</u>.*

4. I asked Inspector Muller to pay you a courtesy call and check on your progress. He discovers you in bed at 10 o'clock, lying in sin with some sort of half-dog, half-human – 'a disgusting abomination of Nature' – in some sort of flophouse littered with bottles and overflowing ashtrays. You have been leading a life of <u>depravity and hedonism</u> at the expense and in <u>mockery</u> of the Reich!

5. I sent a copy of your book to Professor Gebhardt, your former tutor at Heidelberg University. His reply was polite but shocking. He could barely contain his surprise and amusement, saying your book certainly reflected well on the quality of teaching at Heidelberg – he was delighted that even the least competent 'third-rate' students were now able to find publishers for their work. Parzifal is an almost verbatim <u>re-gurgitation</u> of your final university thesis for which you received the lowest mark in your class. You have <u>humiliated</u> me!

This catalogue of your transgressions and delinquencies leaves me with no choice but to issue you the following ultimatums.

i) Bring me the Holy Grail as aforementioned – and all

your <u>indiscretions</u> will be wiped from the files, and your case closed.

ii) Instruct your father to take the proper, <u>patriotic</u> course, join the party, sign up to the National Socialist Teachers' League and fulfil his <u>duty</u> to school the children of Michelstadt in imparting to them the <u>wisdom</u> of the new curriculum.

I warn you that failure to comply and execute either of these obligations will invite <u>the harshest reprisals</u> of the Reich against you and your family.
Heil Hitler!

I dropped the letter between my knees and slumped back against the wall, heart hammering my ribs. Holy shit! My luck had well and truly collapsed over the finishing line, and time was racing down the final straight. I gathered up the letter and read the last paragraph again, blowing out deep breaths and trying to calm myself. *The harshest reprisals of the Reich!* I did not know exactly what that meant right then but I was able to take a fairly good guess. I had to assume that the reprisals already visited upon my father did not fall into the category headed 'Harsh'.

No, 'harsh' must mean what Father said they call 'protective custody' – a benign term, he explained, until you work out the sinister nature of its true meaning: the state being protected from the inmate! Protective custody meant Dachau. My father and I were heading to the camp. Heini probably had the papers and warrants for our arrest already signed and ready for immediate dispatch. One thing he was not was a slack bureaucrat.

My father's letter was shorter – just one paragraph. He was not going to back down. Noble old fool!

The sun had gone and the night air was filling with cold under a cloudless sky and a web of stars. I put on my jacket, pulled in my knees to my chest and buried my face in my hands. Hunger nibbled at the pit of my stomach and a northerly wind was starting to stab at the peak. But I was not coming off that mountain until I had come up with a plan of action.

•◄•

I woke with a start to the liquid trill of the blackbird's flight call, my neck stiff against the canvas knapsack. I was shivering, my jacket damp with dew, and I huddled myself into a tighter ball. For once, Ingrid was not my last dream or my first thought. Instead, it was something close to a nightmare from which I emerged into a foggy consciousness – a terrible vision of the last Cathars tramping from the castle down to a giant pyre flaming in the field below, the crusading army lining one side of their route in full armour but wearing SS caps and helmets, the Pope at the foot in a hugely oversized mitre but, with his toothbrush moustache and pince-nez, he was Himmler too.

It had been a painfully vivid dream, almost tangible, physical, and I fancied I could smell the woodsmoke and hear the cries of those the martyrs left behind in the castle, the ones they had given up their lives for. But it was a vision made all the more distressing because it was my father leading the procession, holding out a book before him, taunting his executioners all the way down, my mother trailing and wailing in his wake – and, weirdly, Berthold from The Three Hares handing out glasses of Pils to a silent crowd of eyeless, open-mouthed regulars on the other side of the path.

I sat up sharply, shook the images from my head, rubbed my face with numb hands and struggled to my feet, joints creaking. I stood panting, hands on hips. A belt of copper ran below the greying horizon, heralding the sun's emergence. My eyes adjusted and there, beside my knapsack, sat a soft leather bag. I stared at it non-plussed for a moment then reached for it, untying the tassels and pulling it open. A smile broke over my face as I removed the items. There was a corked bottle of milk, a stick of baguette, a small pot of honey and a parcel of waxed paper containing thick chunks of ham, as many slices of hard cheese, a wedge of butter, and cutlery wrapped in a large dishcloth. Poilu – you furry little angel, slayer of demons!

I crossed through the roofless shell of the castle and sat down on the steps of the gatehouse, laid out my breakfast and waited for the day. I ran through my plan – my plans rather, checking they stood up in the light of day, free from the agonies of the night. The priority was my father (and therefore my mother too) but to address that problem I had to deal with Himmler at the same time. Even if I were able to persuade Father to concede, he remained a *mischling* and therefore still at risk if I failed to neutralise the Himmler threat. The two problems were bound as one and they must be solved as one.

The sunlight was inching down the slopes towards the village when I began my own descent on the steep narrow path – the locals insist it is the very one taken by the doomed Cathars. A bag swinging from each shoulder, where I could walk I hung on to shrubs and branches of the gnarly trees, levering myself down the steeper rocks through which the ancient route had been carved. I was impatient to get on, but wary of tipping headlong into the jagged rocks.

I tumbled out of the undergrowth into the meadow and my momentum gave me no choice but to keep running. It was only when the terrain evened out and I was able to slow myself to a walking pace that I saw the unmistakable figure perched on the upper bar of the fence facing up the mountain. Had I not known better I'd have thought I was looking at a dog with a bucket on its head.

Poilu sprung from the fence, took off his beekeeper's helmet and, as we converged, he broke into a grin wide enough to see off an army of cats. I put my arm over his shoulder, pulled him tight and we headed through the gate and into the lane.

'You feeling better?'

'The bread might have been fresher, and you might

have thought to leave me a pot of coffee, but the honey was first-rate. I'll give you that.'

'But the coffee would have been cold by the time I reached the top.'

'Yes, I suppose you're right.'

'You are walking very fast – what's the plan? Post office or Father Pietro?'

'Both – but first I need to speak to your father.'

. ✦ .

'I hope you are not cross with me for speaking frankly yesterday. I was so upset for you, Otto. I am sorry.'

Beatrice laid down the tray on the terrace table, handed me a cup and saucer and laid out the steel coffee maker, hot milk pot and bowl of sugar.

'Not at all. You were right. I have a lot on my mind at the – '

'I was expecting you to come off the mountain holding hands, and then to see her striding twenty metres ahead of you, I could have cried … '

'Yes, yes. Please, Beatrice, now I just want to – '

'You Germans are as bad as the British in your coldness. Why be embarrassed to love?'

I poured myself a coffee. 'Yes, yes. Anyhow – '

'And she is so beautiful.'

'Yes, yes. She's exquisite. The thing is – '

'And intelligent. And what a smile! She even smells like a field of lavender.'

'Yes, yes, she smells lovely but I – '

I turned away, looking down over the rooftops, and watched Raymond close the gate to the meadow, Poilu shooing the last of the cows from the dairy.

'And such a perfect figure, like a mannequin. She could be a fashion model or a cabaret dancer.'

'Yes, yes – a model, a dancer.' I added a lump of sugar and stirred the cup noisily, tapping the spoon on the rim, trying to call time.

'And you must write her letter – a passionate one, not a courteous one.'

'Yes, yes. Passionate, yes, but it's – '

Raymond, the size of a toy soldier, appeared at the foot of the alley that ran to the top of the village and I willed him to step on it.

'And so well read and such a warm lovely laugh. She's almost the perfect woman – '

I held up my hand. 'Beatrice, please! Enough! Ingrid and I will always be friends but right now – well, right now…'

I threw up my hands then went at my scalp like I had head lice.

'Ingrid is the least of my troubles right now. Beatrice, my family and I are in danger. Grave danger. I'll explain when Raymond is here.'

Her face dropped and she slumped into the chair opposite, a hand over her mouth.

'Oh, Lord!'

She leant forward, laid her hands over mine and I gave her the rough outline of the situation. Raymond came tramping up the steps, his boots plastered in dung, a small churn swinging in one hand, a Gauloises in the other, a grin from ear to ear. He laid down the churn with a thump, milk slopping onto the gravel, and slapped me between the shoulder blades.

'So you're back? I thought you'd be chasing that beauty all the way back to Berlin.'

Beatrice said: 'Raymond, sit down. You're not the only one knee-deep in the shit this morning. Otto's up to his neck.'

•→•

Raymond sat with an elbow on the table, massaging his beard, face folded in thought, a fresh cigarette curling smoke from the ashtray.

'But surely the chalice at the Last Supper would be made of something grander, more precious – metal or glass?'

'No, almost certainly not. The disciples were poor people living a simple itinerant life. Unless you were rich, most utensils will have been wooden or stone. Glazed earthenware, maybe marble at a stretch.'

'What type of stone?'

'Alabaster if you have any, but Jerusalem Stone, a pale limestone, is just fine. The Wailing Wall is made from it. It's been used in Jewish ceremonial art since the days of the Old Testament.'

'Well, I certainly have enough pale limestone! And it's soft, easy to work.' Raymond threw out a hand and swept it over the Pyrenees. 'We have mountains of the stuff. So, what about the design?'

'Okay, in a way that doesn't really matter. No one knows anything about the chalice, so we can make it up. Jews were wary of graven images, of art being used for idolatrous purposes, but I've got some examples upstairs of the few they did use. Also, we have the great expert, Father Pietro, to advise. Is he back yet from his solitary retreat in Andorra? And I have this too.'

I reached into the bottom of my knapsack and handed Raymond the Death's Head ring. He turned it over in his huge fingers a few inches from his face.

'What the flaming hell is that? Surely you don't want the skull and crossbones on the chalice.'

'No, just some of those runes – do you have a magnifying glass? – plus maybe a couple of primitive swastikas. It's the ring Himmler gives his gangster warriors in the SS as a seal of their loyalty.'

'Himmler's not going to fall for that, is he? Swastika! It's too obvious, no?' Raymond took a heavy draw on his cigarette and blew the smoke up into the vines.

'Not at all. The swastika has been appropriated by the Nazis from Eastern religions and cultures – Buddhists, Jains, Hindus – it has been a common feature in world artwork back to pre-history, a symbol of good luck and prosperity. Himmler's eyes will light up. He'll take it as proof of the link between Nazism and Aryanism and Jesus.'

He placed the ring in the long front pocket of his

dog-eared blue smock. 'Sounds like that arsehole son-of-a-whore will believe anything that plays into his pigshit theories.'

'Correct – and elegantly put. Oh, and I'll need that ring back when you're done.'

'Okay, fine, let's get going. I'm no artist – it'll be crude. How quickly do you need it?'

'Nor were they – crude is good. And the sooner the better. I need to move fast.'

'Poilu – go and fetch Father Pietro – yes, he came back on Tuesday – and tell him there's a bottle of pastis waiting for him. Otto, please bring me the book with the examples. If I start now, I can finish it today.'

Raymond drained his coffee, ground out his Gauloises and disappeared around the side of the house to his workshop. I went up and fetched my book of ancient symbolism and my writing set from the terrace. Raymond had his back to me, bent over the great heap of quarried stone that sat in the back yard, hurling rocks and small boulders to either side. Clambering up the heap, he picked out a piece of stone about twice the size of a football and raised it above his head in triumph.

He bellowed: 'Look, I found the Holy Grail!'

I placed the book next to his chisels and hammers on the long stone workbench beneath the awning against the rear of the house. Raymond struggled down the heap and waddled over, clutching the lump of limestone to his belly, and dropped it with a thud on the bench, wheezing from the effort.

We went through the book, turning down the corner of pages and pencilling around the illustrations of symbols and images for him to follow. Raymond pointed to a Star of David and said: 'What about this? And the candelabra thing? They're pretty Jewish, no?'

'The Menorah – no. We want to avoid all the really obvious Jewish symbols. That'll enrage him – he'll probably smash it against the wall. Stick to the ones I've ringed and whatever Pietro might suggest.'

Raymond fired up a Gauloises and stuck it between his yellow teeth, picked up a metal pail and plunged into the trough next to the bench, then poured it over the lump of limestone. I threw him a quizzical look.

'You wet the stone first because it makes the natural bed line of the rock more visible. It comes apart easier if you follow the lines. Watch this.'

He took the pitching tool in his left hand, laying it about 45 degrees to the stone, and brought down the hammer on the base of the handle with a sharp, heavy blow. A chunk of stone flew from the table, terrifying the cat curled in a flowerpot. The cat screeched and was over the wall in a blur.

'And they said it was impossible to find the Holy Grail when all the time it was sitting right under our noses!' Raymond threw back his head and roared. 'I'm going to enjoy this.'

I gave him a slap on the back. 'I'll be on the terrace if you need me.' I went back around, settled down at the table and opened the pad of writing paper. I began

'Dear Ingrid' then tore out the page, screwed it into a ball and started again. *'My dearest Ingrid…'*

I said all I needed to say in half a page, folded it into the envelope, then set about the letter to my father and the wording of the telegrams, Raymond chiselling, laughing and cursing at the rear. When I was done, I pushed back on my chair and blew out my cheeks. It was all out there now. The honesty felt good. It was true about breathing easier: It was what it was, I am who I am, it will be what it will be.

I swung forward and got to my feet, sliding the correspondence into the inside pocket of my jacket and felt for my wallet.

'Ah, the man who found the Holy Grail!'

Father Pietro's heavy Sicilian accent was unmistakable, but turning around, I barely recognised the face beaming at me as he came up the steps two at a time. There was colour in his freshly shaven cheeks, the mess of wiry grey hair shorn to a neat town-style cut, the puffy bags beneath the eyes had gone, and the big olive eyes were wide and sparkling. He looked ten years younger.

I muttered, 'Good Lord!'

'I hear you spent a lonely night on the mountain, Otto? Well, I spent 14 nights.' And he pointed towards the distant peaks jagging into a blue-blank sky. He took my hand and my elbow in his other and leant into me.

'I want to thank you.'

'What on earth for?'

'For snapping me out of my self-pity, making me realise I'm not the only one with troubles. I feel, well, almost Christian.'

'I'm glad some good has come from this fiasco. But it's you who have given me strength – '

'Shut up – you don't need to say anything. Come on, let's go and see how the master craftsman is getting on with the Grail.'

Poilu, helmet on again, was leaning into the mass of scarlet hibiscus along the front wall of the house, turning his head slowly left and right.

'Poilu.'

'Yes.'

'What are you doing? Are you alright?'

'I'm watching one of my bees rub its body hair against the stamen.'

'Excellent, but when you – or the bee – are done, will you grab a bottle of pastis, some water and a glass for Father Pietro.'

Poilu pulled his head out of the shrub and took o the helmet.

'Father Pietro no longer drinks. He had an experience in his mountain retreat.'

'What?'

'It's true – sort of,' said Father Pietro. 'I drink a little still, but only after dark and I don't get drunk any longer.'

'And he has given up the cigarettes too.'

I crossed myself. 'This is turning out to be quite a

day for holy works and miracles.'

'On which subject,' he said, leaning into me again and laying a hand on my arm. 'When all this settles down and you are out of your current mess, I have a surprise for you.'

'You have?'

'I sure have. A true gift from God. Does Tomar mean anything to you?'

'Of course.'

CHAPTER EIGHT

The dining car was full, middle-aged men returning from Paris on business in the main, one on the adjacent table holding a cigar under his nose and rolling it back and forth in his sausage fingers. Wealthy Americans and British on touring holidays made up most of the rest, the former conspicuous by the loud volume of their voices and clothes, the latter by their more muted tones.

On the table one down from me and across, a young couple atwitter with fledgling love were putting on a spectacular courtship display. They might just as well have been blowing heraldic trumpets and holding a neon gas sign above their heads flashing, 'Look! We're in love!' They were leaning forward, elbows on the table, faces almost touching, fingers entwining and caressing cheeks, eyes ablaze, food going cold. They were virtually in my line of vision and I observed them half in disgust, half in envy and joy for them. Their faces were so close you feared they were going to start rubbing noses like Eskimos.

My mind wandered to Ingrid, and I pictured her in a restaurant on Friedrichstrasse perhaps, twirling the stem of her cocktail glass, staring into space, blowing smoke over her head, across the table from some species of crop-haired military or civil servant character talking her through the shame of Versailles, the iniquities of the Jews, the barbarism of the Slavs, the perfidy of the French, the stopping power of the Mauser and the unrivalled speed of the Messerschmitt 109. I smiled at all the stories she told of her disappointing dates. Suddenly, an image of her in a suitor's clutch jumped in, and I gestured to the waiter for the bill.

'Another cognac, sir? More coffee?'

'Thank you, no. Any more and I won't sleep. Just the bill. Excellent dinner, thank you.'

'Very good.' The elderly French waiter pulled a notepad from his waistcoat, added it up with the point of his pen, tore off the page, laid it under my brandy balloon and bowed his head. 'Very wise, sir. One needs all one's faculties in perfect working order for such an important meeting.'

He smiled and turned to leave but I stopped him, his remark taking a moment to register. 'I beg your pardon? How on earth do you know I have an important meeting?'

'Forgive me, sir, but it's as plain on your face as the coffee cup on your table. I have been observing the machinery of your mind in your expressions.'

'You have?'

'Yes, sir, I can almost see your headache. I am yet to meet a man who rubs his temples for fun. I wish you all the best tomorrow.'

I did have a headache. 'Why, thank you.'

The businessman with the cigar summoned him with a theatrical clearing of the throat. The waiter turned to leave, adding over his shoulder: 'Be bold, show no fear. Thank you, good evening, sir.'

I hadn't laughed since leaving Montségur, my head being full of Ingrid and Himmler, prison cells and stale black bread. I scooped up the last spoons of crème caramel, tucked a wad of francs under the dessert bowl and sprung to my feet.

The train was thundering now towards Berlin and I headed down the carriages in the same direction, my shoulders bouncing off the walls and windows, the night flickering past the windows, a blur of telegraph poles, like a croupier rifling a deck with his thumb, a stream of stars and distant house lights beyond. The cabin was cramped and it was a relief to have single occupancy, my belongings spread out on the lower bunk opposite. I took the leather grip bag and pulled out the chalice, laid it on the bed and unfolded the woollen shawl in which Beatrice had wrapped it.

Holding it aloft in both hands, like I was Pope Pius himself on Easter Sunday, I revolved it slowly in my fingers. Raymond had done a magnificent job, that was for sure – the carvings crude, a little scuffed and flaked but distinct enough to be identifiable, even to an inexpert eye like Himmler's. There was the engraving of the boat – the Ark – the zodiac, Helios the sun god, three runes taken from the Death's Head ring and two swastikas – more curved and flowing than the angular Nazi version, but swastikas clearly nonetheless.

The stone was rough, as though worn by age, and he had stained the lower half of the bowl with diluted fencing creosote, giving the impression it had indeed once been a receptacle for wine. The rim was chipped in places and, entirely by accident and to his great dismay, Raymond had even achieved a light jagged crack, corroborating the sense of its antiquity and authenticity. It was a masterpiece of forgery. Were it to be sat inside a glass display at Berlin's Pergamon Museum, the visitor would surely stand there in awe, blowing hard and thinking, *Oh my God, the chalice from which Jesus Christ and the disciples drank the holy blood!* But whether the experts would be fooled…

I placed the chalice back in the bag, changed into my night clothes and slid into the cold, crisp linen of my narrow strip of a bed. Lulled by the rhythm of the train, as if rocked in a cradle, I surrendered to my fatigue almost at once. The very next I knew, there was a crisp knuckle rap on the door and a hearty '*Bonjour, Monsieur! Guten tag! Une heure à Berlin Potsdamer Bahnhof! Eine stunde nach Berlin!*' from behind it.

I dressed in a hurry and made my way back to the dining car, thick-headed and a little fretful, as I so often found myself in the morning. It was only when I sat down and ran my eyes over the menu card that I became aware how my anxiety was not the usual residue of anxious thoughts stirred in my deeper mind during the night – it was a fresh anxiety and a keen one.

In a few hours from now I was going to be back in the headquarters of the SS and I was going to be presenting its leader with the Holy Grail – the Holy Grail, how absurd! – chiselled into existence by a chuckling half-drunk French farmer and part-time stonemason just a few days earlier. My next breakfast might not be like this one, chosen from an ornately written card and eaten with silver cutlery on a fine tablecloth. It could well be that I would be eating from a wooden bowl in the damp, windowless cell of a basement in Prinz-Albrecht-Strasse or perhaps Columbia-Haus, the notorious police HQ in Alexanderplatz, or, God forbid, in Dachau, prison of prisons. My stomach was tight, my mouth a little dry. Away in my dark imagination, I had failed to notice that my friendly clairvoyant waiter was standing at my side.

'And, sir, some eggs? I can recommend the poached with some Hollandaise sauce. The chef calls it his *signature*. Fortify you for the encounter perhaps.'

'No, thank you. No, I think not. Just a pot of coffee. Strong as you can.'

'Empty stomach – good thinking in fact. The blood will not rush to aid your digestion and dull your acuity.'

The pencil-thin American woman across the aisle snapped open her lighter, fired up a cigarette and blew a long stream of smoke in my direction. I had not smoked in almost three months, but right at that moment I felt a very powerful craving for that dirty hit to the back of the throat. What if Himmler just picked up his phone and summoned one of his experts to come and examine Raymond's phoney Grail there and then? He could turn it over in his hands a few times and say, 'Bullshit, this is a fake.' What if he just took the chalice – that's all he wanted after all – and then had me taken away, to be disposed of and forgotten about? I carried his dirty secret like a sidearm after all, a weapon to assassinate his character. He was chief of police for all Germany. He could dispose of me with no more thought than chucking a ball of paper into his waste basket. And what of my father, and perhaps even my mother – what might become of them if the ruse was rumbled?

I tipped my head back and emptied the last of my coffee, ran the napkin across my mouth and, tossing it over my cup and cash, got to my feet. The American woman was smiling at me, not in a flirtatious way but, I fancied, with kindness and encouragement. The elderly waiter scuttled down the aisle and took me by the hand, shaking it with vigour, patting my arm with his other.

'Remember, fear is natural,' he said. 'Courage is not. It's a decision.'

'Yes, I have heard that before somewhere.'

Were my anxieties really so transparent or was I in a carriage of mind-readers? Would Himmler read me so easily? The woman was still looking at me as I turned to go and I saluted her with a touch of the forehead. The slow nod that she returned carried a regal quality, like she was giving me her blessing, her divinely ordained assent to my endeavour. I stood a little straighter, to attention almost, gave her a grateful smile and made my way back to my cabin.

I took the uniform from the suit carrier and, starting with the shirt, began to transform myself before the full-length mirror on the door. Beatrice's alterations were faultless. It fitted me like a glove. I brushed myself down and pulled the cap over my short-cropped hair – years of grooming had made Poilu a barber of the first rank – and the additional padding Beatrice had sewn into the cap's lining made for an equally close fit. The train was slowing to a crawl, brakes screeching and whining. I pulled on the knee-length leather boots, fastened the cross-belt over the black tunic, slipped on the Death's Head ring and wriggled the cap into position. Thrusting out my jaw, I cracked my heels together and threw out my right arm at the mirror.

It is one of the curiosities of uniforms and costumes that merely by altering the outward appearance, a slight change in the inward character of the wearer is achieved. To look at that strange figure in the mirror, I am obliged to confess again, was both thrilling and unsettling. I couldn't help but wonder whether the character of an entire nation might be changed simply by putting on a uniform. Was it really that easy to become someone else, to become a different country??

I snapped shut the suitcase, zipped up the grip-bag

and turned back to the mirror. I eyeballed myself, trying not to blink, sizing myself up. What is it they say? If you want to defeat your enemies, you have to become like them. Would Himmler now look upon me differently, as one of his own? Could I carry my new self with the necessary conviction?

We came to a gentle halt, the train exhaling in relief. Porters and platform guards cried out, doors slammed, whistle blasts pierced the clamour of a station in full spate. I sat on the bed and waited. I did not want the embarrassment of my American muse from the dining carriage seeing me in my regalia.

I watched the second hand of my watch lap a few circuits then seized my bags and headed along the corridor. Leaning out from the footplate, a thousand hats and caps dipped and bobbed in the cross-current of passengers under a churning cloud of steam and soot. I waited for an opening and stepped down into the flow. In my boot heels and high-brimmed cap, shoulders out, it was as though I had grown by a head.

A large formation of Hitler Youth, as many as two hundred, held centre stage on Potsdamer's small concourse, heavy haversacks tugging at their slight shoulders, porters loading up their tents and equipment bags onto trolleys. A few standard-bearers, their eager faces straining to smile under the effort, swayed the party banner on long wooden poles.

That awful 'Horst Wessel' song, the stormtrooper anthem we heard everywhere, boomed from the loudspeaker public address system, *'Raise the Flags! The Ranks Tightly Closed!'* and the young boys sung along – or rather they tried, most looking unsure of the lyrics, just moving their mouths up and down and glancing about.

The crowd was dense, roiling as one around the troop of youths. Streaming apologies and curses, I muscled my way against the flow.

'Clear the streets for the brown battalions! Clear the streets for the storm division!'

The song had looped into a repeat performance when I fell through the heavy swing doors into the Left Luggage office. I handed over the Reichsmarks, took my ticket, and the tubby little bespectacled clerk heaved my case off the counter and swung it up onto the shelf behind. Sliding a label through the handle, he swivelled about and shouted: 'When will you return to collect, sir?'

I stopped and thought for a moment. 'You know what? I honestly can't answer that question.'

The clerk gave me a quizzical look, and said: 'Suit yourself, sir.'

I nodded and headed out the other door into Potsdamer Platz. A spectacle further removed from the tranquillity of Montségur or Michelstadt was hard to imagine. The busiest transport centre in all Europe stood at a standstill under a web of cabling, the motor buses and electric trolley cars and automobiles of all descriptions and a hundred bicycles, converging from Berlin's five busiest streets. They choked the square, the lights of the traffic tower at its heart rendered useless, horns blaring, bells ringing in plaintive vain.

The pavements were spilling over, especially outside the domed monolith of Kempinski's Haus Vaterland. Shoppers and sightseers thronged into the famous old pleasure palace and its labyrinth of shops and cafes. There was no rush for me – I had made no appointment – and I slowly made my way through the crowds over to the far side, past the Pschorr beer house, a favourite haunt in my student days, and headed south.

The Hotel Fürstenhof was disgorging uniforms and suits from the main entrance, the fountain jetting water in the interior courtyard behind them. The pavement was opening up for me now – or rather for my uniform – and I was in full purposeful stride when I swung a left off Saarland Strasse into Prinz-Albrecht – and, just as she came into my mind, straight into Ingrid, her head down, me adjusting my cap.

We jumped back, avoiding a collision by whiskers, and exclaimed in a startled duet: 'I am so sorry! My fault!' She took a step to go on, but stopped herself, looked up at me again. I smiled at her, my shoulders still back but my head tilted forward, my face in the shadow of the visor. She leant towards me, a little anxious, and I got the full blast of lavender.

'Good God – it is you, isn't it? I didn't – '

'No, why would you?'

My heart was going some, and I had a powerful urge to itch my scalp, the shock of it. We were throwing shy looks, neither of us quite sure what to say.

'I guess I must look as ridiculous as I feel,' I said, an uneasy laugh attached. 'I am enjoying the boots though. Feel like a real man.'

'You have grown into it. It's scary – you *really* look the part. At Wewelsburg you were a kid in his Daddy's clothes. Now… and taller.'

Our burst of laughter came to an abrupt halt and our faces reset to awkward consternation, our feet to shuffling.

'What are you doing here? You're going to see *him*, aren't you?'

'Yes. Yes, I am. I have a little gift for our master, Herr Reichsheini.'

'Please tell me you're kidding.'

'Nope, got it right here.' I raised up my leather bag and patted the side. 'Who'd have thought the Holy Grail was sitting right there in Raymond's back yard all that time?'

'But – '

'He made it. With Pietro as his consultant. I have to try something because – '

'I know – he's out for your blood. God, Otto – are you sure this is wise? He referred to you the other day as "a deviant degenerate fraud, son of a communist mongrel." Can't you stall him a bit longer?'

'He's blown the whistle, issued deadlines, the balloon's gone up. What else can I do? And my bloody Dad. I have to take the initiative. What would you do in my shoes – my big, new, shiny boots?'

Her smile was an anxious one and she exhaled hard. 'Well, look. Let's hope.' She crossed her fingers and waved them at me. 'It'll buy some time – and if there's trouble I'll help as best I can but once that man makes up his stubborn mind then – '

I held up my hand. 'I really don't want you dragged into this, Ingrid. This is my problem and – '

She held a finger to her lips, stepped closer as though she didn't want anyone else to hear. 'Listen, I can't promise anything right now, it's a long shot – literally – but in here, I might just have something to help you. *Might*. It's a big *might* but you never know.'

'What is it? Go on. A one-way family ticket to Rio?'

'I'm not going to say now, Otto, and raise your hopes. But – '

A woman came briskly around the corner and we stepped against the wall to let her pass. It was Hedwig, all tall and willowy with her nose in the air, clutching her handbag in both hands like a dog on its hind legs begging for treats. Ingrid exchanged icy good mornings with her and I lowered my head to hide my face. She walked on and the two of us swapped looks, blowing out our cheeks.

'The honeycomb sweet turtle dove herself!'

'If you see her at HQ, be careful – she's been fuelling his worries about you knowing about them. Probably ashamed you heard. Who wouldn't be?'

'Will I see you back there?'

'No, I'm heading down to Wetzlar, see Dad at the

Leica factory. I've got some special film to be developed that I can't trust a street shop with. Back late morning.' She reached out and squeezed my arm and I had to stop myself pulling her into me. 'Hey, I – '

'So we are friends again, yes? I don't know what the hell happened but – '

She stepped closer and took me by the elbows. 'Always, Otto. Look – '

'You don't have to say anything, Ingrid. Friends is enough for me. I think you are – '

'Me too. I think you are -'

'Well, look.'

'Well, look.'

I put my arms around her and squeezed her against me, kissing the top of her head. I could feel the emotion rising in my throat and when I let go, see it in her eyes. We stepped back, still looking at each other for a few paces, then we spun and went our ways.

I crossed over to the south side towards the entrance of the Early History Museum, the magnificent Martin-Gropius-Bau, and cut through the queues heading up the pillared steps. I stuck out my chest, the weight of the Holy Grail making my bag swing, and I marched on like I was the top SS cadet in my year. What was it that Ingrid and the night train waiter had said? Courage – it's a decision.

Four guards in helmets, machine guns slung over their shoulders, milled on the steps of Himmler's headquarters, sharing a joke. I slowed my stride and they straightened up, smiles falling from tough-guy jaws.

The clipboard guy was there, I clocked him straight off, but there was no way he recognised the scruffy little civilian he sneered at last time. He shot a look at the pips on my collar and he saluted smartly. Traditional military salute, not the *Sieg Heil* javelin version.

I waited for him to address me, holding his eyes, and he looked down at his clipboard. 'You have an appointment, Hauptsturmführer?'

'No.'

'A social visit?'

'No.'

'The purpose of your visit then?'

'To see Reichsführer-SS Himmler.'

'Excuse me, sir?' And he turned to his colleagues with a smile. 'Forgive me, if you don't have an appointment, I think it highly unlikely the boss will take a drop-in visit from a Hauptsturmführer?'

'What's your name, Unterführer?'

'I'm sorry?'

'I said, what's your name? *Unterführer.*'

'Neumann.'

'Okay, Neumann. Why don't we let Herr Himmler decide whether my business is worthy of his attention? If it's not, I'll see you out here in a moment and you and your meathead friends can giggle and smirk as much as you like.'

I kept my eyes trained on his, jutting my jaw, adding: 'You're a gatekeeper, one up from a guard dog, not the king of the castle.'

'Yes, sir.'

He pushed open the door and I could tell by the way he squinted he was trawling his memory, trying to place me. I made my way up the wide stone steps and clicked across the great hall to the reception desk. Two plank-stiff guards at the foot of the stairs to the left, eyes beneath their helmets following me like ancestral portraits. Same woman as last time, blue-ice eyes, blue-ice manner. Her noodle-thin eyebrows rose by way of asking my reason for standing before her.

'I am here to see Reichsführer-SS Himmler.'

'You are? What is your appointment time?'

'I don't have one. Just tell him Hauptsturmführer Otto Eckhart is here to see him.'

Her eyebrows made another trip up her brow. 'And what, may I tell him, is the nature of your unscheduled visit?'

'None of your business.'

She eyed me for a moment, then picked up the phone, dialled and, lowering her head into the blotting paper pad, I heard her say, 'Hedwig, I have an Otto Eckhart...' She swivelled her chair and continued with her back to me. She swung back slowly and dropped the handpiece from two fingers into the cradle as though disposing of something disgusting.

'The Reichsführer-SS is currently away from his desk.'

'Bullshit. Call Hedwig back and tell her Herr Eckhart has come to discuss some affairs of state. Tell her it would be a terrible shame were this information, vital to the Reich, to fall into the wrong hands.'

She picked up the handpiece again, our eyes in a stand-off, and pirouetted in her chair so fast she had to plant a foot to stop her coming full circle. The exchange was brief, and when she turned back, she replaced the handset in a normal fashion this time and with a smile. No more than a minute had passed when a door swung open and heavy footsteps echoed their way up from the basement.

I turned to face the stairs and two SS guards emerged from the shadows, the shorter of them snapping, 'Follow me, Hauptsturmführer!' He threw out an open hand, gesturing down and I strode towards him, my confident manner belying the fear seizing me. I shadowed him down the stairs, the other one behind me. We passed through a heavy set of oak doors and they snapped shut like an animal trap, killing all noise from the hall above. The squat guard unhooked a fat bunch of keys from his belt. He found the one and slotted it into the lock of the reinforced metal door before which we now stood. Reaching for the door handle, he turned and, a smile creeping up the side of his face, said:

'The Reichsführer has requested you are taken the back way. He thought you might be interested to witness the fruits of our programme of *intensiied interrogation*.'

Using both hands, he leant back and heaved open the door.

A grey corridor ran the length of the building and I

was barely able to see the far end of it. He ushered me through. I waited for him to finish locking the door and he led on. A man in a brown warehouse coat about halfway down was slopping a mop into a bucket and working it over the floor. The guard slowed his pace outside some cells where groans and sobs were clearly audible above the sharp rapping of our heels on the stone floor.

He stopped at the cell where the cleaner was mopping – mopping blood, no question, and lots of it. Adorning the wall to the left of the door was a bloodied handprint, almost perfect, such as a young child might produce with paint in art class, the fingers then smearing towards the frame. The guard slid back the cover and put his eye to the peephole. He stepped back and invited me to look for myself.

'Communist diehard,' he said with a scoff and shake of the head. 'One of the last.'

I took off my cap and put my face to the door. It reminded me of the time I had looked into a diorama at the fairground as a child. But it was not a happy scene depicted, no Alpine idyll of wooden farmhouses, grazing cattle and buxom maidens. The room was barely wider than the corridor, the only light coming from a rectangle of thick frosted glass at the top of the wall. At the foot of it lay a narrow shelf of wood – the only furniture – and wedged at the end of it, in the corner, a ball of human, its shoulders shuddering and a bare foot hanging over, quivering as though tapping out a crazy jazz beat, *allegrissimo*.

'You'd think a teacher – of all people – would be quicker to learn, to know better. Sad really.'

I said nothing, just looked at him blankly, trying to thwart the rush of images of my father wrestling into my mind.

'Come, come – mustn't keep him waiting.' And he hurried away, metalled heels like a burst of automatic fire in an ambush. Through another heavy metal door, we descended a staircase and crossed the delivery area to the birdcage elevator I had shared with Himmler on my previous visit. The vans were lined up outside in perfect formation as last time, the drivers or agents or hired heavies – whoever – huddled under their hats, pulling on cupped cigarettes, a light drizzle now falling from the leaden sky.

Leaving the other guard in the depot, we stepped in and he yanked shut the concertina grille, slapped a brass button and the elevator jumped into motion. I steadied myself with long deep breaths, the hoist ropes jerking us up through the bowels of the noble old building, the motor whining overhead. The lift was as slow heading up as it had been fast coming down and we laboured through all the floors before it clattered to a halt on the fifth. I was looking at the toes of my gleaming black boots when my escort ripped back the grille. I planted one foot out and stopped dead in my stride.

Himmler was standing right before me, long leather coat buttoned and belted, hugging his cap under folded arms. The patent leather of his coat and the skin of his scalp shone beneath an uncovered lightbulb. It was as though he had been immersed in phosphorescence. No imbecile grin wreathing his rodent face today. His mouth was set fast and his eyes were hard behind the pince-nez, boring into mine.

I was still standing one foot in, one out when, at last, he spoke. 'Thank you, Hoffman, I shall escort the visitor from here.'

Hoffman pulled his heels together, thrust out a ramrod arm. 'Sir! Heil Hitler!'

Himmler threw a limp arm in the guard's direction, half heil, half waft, and headed along the short corridor to the back door of his office. He had left it slightly ajar and a slice of light cut into the darkness. I inhaled deep, adjusted my cap and stepped into the darkness, the bag pulling on my arm. I eased the door to with my shoulder and it shut with a faint click. He was in his seat, knocking and shaping a stack of papers into the leather inlay of his desk. He laid the sheaf before him and, using his palms, patted the edges so that perfect symmetry was attained. His mouth was clamped, lips white with the force. He was breathing through his nose as someone might before taking the plunge in an Alpine lake after the Spring melt.

I am no actor – unless you count my performance as a mute shepherd in a school production of Goethe's *Faust* – but the curtain was about to come up and I was concentrating on my performance as though my very life depended on it. As indeed it probably did. I stood before his desk, bag and Grail at my feet, straight arms pressed to my flanks, chin high, looking above his head, but not so far that I was unable to read his expressions and gestures. He was staring at me now, in that way peculiar to him, tilting his head, first one way, then the other. He sat back in the chair, elbow on the armrest, chewing a thumb knuckle.

'So, Eckhart – '

The words had barely left his mouth when I pivoted on the balls of my feet and cracked my heels together – it was a first-class heel-crack, as fine as you'd hear anywhere in the Reich that day – and still looking over his head, I snapped: 'Sir?' And I looked down at him. He said nothing.

I continued to hold his gaze, like we were playing that children's game, trying not to be the first to look away. Half a minute had passed before, in one rapid motion, he hauled himself to his feet and froze. He emerged from his recess, feeling his way along his desk, his eyes still drilling into my face. Keeping his distance, he arced to my right with slow, measured strides, head to one side, like I was a modern art exhibit or a wounded animal. Disappearing from my peripheral vision, he came to a halt directly behind me. There was no movement in the airless room, the only noise his heavy breathing and the dull hum of traffic beyond the sealed windows. The sweat on my hairline triggered an intense urge to scratch but I remained stiff as a waxwork guardsman.

A good minute passed this time before he resumed

his circumnavigation. He reappeared on my left and stopped abruptly. Knuckles on his desk, he stared up at Lanzinger's portrait of the knightly Hitler on horseback hanging between the bookshelves, and rocked back and forth. He swung a semi-circle and took a huge sidestep so that he was standing right before me, his face no more than a pencil length from mine, a muscle twitching his cheek. I gulped but I did not flinch. Still he said nothing, just breathed like people do in their sleep, heavy and slow, chest rising and falling, a sickly-sweet woody stench filling my nostrils.

'You've changed, Eckhart.' It came out mildly, whispered, but riding on a snarl and vapours of vinegar and rotten meat. 'And I don't mean your tan and your new physique. Are you putting on a show for me, Eckhart?'

'Certainly not, sir. With respect. In France, yes, I was. But not here, back, thank God, in the Fatherland.'

'Your meaning?'

'To fall in and win the trust of the locals, sir, I was compelled to assume their dissolute habits. As a moral costume if you will.'

'So, like an undercover agent, going native?' he scoffed. 'Agent Otto, eh?'

'If you like, sir. I needed their help in hunting down the Grail. Hence the drinking, the slovenliness, the lounging – you know the French, sir.'

'I do Eckhart, I do. How very cunning and daring of you.'

In my heels and cap, I had gained a few more

centimetres over him and, leaning in a little, he was so close he had to keep his neck tipped back quite far to look into my eyes.

'And the dog in your bed? How do you – '

'Not guilty, sir. The half-beast freak took a liking to me. My kindness to him won me many favours in the village. Frankly sir, Inspector Muller's inference of bestiality appals me.'

I was aware of his slow blinking, his toilet breath almost unbearable.

'And what of your *book*, Eckhart?' He said it with a slow sneer. 'Your bottom-of-the-class university thesis, rather. And the contempt of your professors?'

'Professor. Singular, sir. Just one of them, Gebhardt. But no excuses, sir, I was a poor student. Immature, lacking in confidence, bullied a little. But sir – '

'But what, Eckhart?'

My mouth was dry now and the words came out in a rasp. 'There is something you should know about Professor Gebhardt.'

He tipped himself even closer and, in a quiet voice, said, 'Is there, Eckhart? Careful now – remember that Hermann is a faithful party man. He has worked miracles in mucking out the Heidelberg stables of social democrats and other undesirables.'

'Understood, sir, but… first, you should know Professor Gebhardt has nothing but scorn for Norse and Teutonic mythology. He delighted in mocking my fascination with our deep German past. Hence the low grades.'

'Do you really expect me to believe that – of a professor of early European literature in one of Europe's finest universities? That's poor, Eckhart.'

'Only "infants and imbeciles" are interested in that nonsense, he liked to say. I'll show you his comments on my essays. It was the poetry, the language alone that fascinated him, sir.'

He put a hand to his chin, glossy with balm, and stroked it over and over, slowly. 'Did he now? Infant? Imbecile? *Nonsense?*'

'And sir, on my honour, my research is solid, my thesis holds. I am proud of the book. I stand by it – for you, for the Führer, for the German people, sir. Other professors may have given me a first.'

I was close to vomiting from the stench and the nerves, and it was a great relief that at this point Himmler took a step back and sat on the edge of his desk, arms folded, legs outstretched, ankles crossed, leather coat squeaking as he made himself comfortable.

I exhaled, saying: 'And, sir, there is one other fact you should know about Professor Gebhardt?'

'Go on.'

'Well sir, this is awkward. How can I put this delicately so as not to unsettle your moral sensibilities?'

'My moral sensibilities? Are they so obviously delicate? I am not an *infant*, Eckhart. Or an *imbecile* for that matter. I am the Reichsführer-SS, the Chief of Police for all Germany.'

'His words, not mine, sir. Very well. Let us just say

then that there was good reason why Professor Gebhardt was known to the students as "Professor Pervert", sir.'

He leaned forward, lowered his head and looked up at me from under his brow, his pince-nez dangling on the edge of his nose, eyes smiling.

'Pervert? What are we talking, Eckhart – prostitutes? Sado-masochism? Fancy dress homosexual orgies? Rope and chain bondage? Erotic humiliation? Fetish art?? Specifics, please.'

'Perhaps, sir. I couldn't comment. I know only of a depravity that is almost unspeakable. Children, sir, some as young as ten. He tutored for many Heidelberg families. In his remote home on the hill above the castle.'

Himmler sprung from the desk, throwing an arm up and exclaiming: 'That is extremely revolting, Eckhart – this is just idle student gossip! You are making this up to save your own skin, and – '

'No, sir!' I shouted it. 'Excuse me, but with respect. Gebhardt has been reported by parents on several occasions – to the university authorities and, I believe, to the police. But such was his reputation... Well, you can make your own enquiries.'

This was all fact, and I was able to say it with the stamp of truth in my voice.

He was pacing the room now, hands behind his back. 'I shall, I shall. That is quite abominable. Children! I have my own little Gudrun and the thought – ugh! You're quite sure?'

Professor Gebhardt – a Nazi before the Nazis, a flagrant deviant and a merciless bully. I pictured him, hands cuffed behind his back, piping his reedy protests, escorted through those ancient corridors of learning out to the waiting *schubwagen* and away to a damp underground cell and a plank for a bed. That was going to be the scene later in the day, perhaps before lunch, and a thrill ran through me.

'Quite sure, sir.'

He sidled past me, whispering, 'If you're wrong, Eckhart, if this is self-serving slander then – then may God and the Führer have mercy on your soul!'

Back behind his desk, he took off his glasses, rubbed his face and dropped into his chair, elbows planted, hands on his head. The phone rang and he let it go for several rings then seized the handset and barked 'Not now!', slamming it back down. He put his head back in his hands.

I saw my moment and, getting down on one knee, opened the leather bag, quickly unfolded the shawl and lifted out Raymond's chalice, trying not to picture him guzzling Ricard and singing blasphemous songs as he worked on it. I lowered it onto his desk, silently upon the leather inlay, and resumed my guardsman's pose, my eyes fixed on him, heart still thumping.

He was nodding his head back and forth, face to the desk, his fingers massaging his stubbled scalp. A shaft of sunlight, bursting from behind a cloud, illuminated his desk. Look up! Look up now! It was the perfect moment, a beam sent from the heavens! I feigned a coughing fit and he stirred, placing his hands under his chin in the prayer position. He was looking straight at me and I smiled at him through the shaft of dazzling sun cutting between us like a spotlight.

His eyes fell slowly to the desk, to the stone chalice. He didn't blink, he didn't move. Slowly his jaw slackened, and his mouth drooped open. He reached out, like he was about to cup a butterfly, and wriggled to the front of his chair. Wrapping his hands around the cup, he raised it slowly, as if in dread of dropping it, and eased slowly to his feet. He held it right out, raising it higher, eyes following it, swallowing hard, punching out breaths now, turning it in his fingers, his face a cartoon of wonder.

'This is it?' He was barely audible.

'This is it, sir.' I gulped.

Still whispering, he said: 'You found it, Eckhart! You found it! And look, these symbols are just like the Hakenkreuz.'

'Yes, very similar – and the runic inscriptions. Nordic, sir. It proves you right. The Aryans *did* spread east. We are the ones, the first true civilisation, the true chosen ones.'

He lowered the chalice gently back on the desk, his face hardening. 'But how do we know it is *the* chalice, Eckhart? I mean, the very one. Can we really stand before the world at Nuremburg next month, and hold this aloft?'

I bent down and took the envelope from the bag and handed it to him.

'It's a letter of authentication from Father Pietro Lambertini, the world's greatest authority on Holy Relics. You'll find all his books in the library.' *Unless you had them burned*, I thought.

Himmler ripped a perfectly manicured thumb under the wax seal of the envelope flap and pulled out the letter.

I continued, 'It's been scientifically dated from the time of Christ, the stone is from the hills of Jerusalem, the carvings are consistent with traditional sacred artwork of the Jews of the early first century. If any chalice can lay claim – '

His eyes darted back and forth, the letter trembling in his hand, his Adam's apple bouncing in his throat.

'No one will ever be able to prove or disprove its authenticity,' I went on. 'But no chalice to date comes even close to meeting the criteria. I suspected all along that Father Pietro held the key to the mystery. He was so evasive but when he found out I was working for you – '

'So he just gave it to you? Just like that. Here you go my friend, have the Holy Grail.'

'He lost his faith, sir. Hates the Catholic Church now and it hates him. They can't bear that a man so immersed in the great mysteries of the early Church has turned his back on them.'

'Well, he's certainly not alone in his contempt for the

Church,' he laughed. 'But I don't understand… Where did he get it from? He just lifted it from the Vatican?'

'Until now, he was the only one alive aware of its existence. He found it in a long-forgotten collection dating from the time of the Crusades, discarded for centuries among a thousand other artefacts. He is certain that, after Saladin's sack of Jerusalem in 1187, the Knights Templar took it from the Church of the Holy Sepulchre and brought it back to Europe. What happened to it after that is anyone's guess, but he's on the trail of that as we speak. He had it tested secretly – never told a soul – and when they cast him out, he walked out with it. It was his way of having revenge.'

'But why you? Why give it to us?'

'Read on, sir.'

The Reichsführer-SS finished the first page and hurriedly turned over the second, his eyes racing over Father Pietro's immaculate italic script, a grin spreading over his face.

He dropped the letter to his side. 'So, he's one of us? He shares our vision!'

I smiled back, picturing unshaven Father Pietro sliding off his bar stool, mumbling profanities and staggering out into the square in Montségur, Gauloises hanging from his mouth.

'One hundred percent, sir – almost a fanatical addict. The Führer is his new God, Mussolini the prophet. He is convinced, like you, Jesus was of Aryan descent – that a sophisticated Nordic civilisation existed long before the Abrahamic religions. That it all began right here.'

I stabbed a finger down at the floor. 'Right here, sir!'

I reached down into my bag and pulled out another envelope. 'It's a personal letter from him to you. I imagine it will make you blush. He's a great admirer.'

Himmler took it and rubbed his finger over the wax seal and slid it into the inside pocket of his coat, face like a kid around the Christmas tree. 'He is? Good heavens!'

He ripped the handset from the cradle of one of his two phones, dialled one number. 'Get me Goebbels. Tell him it's important.' He put the phone back down.

'You were saying, Eckhart.'

'No, sir, I said nothing.'

The phone rang and he snatched at it. 'Joseph! I beg your pardon, right you are… A meeting with Todt, is he now? Well tell him to telephone me as soon as he's free, will you? Yes, yes, Heil Hitler.'

He dialled his secretaries again. 'Get me Dr. Walter Wust – yes, at the Ahnenerbe. Yes, that's right, its new President.'

I smiled. Excellent! He was calling his clowns at the Ahnenerbe, the SS's private scientific institute, the circus freaks I had met at Wewelsburg. I knew from Ingrid that the institute was little more than a department of historical propaganda – a laughing stock amongst serious scientists. So long as they were in charge of verification, I was probably in the clear.

Himmler was in a state of the highest excitement, running his palm back and forth over his scalp, turning and pacing almost on the spot, the phone clamped to his ear. When Wust came on the line he sprung back so violently he almost pulled the phone from his desk. He took a deep breath, trying to calm himself before he spoke.

'Walter! Heinrich here. When can you get over to Prinz-Albrecht-Strasse? Yes, *very* important. Historic. Well, put Bormann off until tomorrow. No, bugger Borman – yes, it's *that* momentous!'

He put down the phone, thrust his hands into his coat pockets and started marching between the south-facing window and his desk, pivoting on his heel as if on the parade ground. I may just as well have not been in the room. I would probably never find him in a better mood – or at least not in one so distracted. I let him make a few more turns then put a fist to my mouth and coughed. Still nothing. He picked up the phone again, held it a moment, then put it back down. He sat at his desk, took a pad of headed notepaper from his drawer and ripped off the lid of his pen. He scrawled a few lines, then dropped the pen, leapt to his feet and seized the chalice, holding it high, shaking his head with a smile of happy disbelief.

'Sir?'

Nothing.

'Sir?' This time I said it louder.

He put down the chalice. 'Yes, Eckhart, what? Thank you, yes, you can go. Is that it? Well done, congratulations. I always had faith in you. Well done, well done.'

'Sir, I have been meaning to ask about – '

Silence.

'Sir, I was hoping to ask – '

'Hope what? Ask what?'

'My father, sir.'

'Your father? What of your father?'

'My father who – '

'Oh yes, your communist teacher father. The *Michelstadt mischling*, Muller calls him.'

'He's no communist, sir, and he is a war hero and today a much respected... Well, I thought you might have a word with Darmstadt Stapo, sir. With Muller. I will talk to my father about it all but – '

'Why? Say what, Eckhart?'

'Sir, I was hoping your intervention might – '

The phone rang and he threw himself at it, snatched the handset, fumbling and juggling with it in his lap. He put it to his ear and stood up, his other hand on his hip.

'Excellent, put him through.' He cupped a hand over the mouthpiece, turned to me and smiled, 'Thank you Eckhart. First-class work. I'll be in contact.'

He pulled his hand from the mouthpiece. 'Joseph! I have the most wonderful news.' He raised a hand at me, waved me off and turned his back.

I walked slowly to the front door of his office and reached for the handle. Himmler turned about. He was smiling and looking straight through me. He pressed the handset tighter to his face and said, 'You are never going to guess what my southern Europe expedition team have just unearthed...'

I stared at him for a few moments. I might have stared for an hour without him registering my presence. I shut the door behind me, and kicked the air. I stood in thought, a muffled Himmler yelping with excitement. The door was open to Ingrid's office and I looked around, checked the doors to the other staff rooms were shut, and slipped in. I picked up her telephone and dialled the exchange.

'Yes, good morning, put me through to The Three Hares in Michelstadt. Yes, in Hesse. Quick as you can.'

CHAPTER NINE

It was liberating to be out of the SS uniform, and I ran up the stairs from the men's room, happy to lose myself once again in the bustle of faceless hats. The early morning hordes had dispersed, and I was able to stride over the Anhalter concourse without recourse to force. I glanced up at the departure board, ran my eyes over the destinations – and erupted into a sprint. The Frankfurt train was pulling out right that instant. To catch the connection and get home that night, I had to be on that train. I had to get to my father, plead with him, explain that the time for protest had passed, that he was putting us all in danger now. If that didn't work, then I had to get him out of Michelstadt for a few weeks, maybe on a walking holiday down in the Allgäu, tell him it was a late birthday gift, the hotels were booked. It didn't solve all the problems, but it bought some more time.

The platform guard's whistle rent the air and I careered around the corner onto Platform 6, sliding like a hapless skater. The couplers clanked tight, the carriages braced and the train ground into motion, declaring its departure with a furious blast of smoke and steam. A Wehrmacht officer was leaning out of the last door of the last carriage saying goodbye to his wife and children. I shouted to him, waving my hat, and he threw open the door. His family jumped back, he took my case and, just as the train was starting to outpace me, seized my wrist and hauled me aboard.

I lurched across the compartment, pulling up just before barrelling into a man in a homburg, pipe smoke rising from behind his *Völkischer Beobachter*. He lowered the paper a little and inspected me over his glasses then yanked at the paper, making it snap. I looked around to see all six seats were taken so I thanked the officer, apologised to the others for my dramatic intrusion. With one foot out in the corridor, I leant down to the man in the homburg and whispered, 'No wonder you're in such a vile mood, reading trash like that.'

I made my way along the train until I came across an empty compartment. I sank into a window seat, my back to the direction of travel, the train rattled over the Landwehr canal into the tree-lined suburbs of Berlin's south-west and away into the flat countryside.

It was almost twelve hours, just before midnight, when the branch line train pulled sleepily into Michelstadt, the brakes sighing, almost yawning, as it came to a halt. Berthold had said he would wait up for me – there was much to report, he said – but there had been a full day's drinking ahead of him then and I feared he may have forgotten, locked up and fallen asleep in a stupor of Pils and schnapps and hard graft.

I tramped up the hill from the station as fast as my heavy case and stiff limbs would allow. Coming over the brow I groaned at the sight that greeted me – a party flag now hanging from the flagpole on the Rathaus. I came around the corner, and there was Berthold rubbing his vast belly under the huge glass streetlamp above the door to his inn, swaying a little and burping a volley of smoke rings into the still night air. He swung around, hearing my heels on the cobblestones and I broke into a half-trot.

'Thank you, Berthold!'

The smile I gave him was not returned.

'Muller and his cronies left here twenty minutes ago.'

'Good, he's the last person I want to see right now.'

'It's not good, Otto – they went that way. To your house – unless it's the cattle helping them with their enquiries.'

'What?'

'They were pretty drunk too. It's getting ugly here, Otto – yesterday they closed down Dr Steiner's practice for all patients except the other Jews in Michelstadt.'

'What Jews?'

'Precisely. Put him out of business. And your father was in the square again this afternoon, handing out anti-regime leaflets, urging support for Steiner.'

'Shit! Here, take my case, will you? I'll come for it in the morning.'

I dropped my bag and ran off down Braunstrasse. I was as fit as I had ever been after all the climbing and hiking in the Pyrenees, and within five minutes I was at the bottom of the shallow scoop of valley where the lane twisted steeply up to the old farmhouse. The ground floor was propped up by flying buttresses of light from the small windows, the door opened and a yell – my mother's – tore into the night. I started running again, car doors opened and slammed, my mother hollered a second time, headlamp beams sliced through the darkness. I reached the wide-open gate, panting hard now. I shouted, 'Hey! Wait a minute!' and I made to block the only route out.

A man looked over, then held down his hat and eased himself into the back seat. The car jerked away before he had shut the door. My mother ran after it but gave up after a few strides, her silhouette motionless in a shaft of dusty light. I stood in the middle of the gateway, putting my arms out at the side. The car gathered speed, spraying stones from the back wheels as it straightened up and fixed me in its beams. I held my ground but the car kept coming. I jumped aside and they flashed past. Inspector Muller smiled, tipping his hat at me from the front passenger seat, my father behind him, his nightshirt beneath his coat.

Our eyes locked for a split second and there was not a flicker of fear in his face. He looked relaxed, there was even a hint of humour in the brightness of his eyes. I turned about, shaking my head – more at him than them – hands on my hips, watching the headlamps zigzag their way through the meadow and over the hill into the darkness. My mother was slumped over a water butt, and I ran to her and took her in my arms. She cried until she had nothing left to cry. Standing back, she rasped: 'Dachau – they're taking him to Dachau.'

• •

We stayed up long into the night and I left Mother to sleep when I headed back to Michelstadt. Swallows plunged amongst cattle tinkling their bells and whisking their tails, heads down over the meadow glistening in the heavy dew. It was a perfect summer's morning, entirely at variance with the winter of my mood. I climbed the hill, bounced along the cobbles and leant my bicycle against the wall. The bell in the steepled Gothic church opposite began to strike the hour and, passing beneath the ancient stone arch, I tramped up the steps into the lobby of The Three Hares, rubbing knuckles into my dry, weary eyes.

I was greeted by the cuckoo bursting from the shutters of its Black Forest house affixed to the wall. I hung my hat on the stand next to it and watched the watermill on the side of the house turning its real water. Dancers in rustic costume revolved beneath a balcony while the oompah band silently worked its tuba, accordion, drum and cymbals, entirely out of tempo with the revolving dancers and the measured call of the cuckoo. It was like a bad joke – sure, that's exactly what Germany is like – and a sensation of mild hysteria ran through me.

In the restaurant, a handful of couples addressed

their breakfast in silence, the room's only sound that of cutlery on crockery. On the ninth strike, the church bell fell quiet and, taking the step down into the stone-vaulted bar, I found Berthold running a foam scraper over a tankard of beer.

'I never drink before nine,' he smiled. 'That's just wrong.'

'Thank God there are still standards left in our great country.'

I pulled a ten Reichsmark note from my wallet and laid it on the bar, adding, 'Berthold, I'm going to need your phone this morning. Never know who will be eavesdropping in the Post Office.'

'Too right – but I don't want your filthy SS money. Buy me a beer when you're done. How did your father cope with Muller and his heavies?'

'Not very well. They took him. To Dachau.'

Berthold took the beer from his lips and laid down the tankard on the dripping mat. He leant his massive hands on the counter, as if to steady himself. 'No – tell me that's not true. Please.'

'I can't. It is. I need to get on that phone.'

'Of course, of course. Use the one at reception. Number here is 374 if you need to be called back.' Berthold lifted the tankard, drained half of it, wiped his mouth with the back of his hand and added, 'Come, come, I'll get you set up.'

I tried Ingrid at her apartment in Charlottenburg but it rang and rang. It was the same when I called Prinz-

243

Albrecht-Strasse. I waited a while then tried both again. There was still no luck at her home and I was about to give up on the office number too when someone picked up. A smooth but exasperated voice said, 'Miss Behringer's office. Karl Wolff speaking.'

Wolff – the Chief of Himmler's personal staff. By his irate tone I had the impression he had jack-booted across the corridor to put an end to the annoyance of my remorseless ringing.

It was then that I remembered that Ingrid was making her way back from Wetzlar and it would be at least two hours before she was back at her desk. I was about to put down the receiver, but fearing that that might somehow throw suspicion upon her, I said, 'Good morning, Gruppenführer. This is Hauptsturmführer Otto Eckhart.'

After a pause, he said, 'Ah, the great historian and Grail hunter no less. I understand congratulations are in order.'

'Thank you, sir, but it was very much a team effort. I would not have been able to accomplish my discovery without your office and the whole-hearted backing of the Reichsführer-SS. It is for us all to feel proud this morning.'

Karl Wolff – a suave, old-school figure born of a wealthy family, according to Ingrid, susceptible to charm and fine manners. 'The Schutzstaffel executes remarkable work for the Reich,' I added.

'Why thank you, Eckhart. How may I help you this

morning? Don't tell me you are calling to report that you have now unearthed the Spear of Destiny?'

I joined in his laughter with as much sincerity as I could muster and when silence returned, I said, 'Actually, I was rather hoping Miss Behringer might put me through to the Reichsführer-SS. I have a small favour I forgot to follow up with him yesterday.'

'Herr Himmler is out of the building this morning, but I am very pleased to tell you that, any moment now, he will be in the company of the archaeology experts at the Pergamon. After that, he heads down to Wewelsburg for a few days.'

My heart jumped and I had to put my hand over the mouthpiece and blow out a breath. 'The Pergamon?'

'Yes, he's very excited to show them your find. By the way he talked, you'd think he had found it himself! He was almost skipping when he left.'

The image of Germany's chief policeman skipping like a kindergarten girl along the Unter den Linden clutching his toy chalice was an unsettling one to picture, and served only to fuel my erupting disquiet. The Pergamon Museum was the one place in Germany I hoped Himmler would not present Raymond's Grail for examination. I had gambled on him keeping it with the Ahnenerbe, inside his SS madhouse. The Ahnenerbe is a sinister circus but the Pergamon is an institution highly regarded around the world. It would surely not be long before their specialists exposed the false claims of the chalice.

My mind raced through the options. I could well have spent the next few days sweating over a scheme to rescue my situation, but it is remarkable how extreme pressure can force the mind into a rapid process of calculations, reaching a solution probably no worse or no better than that achieved from hours and days of mental toil. Half a plan jumped into my mind and I ran with it, not entirely sure where it was going to lead.

'I am so pleased to hear that, Gruppenführer. I am very impressed, but not in the slightest surprised by the exceptional efficiency of an elite institution such as the SS.'

'We do try our best, Eckhart. May I be of any help to you in the meantime?'

'Well, in fact, perhaps – actually, it's nothing really, just a small administrative matter. I most certainly don't want to bother someone of your rank and standing with a silly little –'

'No, please, Eckhart, it would be an honour. After what you have achieved. Such a great coup for the Reich. It's the least I can do.'

'Thank you, and of course I would not dream of disturbing Herr Himmler down at the castle with matters so trifling. I am only too aware of how much that mystical place allows our leader to unburden himself of the onerous weight of his high office.'

'Quite so, Eckhart. Very well put. So what exactly may I do for you in his absence?'

'Well, Herr Gruppenführer, it's really rather

embarrassing. My father, a tremendous patriot and war hero actually, just like you in fact – he received the Iron Cross first class for his desperate actions on the Eastern Front. Well, a few weeks back he picked up some vicious sort of infection swimming in a lake – I saw a herd of cows defecating in the shallows not far from him. Anyhow, it has had a very peculiar effect on his mental faculties.'

'Heavens, I am sorry to hear that Eckhart. How awful for him.'

'Yes, it has led to a great deal of misunderstandings, not least with the local police authorities. He doesn't quite think he's Napoleon Bonaparte or Frederick the Great yet, nor is he drinking from puddles – but who knows, that may just be a matter of time!'

We roared with laughter and then, in a soft voice, when we had died down, I said, 'But, he's got it into his crazy head – if you can believe this of a man like him – well, that our Führer is becoming some sort of despotic monster. Like Stalin. Amazing really because he was the Führer's greatest champion just a few weeks ago. It was all *Uncle Adolf this, Uncle Adolf that.* But I do feel for the provincial police – how could they be expected to understand his health condition, when this bizarre sickness of the mind has baffled so many eminent doctors? After all, they were only doing their duty, these policemen.'

'He has been detained, you're saying?'

I paused, sighed and in a quiet, croaking voice, I said,

'Yes, it's awful, my frail mother is quite beside herself. I am starting to fear for her health as well now.'

'Why, that's appalling, Eckhart! And a war hero and a devoted Führer follower.'

'It is, it is. Terrible. He needs hospital treatment, sir. I fear detention will only aggravate his temporarily deranged mind.'

'Well, quite! Now, do we know where he's being detained? I will look into this at once. You are quite right that we don't want to add to Herr Himmler's burden – he has so much with which to contend right now, what with Nuremburg around the corner and Il Duce's visit. Let me take up the case for you.'

I was having to think very fast, my plan coming together as the words tumbled from my mouth. I could barely believe what I was saying and doing.

'That's so very kind of you, Herr Gruppenführer. Without wishing to make your ears burn, Ingrid did tell me you were a man of the highest honour and kindness.' – a *ghastly, oleaginous bottom-patter* was how she actually put it – 'I tell you what, for I know you are a very busy man too, let me talk to the local Stapo myself. I am sure I can explain the misunderstanding. But perhaps, as a last resort, if there is still some sort of bureaucratic obstruction, perhaps then I might contact you for help. Herr Himmler asked me yesterday to remind him to sort out the error but we were so swept up in the excitement of the Grail, you know...'

'Of course! And of course you must contact me. I am

saddened for you and your family. I shall do whatever I can. I am here for the whole week.'

'You are truly a gentleman, Herr Gruppenführer. It's been an honour talking to you. Thank you.'

'No, thank *you*, Eckhart. You are the hero of the Reich this morning.' Then, with a giggle, added hastily, 'After the Führer, of course!'

'Indeed – and before we part, may I ask you to leave a message for Ingrid, Miss Behringer, to telephone me at The Three Hares in Michelstadt? Number's 374.'

'Of course. Let me just jot that down… there we are. Very good.'

'Very good.'

'Thank you.'

'Thank you.'

'Good day.'

'Good day.'

'Heil Hitler.'

'Heil Hitler.'

I thrust down the handset and threw myself back in the chair. Berthold, who had been staring pop-eyed from the other side of the desk, clapped furiously, his giant belly bouncing with laughter. 'Germany's Clark Gable!'

I looked at my watch – it would be a while yet before Ingrid would call. I headed out into the street, hands deep in pockets, hat down hard over my eyes. I was in no mood for vapid chatter or sympathy or any talk of my father. Half the town, Berthold said, were turning into foot-washing Führer worshippers and sneaky informers.

The flag on the Rathaus rippled in the warm breeze funnelling up the hill. Beneath it, the bürgermeister's daughter – a picture postcard blonde with a winning smile – rattled a tin for the League of German Maidens. I gave her a so-sorry smile and pulled out the lining of my trouser pocket. I had plenty of change clenched tight in my other pocket.

The marketplace looked no different to how I had ever known it, no different to how my father had ever known it, barely any different to how it had looked for three or four centuries – timber-framed buildings, pointed gables, burnt orange roofs, wrought-iron trade signs hanging from the artwork facades, draymen unloading barrels from the horse cart, the entry bell tinkling on the door of the pastry shop, the window box flowers cheerful as every summer, the dark wooded hills beyond. Germany at its most picturesque.

Then I wandered over to the news and cigarette kiosk. Now that was different. *Der Angriff*, *Der Stürmer*, *Völkischer Beobachter* – unapologetic propaganda organs of the state – filled the racks, a few copies of the old liberal newspapers looking sorry for themselves on the bottom rungs. I reached down and pulled out a *Frankfurter Zeitung* – the only vaguely independent paper left, Father claimed, its circumscribed freedom ensured by the Propaganda Ministry to give the regime a veneer of honesty and open-mindedness overseas.

I slipped the coins into the change tray and shot away before Lothar turned around from unboxing his cigarettes. Lothar – an opinionated bore in wartime or peace, lean times or fat – and I had not a shred of forbearance that morning to see me nodding politely through one of his semi-literate philippics.

A pair of rutting pigeons made way for me on the stone basin of the fountain. I sat down, snapped the paper into its full length, and ran my eyes over the headlines: Franco's forces had taken Santander, the Japanese fleet had blockaded the coast of China, Mussolini was going to be given the full ceremonial treatment on the Unter den Linden during his state visit, everything else apparently going from terrific to absolutely outstanding right across Germany forever and ever, amen.

I read the paper like I was playing the accordion, pulling one page after another in the hunt for an honest or interesting headline. I got about halfway through when I folded it in half then into a quarter and, rolling it into a baton, briskly made my way back across the square and rammed it into the litterbin next to the tin-rattling daughter of the bürgermeister, the grin still chiselled into her features.

I looked at my watch yet again, willing Ingrid to reach her desk – every hour counted now – and returned to The Three Hares. Pacing the bar, the restaurant and the lobby, I drank enough coffee over the morning to revive a corpse. Every time I heard the phone ring, I hurried to the desk, only to be disappointed when the caller transpired to be a booking guest, a supplier or someone who had misplaced their hat.

Berthold had been wise not to let on to Frau Voigt – Erma today – about my father, but she was in irritatingly playful mood and she persisted in teasing me about my love sickness for my new girlfriend. It was just before midday when the phone tinkled once again. Erma leant over the counter in a cloud of cheap scent, revealing the mountain pass between her breasts, and presented me with the handset and a wink, saying, 'Friend and colleague, my left foot!' I cupped my palm over the mouthpiece as she had and, returning her wink and smile, said, 'Would you mind, Erma? This is rather private.' She battered her lashes theatrically, blew me a kiss, and disappeared into the restaurant.

Ingrid was almost whispering. 'Otto, *he*'s back, dictating letters to half of Germany to boast about his Grail success before he heads for Wewelsburg. Make it quick.'

I rattled off everything that had happened – the arrest of my father, my conversation with Wolff, my plan to get my father out of Dachau – a plan I hadn't thought through and for which I needed her help from the inside. 'But I have to act now. While he's at Wewelsburg, away from Berlin. I think I can get Wolff to sanction his release.'

Ingrid paused, then, 'Stay where you are – I'm coming to Michelstadt. I'll deal with Wolff, spin him some excuse for my absence. If you want a favour from Wolff, all you have to do is drop something by his desk and bend over.'

'But – '

'But nothing, Otto. Don't do a thing. We might just be alright.'

I doubted the *alright,* but I liked the *we.*

CHAPTER TEN

Growing up, the joke in Michelstadt was that even the wild boars turned on their heel and fled at the approach of my mother. She was a formidable figure for sure, a remorseless organiser, a one-person Rathaus who has done more good in the community over the years than two generations of the fat old men on the town council – a 'toothless tiger… a talking shop… a parliament of fools' she liked to say, made up of 'lazy status-chasers'. She pretended the Rathaus didn't exist, by-passing its occasional motions and trumping its idleness with her ceaseless energy ('Someone has to stand up and do the right thing by this grand old town!') If only my mother had been running the Weimar Republic, my father liked to say, then the National Socialists would have been driven high into the Alps and the depths of the Black Forest.

Among her many initiatives, she had founded a programme called Neighbour Alert, in which citizens looked out for the welfare of the elderly, the infirm and the less wealthy in their immediate neighbourhood. It made sure no-one went hungry, no-one went without medical care, and no family was forced to neglect the education of their children by forcing them into work before they were of age. The unintended consequence of her actions was to create a stronger community.

The case of Magda is a good example of her Christian charity and sense of civic duty. When, to her horror, she discovered that Michelstadt had its very own prostitute – Magda, an uneducated Ukrainian orphan plying her trade *al fresco* down by the warehouses near the railway station – she brought her to live with us, forcibly. Mother arranged intensive home-tutoring and piano lessons and Magda took to both disciplines like a horse out of the traps. Three years later, quite the lady now, Magda won a scholarship to Munich's Royal Academy of Music and today plays second violin in the Philharmonic there. After a few years of Mother's *ad hoc* government, the fat councillors of the Rathaus as good as surrendered, adjourning their meetings early and repairing to The Three Hares, grumbling that 'Freya' would sort it out (they nicknamed her after the Norse goddess of war). When the incumbent mayor of the day finally admitted defeat a few years back and encouraged her to run as his successor, she replied: *'What, and sit around all day eating lunch?'*

It is true that not everyone liked my mother, but everyone respected her, even them, and especially the less privileged and prosperous down at the foot of the village. And now, hearing of her distress at Father's detention, the citizens of Michelstadt came in numbers to support and console, filing over the hill from town, bearing gifts, hand-drawn cards and prayers urging hope and faith.

For two days the yard was full of automobiles and bicycles, even the occasional horse and trap. The kitchen had been transformed into a menagerie of twittering well-wishers, the table a miniature botanical garden and *konditorei*, crowded with flowers and pastries and cakes, the shelves and surfaces a forest of cards. Carted to Dachau, it seemed my father was as good as dead, this was his wake and a pall hung over the house. But the kindness and distraction of friends and near-strangers lifted my mother and by this, the third day, she had recovered some spirit, outwardly at least.

I had fled the menagerie to the living room and was leaning against the windowsill, absently watching two couples a few hundred metres apart making their pilgrimage to the house on foot. Half a dozen cows, motionless at the top of the hill behind, broke into a fast trot away from the lane. A large automobile shot over the crest, travelling so fast its front wheels left the ground.

Shit – the Stapo! It was a very large automobile, official-looking, and swerving onto the grass to avoid the first couple, it dropped from view. I pictured Muller at the wheel, his fat pig-face screwed up in furious delight, a trotter flat to the boards. Surely the Pergamon couldn't have figured out my fraud so quickly, my mother having now to witness her son being carted away as well? Was there a glaring anomaly or anachronism in the chalice carvings? I leant my head against the glass.

When I looked up, the giant automobile reared up the slope and, dropping gears, bucked through the gate, arced across the yard and skidded to a sharp halt right in front of me. I recognised the vehicle now with its roof up – the Mercedes, side-on, magisterial in its sleek lines and deep-waxed burnish. The door sprung open, out stepped Ingrid, and I hurried to the front door. We embraced hard. Lavender with a hint of cigarette smoke filled my nostrils and I took a deep draught. We stood back and held each other by the forearms. She was grinning from ear to ear, her arms outstretched as if taking a curtain call at the State Opera House. I frowned, a little piqued by her apparent merriment, but said only, 'But I thought you were coming by train? Won't they notice it missing?'

'I told Wolff it needed servicing and not to expect it back for a week. I have plans for it. And you.'

She reached into the backseat and pulled out an overnight case then a large jute or hessian bag, almost half a sack. She held it up by the corners, saying: 'Something to cheer your mother. Ethiopian coffee – the best. From the Yirgacheffe region. They remove the fruit, and then wash the beans before drying them naturally. Oh, and I've got something very special for you too.'

She gave me a peck on the cheek and strode off towards the house. I remained rooted to the spot for a moment. This was no time for a quarrel – I was overjoyed to see her – but what the hell with all this cheerfulness? You'd have thought she was arriving at a birthday party.

She turned at the doorstep, coffee sack tucked under her arm, and waved me along, 'Come on! Aren't you going to introduce me to your mother? I'm dying to meet her.' Maybe she had taken too much of her Benzedrine inhaler.

The room fell silent at the entrance of a stranger, and my mother stepped forward, hand outstretched.

'Delighted to meet you, Frau Eckhart. Otto has told me so much about you.'

'Ingrid, yes? From the civil service in Berlin.' Mother was beaming too, her eyes bright now through the puffy sacks.

Ingrid threw me a look and said, 'Yes, that's right. I am so sorry to hear about your husband, Frau Eckhart.'

My mother brushed down her sleeves and straightened her brooch, throwing me a look with startled eyebrows that said, *Why didn't you tell me your new friend was such a sophisticated beauty, Otto?* And I could see her mind working out the seating places at the wedding.

'Yes, stupid man! Stubborn as a donkey stuck in a bog. I hope he'll have learned his lesson by the time they let him out. You can say what you like about the Führer but – '

Ingrid cut in, 'Or perhaps you can't!'

Ingrid's joke fell flat, the room looking at its feet and, seeing my mother's face drop, she said with childlike eagerness, 'Here, I have brought you some coffee beans. Fresh from Ethiopia! One cup of this and you'll be dancing all over the house. It's better than drugs!'

It was my turn to throw a look – at Ingrid – and I hoped she read the message: ease up on the jollity, will you? She did. Her smile collapsed, her brow knitted and her eyes narrowed. She turned from me to Mother.

'Frau Eckhart, I know people in Berlin. I will do everything to find a way to help resolve your husband's case. What we need to – '

My mother lit up and she lurched forward, Ingrid vanishing into her bear-hug embrace. When my mother released her, finally, her cheeks were wet with tears, a smile trying to break out of the miserable carapace her face had become since Father was taken. 'I am so grateful!' she said and dabbed her nose with a ball of handkerchief. 'I am sure when his case comes before a judge…' Her voice trailed off, she blew her nose like a car horn, the room put on a half-smile and shuffled its feet.

I broke into the uneasy silence, tapping Ingrid's elbow. 'Come on, Ingrid, we have much to discuss and then let's make up your room.'

Ingrid nodded to my mother and muttered pleasantries to the room. I led her into the sitting room and shut the door. I spun around, threw out my arms and, whispering but furious, 'What on earth are you doing, raising her hopes like that? Her husband has been locked up in a concentration camp. And what's with all the jolliness?'

She was staring straight through me, nibbling a nail, as though trying to work something out.

'Ingrid, are you listening?'

She turned her back on me, took a knee and, laying her case flat, clicked open the button fasteners with her thumbs.

'Ingrid? What's got into you? Say something, will you?'

She lifted out some folded clothes and placed them on the rug. Then a washbag, some shoes. I was about to speak again, the anger in the back of my throat now, when out came guns – two Walther PPKs, two cartridge boxes, a camera in its case, a stitched leather tube, a hairbrush, and some manila folders with the Reichsadler stamp and filing numbers in the corner. When all the contents lay in neat piles and the case was empty, she unpopped some press studs, peeled back the cloth lining and took out a large white envelope. She stood up, still grinning, and handed it to me. It was stiff and heavy.

'Well, don't just stand there, Otto. Actually, you may need to sit down.'

I remained on my feet. The envelope was unsealed and I put my hand in. I felt the glossy finish of photographs. I was looking at her as I pulled them out. She was smiling so hard her cheeks were going to fly off. I laid the envelope down on the reading table – eyes still on her. Then I looked down at the top picture. My mouth didn't so much fall open as sink. I found myself sitting in the armchair, struck dumb as I worked through the pack.

I rifled through them again, laughing nervously now, and said, 'But how? You can't have been in the room surely?'

'Roof of the church tower. Latest long-range lens from Leica. Dad gave it to me. Straight from the lab almost. I didn't know if it would work.'

'I'm not sure whether I should be disgusted or overjoyed.'

'Be both!'

I stood up and pulled her to into me and it coursed through me like fire, the love, the hope, the courage, the whatever.

• ➤ •

The last of the sun slanted into the kitchen, catching the steam from the sausage casserole on the stove – the 'Last Supper' as Mother kept insisting on calling it. Ingrid sat at the kitchen table, a mass of paper and a half-full ashtray before her. She laid down the pen, took off her glasses and shook the stiffness from her hand. I shut the front door and made my way around Mother's two travel cases and big bag of coffee by the front door, the floorboards cracking under her slow footsteps directly overhead.

Ingrid said, 'Yeeha cowboy, how'd it go? Sounds like you killed a lot of Indians out in those woods.'

'Seven to be precise. Then I ran out of ammo. I am lucky to be here.'

Ingrid blew out a long breath. 'Right, I'm down to my last too. If I do one more of these, I am sure to sprout a toothbrush moustache, grow fat little squirrel cheeks and start blaming everything on the Jews.'

She handed me her latest efforts, a whole side of jagged black script, his name scrawled again and again, all of them almost identical. 'It's actually the easiest signature to forge – the I, the Ms, the L – they're just diagonal lines, a kid's sketch of a mountain range. Even the E is more of an N. The only tricky bit is the flamboyant strike he does through the H of Himmler, a big teacher's tick, like he's giving himself full marks for being a good little Heini.'

I picked up the copy of a letter she had brought bearing a real signature on it and held it up next to the forgeries.

'Amazing – you should work for a criminal syndicate.'

'I think I already do, don't I?'

I flopped the papers onto the table, took the handgun from inside my jacket and laid it down.

'You were right – it's easy – easy as, well, shooting someone. Up with the safety catch, pull and *bang*! I even managed to hit the tree stump six out of seven times.'

'Were you standing next to it?'

'Very funny. Don't tell me – you can hit a birch sapling at fifty paces.'

'Well, actually, yes, I can. Classy sidearm the Walther PPK – a thing of beauty. Blue-steel finish, nice and compact for a concealed carry, no snags when you draw. Double-action option on the trigger, meaning it can de-cock the safety and release the hammer in one pull. And the point 32-calibre is a capable round – you're not going to take down a bear with it, but it does the job. There's not a finer semi-automatic out there.'

She was practising more signatures as she spoke, her face tense with concentration.

'What's semi-automatic mean?'

'Able to fire repeatedly thanks to an automated reloading system requiring alternate release and pressure on the trigger for successive shots. Self-loading to you, but you have to keep pulling. It's not a machine gun where you just keep the trigger depressed.'

'Where do you learn all this man stuff? Cars and guns and cameras?'

She looked up sharply, as if shaken from a trance, her cheeks reddening a little. Squinting her eyes, she leant towards me, whispering, 'Because I am a secret agent of the state police tasked with ridding the world of evil young academics with a special interest in medieval history.'

'Come on, really.'

'I told you – I've been on a lot of dates. It's all men are interested in these days – guns and girls, war and sex.'

'I'm not – war and guns, I mean.'

She looked up and threw me a smile.

'I can't believe we're doing this.'

'I've got the easy bit. It's *you* doing this, Otto.'

I scratched at my scalp with both hands and she added, with doubtful cheer, 'You'll be just fine – and you said you used to do a bit of acting at school.'

'Yes, who will ever forget my mute shepherd?' I sat down at the table, opposite her. 'I've been trying to picture how it's going to play out. I'm half excited and half terrified. It really is jackpot or bust, isn't it?'

Ingrid lit a cigarette, blew out a long jet of smoke and said, 'Yup, two days' time, it's going to be heaven or hell, champagne cup or turnip soup for you. There's no middle way.'

We sat in silence, looking at each other through her smoke. 'I'm worried for you, Ingrid.'

'Oh, stop it – I'll be fine. I've wanted out of that hellhole for years. I have cousins all over the globe and – thanks to poor old Mum – I have my Swiss and US passports. And of course my contacts in London will – '

I turned to her and raised my eyebrows.

'I keep telling you, Otto, I can go anywhere I like.'

'Your contacts in London, Ingrid?'

'Oh nothing, I mean I have some very useful good friends there.'

'Oh yeah?' I was smiling at her but she was looking away.

'It was a poor choice of words, Otto, that's all. Don't let your imagination run away with you.'

'Fine, let's leave it there. For now. And you're absolutely sure about your father?'

'He is off to Cherbourg on Thursday, starts at Kodak next month, contracts all signed. He'll be mid-Atlantic by the time they think of coming for him. *If* they think. Thinking's not their greatest strength. It's exciting – I've never been to New York. I have an excuse now. I'm more worried about her.'

Ingrid, hand cupping one elbow, waved her cigarette towards the ceiling. The floorboards creaked towards the bedroom door and we heard her making her way down the staircase, the sadness audible in the sombre tread. I got to my feet, opened the door and took the suitcase from her.

'A third one, Mother! You'll be packing the hens next.'

'It's for your Father.'

'Of course – good.'

'If he'll be joining us, that is.'

Ingrid and I flung each other a look. Mother went to the stove and plunged a wooden spoon into the pot, stirring it hard, like she was cranking in a winch.

'Mother, everything's going to be fine. Berthold and Erma will look after the house as though it were their own. And, come on – look on the bright side, half the payments they get from renting out the rooms will go straight to you and Dad. That'll be very good money.'

She walked to the window over the yard, put a hand to her mouth and sighed through her nose. 'I have lived in this house for forty years. And you won't even tell me where we're going.'

She had repeated that all afternoon – since we told her the rough plan – and I was at a loss for a meaningful reply, or evasion. Ingrid shot to her feet. 'What about a celebration drink then – to your return. You'll be back soon enough, Eva. So will Germany. Look at it as an extended holiday courtesy of the state – part of the *Strength Through Joy* programme!'

I went to the larder and fetched a bottle of Riesling, took three glasses from the dresser and poured. Ingrid and I raised ours, clinked and held them out, waiting for Mother. Finally, slowly, she raised hers and not so much clinked as clunked our glasses.

Her eyes narrowed, darting back and forth between us. 'You two better know what you're doing or there's going to be hell to pay.'

'Come on, let's eat, get an early night. It's a long old ride to Dachau.'

CHAPTER ELEVEN

'They've built these autobahns, wonderful, but why are we the only ones on the road? Apart from a few trucks.'

The question, accompanied by a rap on my epaulette, roused me from an uncomfortable half-sleep. I twisted in the passenger seat to face her.

'No one can afford an auto, Mother. You've heard the jingle on the wireless – *If you want to drive your own car, put five marks a week in your jar!*'

Ingrid took a hand off the wheel, wound down her window a little further and fired up a cigarette. She took a deep drag, blew it sideways. The little clock in the polished wood of the dash said five past three. I had been asleep for over an hour, since the sight of Ulm and the towering spire of its minster. Seemed like yesterday Ingrid had said, 'On a clear day you can see the Zugspitze 150 kilometres away from up there,' and I drifted away, dreaming of the Alps, a happy dream until Himmler turned up in his bundhosen and badger-fur Tyrolean hat.

Ingrid leant back now, half-turning her head, raising her voice over the rushing air. 'You'll see the Führer cutting the tape on a new synagogue before you see an autobahn full of Volkswagens, Eva. Uncle Adolf decided they'd cost just 990 marks, just plucked a figure, and it was doomed. Even five marks a week, that's four years. And besides… '

'Besides what?'

Ingrid took another drag, wound down the window further and the air roared in. She leant towards me and said, 'Because the autobahns are not really for us.'

'Huh?'

'They're for the military. For the rapid movement of troops and *matériel*.'

'You serious?'

'I hear it all.'

Ingrid took three rapid draws on her cigarette, tossed it through the window in a blaze of sparks and cranked the handle. The giant luxury Mercedes powered out of a range of low wooded hills and into the flatlands of Upper Bavaria.

'How we getting on?'

Ingrid raised a finger off the wheel and the road sign, tiny in the distance, quickly rose to meet us (We had barely dipped below 120 since hitting the road.) Forty-one kilometres straight on to Munich, fourteen to Dachau. I opened the glove compartment, lifted the chamois leather and pulled out the documents. I shut the compartment before Mother laid eyes on the two Walthers. Ingrid and I raised eyebrows at each other and blew out our cheeks. She gave me a pat on the knee.

Another five minutes and she slowed, taking the turnoff into a cubist patchwork of golden and green crop fields – rye and potatoes mainly – the narrow road bending to the south, the red-roofed Palace of Dachau on its hill the only landmark breaking a horizon flat as an anvil from north to south. I pushed myself back into my seat, breathing deep through my nose, and found myself placing two fingers on the pulse on my wrist.

Ingrid threw me a look: 'Remember, Loritz is going to be a lot more nervous than you when he sees that letter from Himmler.'

Just south of the town, she pulled into the yard of a derelict farm building, its roof punched in, one barn door left, splintered and hanging from one hinge, the other lying face down in the dirt.

'Right, let's get official.' She reached over to the glove compartment and pulled out the chamois leather and two party flags on little silver poles, handing me one. 'You do that side. Just screw it into the thread hole behind the headlamp.'

Back in, I watched Ingrid running the cloth over the coachwork, working her way around to the back. I shuffled through the documents, Mother fidgeting and murmuring behind, and Ingrid climbed back, tossing the chamois into my lap. She pulled out a lipstick and applied it in the rear-view mirror, dropping it back into the handbag in her footwell, and fired the engine. A heavy shiver ran through the chassis, the little flags stirred by a gust of wind.

'All set?'

I threw a hand over the back of the sofa seat and twisted to face Mother, forcing a smile. 'You've always told me to put on a brave face. Your turn now.'

She leant forward and squeezed my hand. Her eyes brightened, she smiled and, bouncing her head side to side, started singing... *'Dear God, make me dumb that I may not come to Dachau... Dear God, make me dumb that I may not come to Dachau...'*

I had heard the jingle a few times since my return – Ingrid said that actually it was the authorities who had started it. They wanted word to get around, for everyone to shut up and get scared. Ingrid laughed and made it a duet, pulling back onto the road. I added my voice too, the three of us repeating it over and over like a nursery rhyme – nervous energy having a peculiar effect on human behaviour.

'Dear God, make me dumb that I may not come to Dachau... Dear God, make me dumb that I may not come to Dachau...'

Then we reached the edge of the town and fell silent.

We pulled into a long straight road, freshly surfaced by the look and smell. We accelerated towards the red-tiled palace surveying its former realms, the tree crowns stirring above the walled garden. At the river below it, Ingrid turned and we followed its lightly winding course, passing under a railway bridge. The town was going about its everyday business, shoppers and dog walkers and cyclists, mums and kids throwing bread to ducks, a few heads turning to admire the Mercedes, builders on roofs, a truck tipping dirt. Most of the houses and commercial buildings on the flat skirting the Old Town were new constructions, the trees mere saplings, the gardens undeveloped, some not even grassed yet, the party flag on a house front here and there, an air of fresh prosperity and self-congratulation pushing through the shabbiness.

At the high school, we turned right again. Ingrid accelerated, a cattle market to our left, farmers in hats and shirts sleeves leaning over the enclosure. Ingrid slowed hard, dropped a couple of gears, the Mercedes bucking. Mother sucked in a breath, placing her face and a hand against the window. A vast building site lay before us – skeletons of low-rise factories or workshops, half-rooved storehouses and housing blocks and rank upon rank of wooden barracks, piles of debris and dirt, cranes and plant equipment, stacks of stone and brick and wooden planks and tiles, hundreds of beetling workers, thousands maybe, kicking up a cloud of pale dust glowing in the hot afternoon sun. No effort to hide the place, that was for sure. Half the size of the town, right there for all to see, proud of itself.

Ingrid, throwing glances outside, said, 'Welcome to the future. A new camp for 6,000 more undesirables, sub-humans, enemies of the state... And there, right next to it – that area with the decent buildings – that's the training camp for the SS *Death's Head* Corps, Heini's special guards to run the next camps. Prinz-Albrecht-Strasse is very proud and very excited.'

We stopped at a T-junction, all looking left, my heart starting to really hammer. Minutes now. Ingrid blasted a heavy sigh.

'...And this here is the original, the first *gulag* in Western Europe. You know, anything Comrade Josef can do, Uncle Adolf and Uncle Heini can do better. God, I can't wait to get out.'

I thought she meant get out of the car, then I twigged. I felt my mother's hands on the seat pulling herself forward to see better. A row of poplars flanked the longer perimeter, stretching away to pan-flat farmland quivering in the heat. Along its lower side, the width, ran the back wall of a U-shaped building, watchtowers at each right angle, helmeted guards beneath the open-sided roofs.

A lookout in the tower nearest was propped on a heavy machine gun trained at the construction site, cigarette sagging from his mouth, helmet pushed up over his forehead, belt of ammunition trailing from the gun. He turned towards us, stared for a moment and, tossing away his butt, pulled himself up, straightened his helmet and tapped the other guard on the shoulder. The colleague, swinging our way, put binoculars to his face. The machine gun guy crouched and began scanning the work site, arcing the range of fire, his mate slowly lapping the small observation platform, making a theatrical show with his binos, hunting out wrongdoing amongst the inmates; Communists and Social Democrats in the main, Ingrid said, plus a few turbulent priests, unapologetic homosexuals and recalcitrant Jehovah's Witnesses – the latter's vision of Armageddon and the Thousand-Year Reign being somewhat out of step with the National Socialist version.

Ingrid swung into the dirt road and we headed towards the guardhouse and camp entrance, the hot wind yanking at the swastika flags on the fenders. On the other side of the road, a canal ran alongside the camp between the swaying poplars and a high wire fence crowned with barbed wire. We reached the front of the guardhouse, its archway topped with a watchtower leading into the camp. Ingrid slowed, looked left towards the work site. Five files of men, far as we could see, tramped their way towards us, knee deep in dust, heads nodding like workhorses, a few propped up by their neighbours, guards on either side wobbling on bicycles.

Pulling away, Ingrid said, 'We'll let them pass. Drive around or to the top and back, make it appear we're inspecting the place. The watchtower guys are bound to call in.'

Mother spun around in her seat so that she was looking through the rear window and then pulled herself onto her knees. 'Look! It's him. There he is! Otto, it's your father! Dear God.'

I swivelled and squinted at the men now sloping out of the site and onto the bridge over the canal to the archway into the camp. The strong sun beat down on the back of the car making it hard to see. Plus we were moving away from them, and anyway, they all looked the same with their shaven heads and striped trousers, their shirts – their own it seemed – caked in white dust, the rabble cohort shuffling, tripping, swallowed by the arch and lost to view.

I counted seventeen barracks on our side, making thirty-four in all. At the end of the fence Ingrid halted, faced with a tight turn. Both hands on the right of the leather grip, she hauled down on the spoked steering wheel, muscles tautening in her slender forearms, the wheels of the four-ton vehicle twisting and scratching in the hot gravel dirt. She blew out a long breath from the effort, and we made our way along a sort of market garden at the back of the barracks, the size of two football pitches at least. A large glasshouse, its windows fogged with condensation, sat in the middle of row upon row of vegetables, all arranged with the precision of a Prussian parade ground, each plant and row perfectly spaced from the next. Roughly two dozen men worked the plot, most hoeing, some wheeling barrows, a couple of guards leaning against the back of a barrack, keeping out of the sun.

Mother gushed, genuinely thrilled, 'At least they're feeding him well!'

Ingrid threw a look over her shoulder, made sure Mother was looking out the window still, leant towards me and said, 'They work the garden – and all those fields – but they don't get a bean.'

Moving slowly, all our windows fully down now, I tugged at the collar of my worsted tunic for some relief. A watchtower sat in the middle of the fence looking straight down a dirt road, broad as the Linden, dividing the two columns of long, light-green barrack houses. The labourers, lead soldiers from that distance, were forming up at the far end. The place was faultlessly clean and ordered, you had to give it that. Not so much as a shoot of weed or a scrap of litter.

We passed the tower, and a guard emerged on our side of the observation platform, craned his neck as though not quite believing his eyes, thrust out an arm, and stood stiff as a statue, chin up to the sky.

Ingrid laughed, 'Go on, then! Don't let him down.' I gave her a look, exhaling hard, and threw my arm out of the window, holding it till we passed. Mother was making gasping noises now, dragging herself over to the window behind me. It was certainly a sight to gasp at and Ingrid slowed up.

At the rear of the second column of barracks lay an enormous pen, a pen within a pen, and inside it, a fence-to-fence carpet of rabbits, hundreds upon hundreds of them, white ones and brown ones, thousands maybe, running and bounding, noses twitching, nibbling what was left of the grass, a vast lightly rolling sea of fur. A bank of hutches was stacked six high against the back wall of the last barrack and half a dozen prisoners were engaged in trying to get the rabbits back into them. Bent over, arms flailing, the prisoners hurried here and there, gathering them up – or trying to. Every time an inmate crept up and swooped to grab one, the rabbit took a few hops and the prisoner stood hands on hips or head, or burst after it, scattering the others in its path. One man, almost berserk, a rabbit secured under one arm, was sprinting in a tight circle scooping his hand to bag a second.

'What the – ?'

Ingrid sighed, 'Yep, you better believe it – bunny barracks. It's exercise hour for the Angoras.'

Mother leant back in from the window. 'Are they for the labourers? Food?'

Ingrid frowned, weighing up whether to tell the truth, then, 'No, the Angoras are Himmler's pet project. One of them. He wants to harvest the wool for Luftwaffe flying jackets and socks for the Kriegsmarine. Give us the edge on sea and air.'

We turned again, Ingrid straining at the wheel, and made our way down the other length of the perimeter, more fields to our left, towards the long white building at the end of the camp. On the parade ground before it, the detail of prisoners now stood in a phalanx of a dozen or so rows, each about thirty, forty men long. A guard on a bicycle pedalled between the rows and another circled the group. Four footguards stood at each corner of the square while a machine-gunner in the watchtower on top of the guardhouse across the way ran his weapon slowly back and forth over the great block of men, stock-still in the beating sun, eyes fixed on the head of the man in front.

We completed the circuit in silence but for Mother's sighs, accelerating along the back of the main building, and turned up towards the guardhouse, pulling up just before the bridge. Ingrid yanked at the long brake stick in the footwell, switched off the engine and shook out her hands.

I twisted around and Mother handed me my visor cap. She had her brave face on, but some excitement, some hope, appeared to be breaking out around her eyes. I clutched the door handle, Ingrid's hand soft on my knee, a little dust devil working its way towards us.

I threw open the door and stepped out, brushing down my uniform, and worked the cap onto my head. The two guards in the watchtower above the archway stood to attention and heiled. Eyes drawn to the big Mercedes and the flags, they probably hadn't noticed my three little pips. I heiled back, gave them a business-like nod, slammed the door and strode fast onto the low cement-walled bridge, pulling on my tight leather gloves like I had been cooped in a motor for too long and hadn't got to strangle anyone all day.

Faces came and shot from the windows, a man scampered from the offices on one side of the arch to the other, buttoning up the top of his tunic, throwing me a look, the prisoners beyond him side-on, facing the barracks, perfect lines between them, dust stirring at their boots.

I stopped under the arch before the heavy wrought-iron gate, latticed in a diamond pattern, a smaller gate in the middle of it the size of a regular house door. At the top of the inner gate, the words, in twisted iron, 'Work Will Make You Free'.

A guard, negotiating a corner, stood up on his pedals and snapped an order, quickly correcting his front wheel to stop him toppling. The prisoners stiffened a touch more.

I turned to the door to my left, the sign reading 'Commandant's Office', and reached for the handle. I went to turn it but the door eased open, revealing a junior officer, high-school face, one pip on his shoulder, head bowed a little. He took a step back, taking the door with him. I gave him a brisk nod and stepped in, the door clicking behind, silencing the wind amplified in the long arch.

A woman in a baby-blue blouse, white Peter Pan collar and cute little necktie glanced up from her typewriter at the desk straight ahead, mouth twitching a smile. A bank of wooden filing cabinets sat behind her, above them a long portrait of Neuschwanstein Castle, a sad pot plant and a calendar nobody had turned since April. To the right, the party flag on a pole – why bother when it just hangs down like a big towel? – more filing cabinets, and in front of them two desks, one empty, one with a man at it. He was about ten years my senior, a mini-Himmler, little round glasses, Charlie Chaplin moustache, head too small for his body, two solid slabs of dark hair split by a pronounced side parting. Three pips on his epaulettes, a Hauptsturmführer, same as me.

He scratched at some sort of ledger, turned his pointy little face towards me, the face of a man long unpromoted, soon to head home to a disenchanted wife wishing she hadn't married such a jerk. He kept his pen at a hover, his head tilted, acting out he didn't know there was a Mercedes Grosser with flags on it sitting outside his window. No doubt he'd heard the excitement, dashed to the window then clocked it was just a commonplace Hauptsturmführer like him coming along, a couple of women in the car, secretaries most likely, out for a joy ride on a mere errand in the boss's auto, probably up from party HQ in Munich.

He arched his eyebrows high, getting his power thrill for the day, a face demanding to be punched, it saying to me, *And yes, how may I help you, Hauptsturmführer? As you can see, you are disturbing me at my important file work for the Reich.'*

I approached the desk, peeling off my gloves, steel heels cracking the silence, heartbeats pummelling my ribcage. He looked up, eyebrows nudging a fraction higher, pen still floating above the document. But the power was all mine, him sitting, cap-less, really having to bend that neck, me high above him under the shadow of my visor. And with my leather gloves. I brushed them over the edge of his desk, slapped them in my palm and leant forward a little, squinting at the form he was completing.

He rose to his feet. I had a few centimetres over him. He executed the eyebrow elevation manoeuvre again and piped, 'Yes, how may we be of assistance this afternoon?'

'Commandant Loritz – I would like to see him.'

'Commandant Loritz, you say?'

'I do say Commandant Loritz.'

'No appointment, no?'

'No appointment, no.'

'May I enquire as to the nature of your visit?'

'No.'

'Your name, then?'

'Tell him I have come with orders from Berlin, from Prinz-Albrecht-Strasse, from the office of the Reichsführer-SS. Actually, tell him my visit relates to the camp's accounts.'

'The accounts? Very good, Hauptsturmführer.' He jumped to his feet, picked up the ream of papers on his blotting pad, hurried them into a neat block, put his pen back in its holder. All of a panic now, brushing down his faultless hair, hunching his shoulders, making himself small, throwing me pursed smiles and blinking eyelids, a pathetic display of animal submission before a predator. He scurried towards the corridor leading from the office, spun around and waved to the secretary.

'Grete! Coffee for the Hauptsturmführer.' And then to me, 'You would like a coffee, wouldn't you?'

I tilted my head and held up a hand to her. 'Thank you but I need to get back to Berlin. I report to Prinz-Albrecht-Strasse first thing. To Herr Himmler.' *Berlin*, the seat of power, Valhalla to a pipsqueak backwater pencil-sucker. *Prinz-Albrecht-Strasse*, the inner sanctum. *Himmler*, a living god.

'Very good.' He shot up the stairs just inside the corridor. I turned to the woman on the typewriter.

'Looks a whole lot of fun working here. What's his name?'

A smile burst across her face and disappeared just as fast.

'Bratfisch.' She screwed up her face, thinking of something to say, to be civil to the visitor from out of town. 'He's amazing with figures. Give him any five numbers up to a thousand, and he'll give you the total just like that.'

I walked to the window, a view straight down the rows of prisoners, still and neat as wooden crosses in a military cemetery. As skinny too, most of them, now seeing them side-on and close up, but a couple of fat guys too, very obvious amongst the others. 'Amazing. I guess a facility for numbers comes in handy here.'

She nodded eagerly and I added: 'How come that man there looks, putting it politely, so well fed?'

She put her hands on the desk and craned forward. 'Oh him, he's new. He arrived on Monday with the Stuttgart delivery.'

I could hear Bratfisch hurrying down the steps, almost running. I turned to face him so that my eyes were waiting for his. He brushed imaginary hair from his brow and shot out a breath, his chest rising and falling.

'The Commandant will be delighted to see you, Hauptsturmführer …'

'Eckhart. Otto Eckhart.'

'Please, this way.'

I followed him up the stairs, down the corridor. Bratfisch rapped lightly on the painted door, stepped in and stood aside for me. A long desk sat straight ahead, two long wall shelves behind, but not one book upon them, just a neat stack of newspapers at the end of one, a couple of trophies and a porcelain of Bismarck the Blacksmith in his apron over his anvil – the one grandmothers have on their mantelpiece.

A squat, powerfully built figure running to fat turned from the window overlooking the roll call parade and strode towards me, hands behind his back, sweat patches leaking from under his arms towards his braces. He thrust out a hand.

'Hans Loritz. How do you do?'

Oberführer Hans Loritz – rewarded with the plum of Dachau – *the* job in concentration camp work – for his tireless efforts up at the Esterwegen camp, then for forming and training up the SS unit down here with equal zeal. A rising star in the SS. Or was. Ingrid dug out his files and turns out he is under internal investigation for embezzlement and smuggling out camp labourers to build his villa down in Austria.

'Hauptsturmführer Otto Eckhart. Pleased to meet you, sir. I have heard a great deal about you. In Berlin.'

Does every uniform make its wearer look much like

another? First, baby Himmler downstairs and now Loritz, Inspector Muller's long-lost twin with a hint of Hermann Goering. Same squat body as Muller, bristly brown hair, boiled ham face, deep-set pebble eyes, chin draping over the stiff collar – the only difference the splayed ski-jump nose, not the flat pig's nose like Muller's with its cavities begging for two fingers up them. Loritz's was heavily flared, like you see in the cartoons ridiculing Africans. Worst nose I had ever seen, made you want to look away – but I kept my eyes right on him. His expression, suspicious eyes and an end-of-mouth smile, caught in no man's land between intimidating and intimidated.

'You have?' He asked it quietly.

'I have.' I flashed another smile, surveyed the room, swatting my gloves into my palm. 'Quite a camp you have here, Commandant. So orderly. I'll be sure to tell them back in Berlin.'

'Do take off your cap and take a seat, Eckhart.' He motioned towards a cheaply produced wooden chair with a seat the size of a dinner plate, incongruously small before his landing strip of a desk.

'Thank you, I am fine. Been sitting all day.'

He quickstepped to his desk, opened a drawer and shut it almost at once, like he was checking it still worked. He closed the file on his desk, opened it again then re-angled a picture frame a fraction. It was of him meeting a Nazi bigwig – Bormann from where I stood – with Loritz grinning like someone was feathering his testicles.

Straightening his shoulders, he stuck his thumbs in his braces.

'Bratfisch mentioned something to do with our accounts.'

'You can relax, sir. I merely implied an irregularity in your clerk's filing, and suddenly I get all the manners and help I wasn't getting a moment earlier.'

Loritz's shoulders dropped and he threw out his hands and a broad smile. 'A cheap trick but I like it! Bratfisch is a good sort but you lose your social skills pretty fast down here. It's not like Berlin.'

'I can imagine.'

'So, to what do we owe the pleasure of your company, Hauptsturmführer?' Sarcastic now, heavy stress on the Hauptsturmführer, thinking he's off the hook, having his time wasted by an upstart four ranks his junior, flicking through a file like he had better things to do.

'There has been an error of another sort, Commandant.'

'Oh, yes?' Snorting, not even looking up, like they don't do errors at Dachau, at least not on Hans Loritz's watch.

'Yes.'

I walked to the open window, prisoners motionless still, the bicycle guards lapping. Who's more bored, you wonder.

'Go on.'

'A recent arrival has been interned in error and I have been tasked with overseeing his immediate release.'

He leant on the desk with his knuckles, gorilla-style.

'You have, uh? By whom? Normally the Gestapo send someone.'

'Our boss.'

He laughed. 'Our boss? Herr Himmler?'

'Yes, sir, the Reichsführer-SS.'

Loritz dropped into his chair and cupped his chin, a smile curling up one cheek.

'I have been in this racket for four years, my friend, and I have never known the Reichsführer to involve himself personally in the case of an inmate.'

I held his stare then shrugged. It was quicker than saying, *So what? Now you do.*

'He tends not to consort with the type we get in here, Eckhart. You know, anarchists, degenerates, cock jockeys, religious freaks…'

He chuckled, pleased with his joke, and I smiled. 'I'm sure, Commandant, but this is a personal favour for me.'

Loritz, stirred now, craning his head towards me, mouth and eyes wide open, mocking. 'A personal favour to you? Forgive me, *Hauptsturmführer* – '

'The inmate is my father, Commandant – Friedrich Eckhart.'

'Your father?'

I nodded.

'My – this is quite something. Son walks in out of the blue to release his father on Himmler's orders. I ask your forgiveness once again but… Why would the

Reichsführer, the busiest man in the Reich they say, find the time to intercede on behalf of – if you'll excuse me, a *Hauptsturmführer?*'

'I work for him.'

He sat back in his chair, rubbing his hand all over his face, his head following me across the room.

'*You* are on the Reichsführer's personal staff?'

'In a manner of speaking. I answer to him, yes. Directly.'

I laid my fingers on the cold radiator. Mother's face was up against the near window, Ingrid blowing smoke out of hers, another battalion of labourers forming up in the swirling dust.

'And are you at liberty to disclose the nature of your service to the Reichsführer?'

'I carry out a variety of work for him, overseas mostly. But, officially – when I'm on assignment, I travel as an historian.'

'An historian!' He gave me a wink. 'I haven't heard that one.'

I turned and sat on the windowsill, ankles crossed. Loritz tipped himself sideways and pulled at a deep drawer below his desk, running a finger over folder dividers like a xylophone. He groaned with the effort of righting himself, held up a buff-coloured file like he was holding the Olympic torch. FRIEDRICH ECKHART in large capital letters on the cover, prisoner number stamped in the corner above a down-turned red triangle.

'Right, here we are: the order of protective custody.' He stood up, held it out like an actor in rehearsal and started reading.

"'Based on Article 1 of the Decree of the Reich President for the Protection of People and State, You, Friedrich Dieter Eckhart, are to be taken into protective custody in the interest of public security and order. Reason for detention..."'

He cleared his throat, our eyes holding for a few moments and then continued.

"'Reason for detention: Suspicion of activities inimical to the State. State and Gestapo police evidence shows Eckhart's behaviour to constitute a danger to the existence and security of people and state. It is feared that if released Eckhart would continue his illegal endeavours to undermine the Reich..."'

'Blah, blah, blah...' Loritz ran his eyes over the rest, stood up. Pausing as though a deep thought stopped him in his tracks, he walked out from his desk, slapping the file in the other hand.

'And the Reichsführer-SS wants to let him go? So soon?' Sounding jolly and friendly now. 'Extraordinary. No mention of temporary insanity, no unstable mind, no mention of illness of any kind in fact.'

I shrugged again, trying to stay fixed on his eyes not his nose, now just a couple of feet away. Trying to get the thought out of my head: you could go caving in there, maybe get lost and have to be rescued. He went on: 'The detention processing system here is pretty unoriginal, Eckhart. Everything is standardised, kept simple and regular, easy to follow, no surprises, so everyone knows the form. It has to be. In the interests of efficiency.'

'Of course. I understand.'

'And usually – always – we receive a doctor's report if the inmate has displayed even the slightest signs of unstable or delinquent behaviour. As a matter of course. Why? Because the lunatics have their own institutions. We don't rehabilitate them here.'

He turned, sat on the edge of his desk, legs outstretched, straight arms propping him up, bunching his chin fat.

'I'm not here to argue with you, Commandant. I am here to carry out orders.' A line of reasoning I hoped he would understand.

He pushed away from his desk, took a couple of strides back my way, a little pause.

'I hope you have brought some good paperwork with you, Eckhart. Because this is a little irregular. You have the correct documentation?'

I took my time unbuttoning the lower pocket of my tunic, unfolding the documents, put one back in the pocket and handed him the Certificate of Discharge and Himmler's two-line letter – Ingrid's two-line letter. He shuffled and read them again, breathing heavy through his smoke-stack nostrils, my eyes drawn to the signatures, thinking of Ingrid practising the big teacher's tick through the H of Himmler. Over and over, not quite happy with it.

He looked up, squinting and nodding, then very quietly, like it was a secret between me and him, 'You know, Eckhart, I have been running Dachau for almost a year and a half now. We run a pretty good show here. This is his marquee camp. He opened the place and I hear he's as proud as ever. I have…'

'He is, Commandant, he is. Very proud.'

'… Never met him, never been invited to Berlin, never even spoke to him. I've had all the official memos and directives of course, handwritten signature and all, but I get it – he's a very busy man. You can imagine then how proud, how happy – how relieved! – I felt when I received this.'

He pointed over his shoulder then skirted his desk and slapped the glass of the picture frame with the papers. 'Come,' he said. 'I read it every morning before I get down to work.'

The breath was caught in the back of my throat. I coughed into my sleeve and rounded the desk, praying the anxiety wasn't showing. We stood shoulder to shoulder, reading it. I scanned it quickly, not really taking it in, seeing a whole lot of numbers amongst a hurried scrawl of gushing adjectives and exclamations of patriotism, not the usual zigzag neatness.

And then, at the foot, the signature – and I stared at

it, another big lump creeping up my throat, Loritz now looking back and forth between me and his letter of commendation. The signature, like the commendation, was clearly written in haste – but how would Loritz know that? The signature bore a resemblance to Himmler's regular one but only some. Similar but not the same.

Loritz looked at the Certificate of Discharge, then at Himmler's letter, then tapped the glass frame, his fingernail just below Himmler's signature.

'Tell you what, Eckhart. As the Reichsführer has taken such a personal interest in your father's case, I now have the perfect opportunity to telephone him, hey?'

He turned to face me, smiling, obliging me to turn too. The ball sat uncomfortably in my throat and I gulped. I tried to hold it a second or two longer but I couldn't. My larynx bounced and he saw, no question. Maybe I showed some nerves in my eyes too. My father told me he'd read a psychiatrist study saying only a small fraction of our communication is verbal – most of it is in our facial expressions and body language. Maybe Loritz wasn't that sharp, but he was beaming now – whether at the prospect of talking to his hero or, suspecting he'd been smart and rumbled me, I had no way of telling.

'Sure.'

He sat at his desk, took out his address book and pulled over the phone. From the other side of his desk, I watched him dragging at the rotary dial, throwing me looks, smiling like a nervous child, flicking his eyebrows.

He planted both elbows on his desk and I could hear it ringing in Berlin, then a click and a soprano voice.

'Put me through to Berlin six-nine-four-eight,' he said, switching to a deep voice. Then softer, 'Good afternoon, Commandant Hans Loritz here. No, Dachau not Buchenwald... I was hoping to speak to the Reichsführer-SS... Oh, in Wewelsburg... He's not back till next week...?'

His shoulders deflated and he looked up at me, grimacing. 'Might I get hold of him down there then? Do you have a number for the castle?'

My turn to grimace. I leant forward and whispered, 'Ask for Wolff.'

He cupped the mouthpiece, scowling. 'What?'

'Ask for Karl Wolff, his chief of staff.'

He waved me away. 'My apologies, I was saying, how about I contact Herr Himmler at the castle?'

My fists tightened behind my back.

'Right, I understand... No, not strictly urgent, no... Fair enough... Then Wolff, Gruppenführer Wolff... Excellent... if you could, thank you, yes I'd very much like to talk to him.'

I turned away and went to the window on the camp side, watched the prisoners in statue mode. God, it was boring just to watch. Enough to make you run for it, risk getting shot, working and working, then standing and standing, most of them all coming from useful everyday jobs, professionals a great many of them. Silence behind me, just the tapping of his pen on the desk and the swing of the pendulum.

Then, 'Good afternoon, Gruppenführer… Yes, everything in good order down in Bavaria, thank you… Yes, clockwork, all running like clockwork… Good, good… Yes, I see, a meeting with Goebbels. Fine, then I'll be quick! I have a Hauptsturmführer Otto Eckhart with me carrying release papers for his father signed, it appears, by the Reichsführer himself. I just wanted to confirm, it being a little irregular, Herr Himmler stepping in like this, his son affects his release…'

My name being mentioned, I turned around. Loritz's head was fixed my way, telephone pressed to his head. 'Yes, right you are. I hear you… So you'll telephone Wewelsburg and telephone me back? Perfect… Yes, the number here is Dachau 667… Yes, almost – one number off!'

Laughing as he replaced the handset, he sprung from his feet, all pleased and excited. 'He's contacting Himmler down at Wewelsburg. One of them's going to call me straight back.'

I'm not sure how long I stood there, dumb and motionless as a prisoner outside. Finally, I slung my thumbs in my belt, pushed myself off the windowsill and said, 'Right. Sure. Of course.' And we kept looking at each other for a while longer, nodding and lip-pursing, playing face poker.

On the spot now, tough to know how to play this scene – did he suspect chicanery or did he just sniff an opportunity to talk to Himmler, aroused about feeling some real power, drop it in casually over a beer in the officer's mess later and then over dinner with the wife? *Hey, sweetheart, how was your day? … A bit boring, uh? Don't forget we have the opera in Munich at the weekend… And look, the chalet down in the Tyrol is coming along nicely, we'll get down there soon and, Oh! I almost forgot, Himmler called up today… yep, yep, very friendly, nothing really, just a chat, but my God that man goes on, had to shake him off in the end, I could still be there now…*

I walked over to the desk, buried my hands in my trouser pockets, dropped into the little chair opposite him and pushed back on the rickety legs, meeting the situation halfway, submissive but nonchalant. Not much to say now, the call-back dominating everything, both of us shooting sideways looks at the phone, the pendulum swinging and ticking behind him. Hitler right next to the cheap clock, looking deep into the future, deadly earnest about the history he was going to make. Loritz rolled the sleeves up his fat forearms, started tinking a teaspoon on the saucer. I tugged at my collar, a rattle of wind on the sash window, some small talk about the exceptional heat for this time of year, probably getting a thunderstorm later.

Tink, tink… tick, tick… tink, tink… tick, tick…

Please, Heini, please be humping your secretary or conducting a seance, chatting with Henry the Fowler or Karl the Great, maybe browbeating his engineers about that new submersible for Atlantis. Find those Aryans, shut up the sceptics…

The phone rang.

Loritz ripped it out of the cradle, then elbows back on the desk, chewing and twirling a pencil in the corner of his mouth.

He was saying, 'Yes, Gruppenführer.' He was saying it a lot.

Wolff, not Himmler!

Then, 'Oh well… Shame… I understand… Business first, it happens… You just don't know… No telling, is there?' And throwing me looks from under his brow, like he was checking I wasn't going to run for it. 'Yes, a very difficult situation, Gruppenführer. No problem, we'll deal with it. I've got him right here. Of course, of course.'

He put down the phone, dropped his hands onto his thighs and stared at me. I swung back on my chair again, hands still deep in my pockets, trying to play it all relaxed, forcing out a half-smile.

'All good?' It came out a little too high and reedy.

'That was Wolff. Says the Reichsführer is not to be disturbed for the rest of the day. Something to do with Tibet and skull size. He's back in Berlin tonight. How about we put you in a guesthouse in town overnight, speak to him in the morning?'

I gave it a few moments, held the stare, then. 'No, that won't do.'

Loritz leant right forward, spreading his forearms, chewing off his lower lip. 'I beg your pardon, Hauptsturmführer? That *won't do*?'

I pushed back a little further on the chair legs to unbutton the tunic pocket, pulled out the square of papers, tossed it onto the desk. It skimmed over the dark oak and lodged under a forearm.

He kept staring, picked up the wedge, then unfolded the papers into a half, warily at first, and then fully open, his eyes widening then darting faster and faster as he worked his way down.

He looked up. I stood up, my face shadowed by the visor.

'You have my father under that archway in ten minutes and I'll make that file in Berlin disappear – I go tonight by train. Give you a chance to straighten out those accounts. How's that sound for a deal?'

Loritz's nostrils working overtime now. He said, 'Or?'

'Or? Or how about I stick a ring in that nose of yours, loop a rope around your neck and get you up to that cattle auction before it shuts. I pocket a thousand marks or so, you start over on a farm.'

•◆•

Ingrid was reversing onto the bridge, then turned the car in the direction of the town. I had Father by the elbow and an arm over his shoulder. He kept looking behind him, at Loritz standing under the arch, hands on hips. I pushed him on.

'I want a word with that commandant. He should be ashamed. It's a perfect disgrace in there.'

'It is, Father, it is. But it's helping no one if I end up

in there with you, and Mother is left by herself.'

'That man should be ashamed of himself – '

'Just keep walking, Dad, and get in the back of car.'

Mother's face was wet with tears. Ingrid was grinning through her cigarette, lightly revving the engine.

'And what on earth are you doing in that appalling uniform?'

'I borrowed it. Mother will explain everything. Just get in the car.'

She threw open the door and I gave Father a light shove into her embrace. I swung into the front seat and Ingrid was around the corner before I had shut the door. I spun about, and through the trail of our dust, there was Loritz on the bridge. Mother's head was wedged into Father's neck and she was cupping both his hands, Father's face set hard, his eyes baggy with fatigue looking straight down the road. His eyes flicked to me and he gave me a smile and a slow nod.

Ingrid tapped the clock in the dash and we exchanged looks. She took the corner at pace then flattened her foot, a storm of dust behind us, tyres yelping around every corner through town, the four of us swinging this way then that.

'So?'

I leant into her, 'It was close. Last resort – told him I'd bin his file.'

She flung a look, 'But, you can't. We can't.'

'I know. It's terrible, isn't it?'

She swerved the car into the station forecourt, pulled

up right outside the entrance, all eyes on the Mercedes and the flags. I leapt out, took my case from the luggage compartment and leant in through the rear window.

Mother leant across Father and, fresh desperation in her voice, said, 'What are you doing *now*, Otto?'

'Getting a train, Mother.'

'A train? Why? And where are *we* going then?'

'Ingrid will explain.'

I slammed the door and jogged towards the entrance, Mother shouting after me. But I wasn't turning around.

The man in the kepi cap behind the glass in the ticket booth looked up from his newspaper as I was adjusting my cap. He tossed away the paper, sat upright and adjusted his own cap.

'Yes, sir?'

'Berlin.'

'Return?'

'One-way.'

CHAPTER TWELVE

The front of the train rattled onto an old iron bridge, so it sounded. I rubbed my face and stretched. Christ, there we were, over the Landwehr. I patted the side of my jacket just to make sure, ran a comb through my hair and rooted into the side pocket of my valise, head clearing, cloud by cloud.

Taking out the little brown bottle, I leant back and held it up to the dirty window, squinting at the label. *Benzedrine* – 'bennies', Ingrid called them. A little boost, give you a little edge, she'd said, finishing our packing back in Michelstadt the night before. Take one and it's like you've drunk a whole cafetière. Take two and you'll be swinging from the trees like Johnny Weissmuller, and they'll clear your throat while they're about it. Then – and then! – I could feel it still, breathe her in – her stepping away from the kitchen table and giving me that long kiss on my cheek, a remarkable kiss, quite close to the mouth, a light palm on my other cheek and squeezing my fingers with her other hand. I was braver than I thought, she'd added. But it's going to be trial of nerves, isn't it?

I rattled the bottle and sighed, my breath steaming the window. Who needed Benzedrine with a stimulant like Ingrid? But why turn down help, today of all days? Why not take both? The intoxicating thought of her, plus the bennies.

I'd be tired after a night in a stiff railway seat, three changes from Dachau – and I was, just as she said, after no more than an hour's half-sleep, all that worrying about her and my parents, willing them to make that long journey of their own, all that way to the south, and in that motor car, that huge, hey-look-at-me motor car.

And now today – only God knew how this was going to pan out. To hell with it. I threw back two pills and drained the last of my hipflask, gazing down at the oily water mottling in the morning sun.

Right there in the canal – that's where they dump the bodies. And that's not just idle rumour. Every Berliner can vouch for that. They'd either seen a floater or knew someone who had. I'd been trying to forget, but Ingrid had told me too many stories. The Reichstag burns down and pretty much the next day the judges throw justice to the vigilantes of the state, the Mullers, and then not even the Lord God himself could expect a fair trial. Or even a trial. A beating, a bullet in the back of the head and a midnight bath in the Landwehr, that's how it works now. That's what she'd said and I needed no persuading to believe it now, after all that had happened.

My neck twisted and my eyes followed the barge

sliding under the next bridge. Maybe that's where I'd be tonight, bobbing along. What did it matter? Rotting amongst the pine trees in a flower-fringed grave plot, an emerald mountain lake below – that's the dream, no? Or face down in the greasy Landwehr with the old oil drums and the shattered pallets, bloating and wrinkling then sinking into the filthy silt? What does the corpse care?

The train pulled through the giant brick arch of the Anhalter, eased to the buffers, doors clattering before it had reached a halt. I hung on the footplate – why rush now? – and scanned the platform. All hats look the same from above, but most of them keep moving in railway stations. So there they were. Four stationary hats, all bunched together near the barrier, pointed this way, one or two tipping up, faces on the lookout.

I won the bet with Ingrid then – Loritz's doughnut brain, once he was over the shock of it, had figured out he had nothing to lose. Even if I was to bin the incriminating file, his case investigator would keep going – top of the class, Hans! – and now Loritz had the chance to sort out his accounts in Dachau, tip off Berlin about our heist, win back some favour there and maybe they'd let bygones be bygones, even give him a pat on the back, turn a blind eye to the anomalies they'd spotted.

I knew in my guts this would be the scene – it was no odds to me if I had to walk to Prinz-Albrecht-Strasse or hitch a ride with the thugs – but what about Ingrid and Mother and Father? Had he put out the alert on them too?

'Right, let's do this.' I said it out loud and stepped out.

The platform had emptied like water down a flood-drain by the time I reached them. They made a move as one, like I was going to jump the barrier and bolt for it, a couple of them reaching inside their jackets. I smiled and threw out my arms, then feigned to run and made them all jump. They formed a line before me, a second barrier, all in raincoats and ties, trying to look like gunfighters, heads tilted.

I dropped my case to the floor, clapped my hands and rubbed them hard, as if before a blazing fire in the dead of a Russian winter.

'Right, we all got our rubber truncheons and cowhide whips at the ready? Let's get cracking, eh? Where do you want to do it? Back of the van? Down there in the freight yard? Or back home in the comfort and cool of the basement in Prinz-Albrecht-Strasse? No place like home, I say.'

'Back of the van.'

I figured it would be him who spoke – the fattest one was always the most senior, the one who'd gone as far as he could up the ranks, knew the fact and had given up on himself, nothing left to life but the fun of beating and eating. One of the juniors went for my elbow and I yanked it away.

'Do I look like I'm running? You can prop me up

when I'm senseless.' I gave him a wink and a smile, let him know I knew he was only following the fat guy's orders, just a callow kid doing his job, earning his crust, putting bread on his table and beer in his glass.

I put a hand on his shoulder, let him know it was alright when he had to follow suit, play his part, launch his truncheon into me. We're all in this. Who knows? The kid might be next – for talking out of line, showing the wrong sympathies.

He brushed off my hand, patted me down while another went through my bag. We took the side entrance into the service area, me in the middle of their diamond. The wagon was right there, driver holding open the back, cigarette hanging from his mouth like he'd seen and heard it all before, probably earlier today or overnight, seizing malfeasants from their beds.

Right, here we go, deep breaths, let's hope the traffic's light. And the bennies start kicking in – fast. They closed in on me, looking for a struggle, but I leapt into the rear like an eager gundog. They followed me in, and the door slammed. The driver shut his and we all squirmed in our seats, getting comfortable, the van rocking a little, our eyes adjusting to the small amount of light from the ventilation slits.

A fist slammed on the metal partition, the engine rumbled and we pulled away.

'Okay, how do you want to do this? Shall I lie on the floor, get into a ball now or do you want to ask me some questions first, make it feel official. I give you some impertinence back, you guys go into frenzied animal mode – you know, *he was asking for it the mouthy little bastard*, blahdy blah, and you can all go home to your wives and girlfriends, maybe stop for a quiet coffee before the U-Bahn, do the puzzle in *Der Angriff*? Is there a puzzle in *Der Angriff*? I guess you'll just put down *Resisting arrest* anyhow. Or even *Suspect fell downstairs*. Actually, can you put that? *Fell downstairs!* Come on, it's a show and – '

If the smallest pocket of the smallest lobe in my brain had held out the smallest trace of optimism that my smart talk might win me a bit of brotherhood and a short reprieve, at least buy some time, the rebuttal to that hope came before we had even left the station concourse. The blow – a fist, I think, because it arrived on the chin and the cheek like a sledgehammer – was so great that, though I was leaning right forward, elbows on my knees, the back of my head smashed against the side panelling, and the recoil was such that I found myself lying in the well between the long benches. Then it was just pain, blow after blow – boots, fists, truncheons, or were they clubs? I think even a whip, a multi-tailed one by the smack of it. I was in my ball, just as I had suggested – we could have saved a bit of time there – and I managed to wriggle so that my head, already protected by my arms, was under the bench.

I cannot be certain whether it was the bennies (unlikely so soon) or nature's own adrenaline and my body had gone into some primitive form of survival mode – but the pain was nothing like the agony I had been anticipating. It would be some exaggeration to claim I was enjoying the experience – all that stamping, belting and punching – but perhaps that was the key: expect the worst and you'll end up pleasantly surprised by the outcome. And by the time we had turned off Saarland Strasse into Prinz-Albrecht-Strasse, the torrent of blows was easing, the lads exhausted by the expenditure of effort and the ebbing of their adrenaline. Job done. Tick.

I played my part to the full – shrieking, yelling, begging for mercy, cursing their mothers – then croaking and panting as the van halted. I could hear the driver thank the sentry on the boom barrier and we drove into the delivery compound at the rear of the building.

A final ankle stamp and a yelp from me before the rear doors flew open. The first two jumped out, each grabbing a foot, and dragged me along the cold, rutted metal floor until I fell upright. They jostled me back and forth, grabbing my armpits, making sure I didn't collapse to the ground. But for the terrific fun of it too, grinning and sneering like tough guys do. The fat guy, carrying my little case, shoved my fedora on my head, tugged down the brim so I couldn't see, spun me around and planted a heavy palm in the small of my back.

'This way, cocksucker.'

'Any chance of a coffee first?'

Speaking, I became aware of the blood in my mouth, then another palm between the shoulder blades and I stumbled towards the wooden stairs.

I spat out the blood, my tongue working over the loosened tooth, the pain like frozen lightning across my skull, the rest of me smarting and stinging under a layer of numbness. But my legs were moving one in front of another, my arms swinging, elbows bending, my fists opening and closing – none of the movements causing intolerable agony, no fractures.

I received a kick in the seat of the trousers – just like I saw that guy in the cloth cap get on my first visit – and I hurried up the creaking steps, limping and holding onto the railing. We reached the heavy metal door leading to the prisoner cells, just me and the fat guy now, the cartoon hard-boiled heavy, failed detective probably, too stupid to solve a case of daylight robbery, makes ends meet with bailiff work in the evenings.

I said, 'Thank you, I can make my own way from here. Will you have room service send down some breakfast? Poached eggs on rye with some ham, hot milk with the coffee.' I spat some more blood onto the floor.

I like to think the guard on the door of the cells was pursing his lips to suppress a smile, but Sam Spade was certainly in no mood for humour. He stuck a thumb upwards, grabbed my upper arm and threw me towards the narrow staircase. We tramped our way up, flight after flight, no problem for me being at the peak of fitness, but Fat Guy was really struggling, his lungs bellowing and wheezing harder and harder. I waited for him on the small landing of the fourth floor, brushing down all the crap from the floor of the van, smiling as he turned the corner. Would he like to sit and rest before we completed our ascent to the fifth? Could I get him a glass of water?

On making the last step, he lunged at me and I skipped away, springing up the next flight, two steps at a time. At the top, I leant over the railing and said, 'Come, on! We don't want to keep the Reichsführer waiting. He may seem mild-mannered – but let me tell you!'

'Shut up you little – ' But he had to pause for a coughing fit. I smiled at the two guards outside Himmler's corridor, but they were miles away, chins up admiring the cornicing.

Fat Guy was purple by the time he made it and there was not the slightest sense of achievement in his expression. I congratulated him all the same, reaching into my inner pocket for the rolled wad of notes. He stumbled towards me, finger pointing up at my chin, neck outstretched, face gurning like a Gothic gutter gargoyle.

I stepped back, peeling off a ten Reichsmark note and I held it out, 'No, honestly, I insist.'

He dropped my overnight case, kicked it into the corner and stabbed a finger in my larynx. Getting his breath back via the nose, then his big, brown-toothed smile, he said, 'I'm now going to clean your room. Last guest just checked out.'

'Please, don't go to too much trouble.'

And I spat more blood at his feet.

·➤·

'Come!'

The guard pushed open the door and Himmler was behind his desk, the Grail before him on his blotting pad, a note clamped to it by a rubber band. His chair was some way back, beneath the portrait of Hitler as Teutonic knight, his slicked-down schoolboy hair appearing to balance the Führer's arse and saddle. His sloping shoulders were pulled out as wide as they'd go, his hands clasped over crossed knees, nose slightly in the air to the side – how a wife might sit, fresh back from flower-arranging in the church, emboldened to confront her husband about the infidelity, indignation clamping the prim white lips.

I pushed back my hat, spun the wooden chair one-eighty and dropped into it, cowboy-style, arms resting on the back, trying not to show the pain, the nerves.

'Excuse the informality, Reichsführer. The back's a little sore from the ride.'

Life or death – that is, the chance of a happy life or the certainty of an ugly death – one or the other, that's how this day was going to end. I needed to get a move on before they dragged me out and it was too late. I started picking at the lining of my suit jacket, like it was a nervous reaction to him, looking up from time to time as I spoke, waffling, spinning it out.

'You didn't seriously believe that's the Holy Grail, did you? The chalice from the Last Supper? Send a guy out to get it, easy as that, like a dog fetching a stick. Christ.'

His face was jerking, the knuckles tightening white. It didn't matter what I said now, so why not try and land a few blows? But this stitching, it was almost industrial, and I plucked away, a little panic creeping over me.

'… But I guess a guy who believes in Atlantis, even sends out an expedition to find it, will believe anything. And an Aryan civilisation in the centre of the earth – I mean, please, Reichsführer! The nobility of the Nordic tribesman, the supremacy of the Teutons – who are you kidding?'

I pushed my tongue against my tooth, the blood oozing still.

'Have you heard of the Sumerians? Next time you're in the Pergamon, look them up. Four thousand years ago they were inventing the written word, the plough, hydraulic engineering, metallurgy, ceramic art – you name it – and what were *we* doing? Sleeping on the forest floor chewing bones and picking fleas off our balls, that's what.'

His upper body was twitching now, his head going from side to side, clenching and unclenching his fists. I was digging a thumbnail into the stitching but Ingrid had done too a fine job.

'Luther, Goethe, Gutenberg, Schiller, Durer, Kant, Bach, Beethoven, Einstein… I could sit here for ten minutes reeling off the names of great Germans. You, we, should be very proud of our culture but…'

His eyes boring into me, teeth pinning his lower lip, he stood and reached for the telephone. My hands were trembling now, and I took a fistful of the silk and yanked, cursing in my head.

He spoke softly into the handset. 'Send them in.'

I kept tugging at the silk. He pulled up his chair, shifted the chalice to one side and dropped his forearms on the desk. He was smiling now. I took out my pen and removed the lid.

'Eckhart?'

I looked up, plunging the nib behind a stitch. He looked at his rectangular watch and said, 'I have a meeting in the conference room in ten minutes. By the time I open it, you will be dead. I could have had you dumped straight in the Landwehr or the Grunewald, but I wanted the thrill of telling you that to your face.'

'Yeah, I figured that. Like your thrills, uh?'

I ran the nib down the lining, ripping a long tear, seized the envelope, spun it onto his desk. The far door opened and a column of boots made its way along the corridor. The office door opened but I didn't turn.

He picked up the fat envelope. I said, 'An early birthday gift. Maybe something for the family mantelpiece down at Tegernsee.'

There was an explosion of heels, and I caught the shadow of their extended arms on the parquet floor either side of me. Himmler fingered the envelope for clues, staring right at me like a bank manager about to refuse me a loan. He opened the flap, started pulling out the wad of photographs. They were halfway out when he froze.

He eased them out and slumped back, his face going from olive to cream to grey. He raised his eyes over the rimless glasses and said to the guards, voice rasping, 'Wait outside, please' and they filed out, the last of them clicking the door.

'Excellent quality, come on, you have to admit it. Ingrid was amazed. She was on the church tower at Wewelsburg one afternoon, trying out her new long-distance lens. Said she almost fell to her death, laughing and retching.'

He narrowed his eyes, looked away when I gave him a big grin and kept on.

'We were trying to work out exactly which of the historical or mythical characters you were seeking to portray. I said your secretary – Hedwig, yes? – was Henry the Fowler, but Ingrid thought the horned helmet made her Odin or Thor. And as for you, I guessed Freya – beautiful dress by the way, love the waist sash – but the long plaits had Ingrid thinking Rapunzel…'

'Shut up!' And he jumped to his feet.

I spun the chair, pushed back on the rear legs, hooked my thumbs. 'I'm all ears, Heini. I've got all day now. And by the way, please tell me she was using the flat of that sword on you.'

He was pacing back and forth behind his desk, four steps one way, four steps the other.

'What is it you want?'

I let the chair fall forward, throwing me to my feet.

'Sit down, and I'll tell you exactly what I want.'

He was so tense I thought his lips were going to fly off. I reached for his wastepaper basket and spat blood into it.

'I said sit down, Heini.'

He sat down. I picked up Raymond's chalice, pulled off the rubber band and read the note. *Forgery* was all it said.

I continued, 'Forgery eh? Just like the version of history you're re-writing. Anyhow, this is what's happening. You do what I tell you, it's all going to be just fine.'

The phone rang and he looked at it, not moving. I said. 'Tell them you're running a little late for the conference. And tell your office to get ready to do some fast work.'

His face was quivering.

I said, 'Do it.'

His hand was shaking when he picked up the telephone and, strangling his fury or tears or whatever it was bursting to get out, said, 'I'm going to be about ten minutes late. I don't know, anything, whatever – get the girls to take out the coffee and biscuits now... I'll explain... Yes, everything is fine. And Hedwig, I'll need you to stay in the office.'

He replaced the handset, his cheeks almost scarlet now, took up a pencil, twirling it through his fingers like a baton.

I continued, 'Copies of the photographs – all securely sealed, don't worry – are currently sitting in the vaults of lawyers in London and in Paris. Further editions are *en route* to Washington. *Par avion*. At noon on Tuesday, the lawyers in those cities will open the packages and follow my instructions. Within the day – I was very clear about that – the photographs will be sitting on the desks of every major newspaper editor and Foreign Minister in those countries.'

I paused, watching him, chewing his lip, running through the scenarios that would ensue.

'Unless?'

I held up a hand. 'I'll get to that. Needless to say, we haven't bothered your newspaper friends here. And I needn't point out that the Führer, not to mention your wife, would be very disappointed to set eyes on those images. Correct?'

'Correct!' He screamed it, slapping the wad of images onto the desk, and they ran out like a pack of cards. He lunged, gathering them, and turned them face down. I chuckled and he hurled his pencil. It ricocheted off the lamp and fell at my feet. Wiping his lips with his sleeve, he narrowed them into a little blowhole and spluttered, 'How dare you?'

I pulled out a second, smaller envelope from the lining of my jacket and flopped it onto his desk. I held up a hand as he leant forward to take it.

'You can open that when I'm gone. It contains the account details for a bank in London – Coutts. Moment I walk out of here you are going to pick up a telephone and start arranging for ten million marks to be paid into – '

'Ten million marks!'

'Yes, ten million marks. Not much really, roughly

the same as an expedition to find Aryans in Tibet I'm guessing.'

We stared at each other, me tossing the chalice from hand to hand, him twitching his nose like an Angora.

'How can I be sure those photographs will disappear?' 'Read the copy of the instructions to the lawyers in there. Soon as the money's in my account, they destroy the sealed envelope, only then will I pay them their very generous fee and you're in the clear. It's all as easy as throwing an innocent man in jail.'

'How can I trust that you won't produce more photographs?'

'The negatives are in your envelope.'

'And what if there are more developed copies you have kept over.'

I leant forward, dropped the smile and said, 'You have my word there are none. I will show you there is still some true honour left.'

I looked at my watch, he looked down at the ground between his legs, exhaling hard, then eyes up at me again. 'And that's the end of the matter?'

'That's the end of the matter. Actually, just one more thing – '

His face and shoulders fell. 'Go on.'

'The fat guy from the van.'

'I believe you are referring to Sergeant Schweinsteiger.'

'Schweinsteiger, is he? My shoes are a little scuffed – look. I'd like Schweinsteiger to run a cloth over them. In the foyer. While I'm wearing them.'

I picked up his handset, passed it to him and when he replaced it, I was at the door, valise in one hand, chalice in the other. I held up the chalice.

'Mind if I keep this? Sentimental value. You know, everyone wants their own Grail.'

I was closing the door behind me but stuck my head back in.

I said, 'That's one thing I've learned from all this — everything, everyone, has some sort of value, even this. Even you are probably kind to animals, or rabbits at least. Anyhow, I'm a better man for having known you so, for that at any rate, thank you.'

'Eckhart.'

I put my head back in again and arched my brow.

'You watch your back now.'

CHAPTER THIRTEEN

Out on the steps of Prinz-Albrecht-Strasse, hands in pockets, waggling a shoe, admiring the shine, my body smarting but my head light with relief, I mused that relief was not an emotion in itself but really the absence of emotion, the airiness left behind once the anxiety or fear is removed.

Old habits die hard, none harder than cigarettes, and I reached into my jacket pocket for my Murattis, like it was those carefree days again, the years of my youth, waiting for my cousin Max to finish his day's study and we'd head up to Kurfürstendamm for the cabaret and the dancing. It would have felt good to lean a shoulder against the arch wall, as I did so often then, cocking one foot over the other, hat down, gassing with whoever, blowing a few smoke rings, swapping tips about the best bars and shows.

It had been some time since I felt this lightness, the hope – everyone out of immediate danger now and just the last and easy part of the escape plan to deal with. But it wasn't quite the same – Berlin wasn't the same and nor was I, the innocence being corrupted by experience and all that. I no longer smoked of course, and the School of Industrial Arts and Crafts was now the most dreaded address in Berlin, probably in all Germany, its front steps occupied not by giddy students brandishing cigarettes and theatre tickets, but by men in helmets with machine guns and daggers.

The duty guard was looking in no mood for a chinwag, that was for sure, his bottom-of-the-class face taut with mental effort under his oversized helmet, engrossed in his clipboard, walking his pencil up and down it, moving his lips like he was learning to read. And when he'd had enough of that, practising the names to himself, he'd be happy just to rock on his heels, airing his chin, admiring the stratocumulus running along the northern horizon like a low mountain range.

But to hell with him and his clipboard and his gun and his square jaw, maitre'd-ing for the Reichsführer-SS – and to hell with that weird little Reichsführer too. You've just been hopelessly outfoxed, Heini, and by a 'mooncalf' amateur historian into the bargain. You have to keep me alive till noon Tuesday and after that, well, good luck to you with that too. If you're planning something, you need to move fast and think hard. I am the one calling the shots now and I am one step ahead.

There was only one person Heini would trust for the job – Muller. He'd probably called the old thug at the Darmstadt Stapo offices before I had even set foot out of the building, before he'd gone down to stammer and flap his way through the conference, his head streaming with shame and images of himself as Rapunzel being sword-spanked by the Viking god of thunder, war and fertility.

Muller was the only of his goons who could pick all three of us out of a line-up – and all he needed was a description of Ingrid's extraordinary beauty and style to clock her in a crowd too. No use sending someone who had to consult photos before he opened fire. He'd have to send Muller. We were sure of that. But Muller would have to find us first. Before we vanished.

First thing Muller would do is go to Michelstadt, find the house closed up, then we figured he'd race back to The Three Hares. Berthold was going to take him aside, give him a beer or two on the house, feed him a few scraps of harmless information and then: 'Hey, Helmut, I don't know whether this is relevant but last time that Eckhart character was in here, I went to bring him his beer by the fireplace over there, and as I approached from behind, I saw he was counting out some French francs and a whole stack of US dollars – I mean thousands of dollars, Helmut – and when I laid down his mug, he quickly stuffed the notes into his pocket. And then, guess what? When he was gone, on the floor below the table I found some document about a liner passage from Le Havre to New York. None of my business really, I'm just saying but I never liked the guy much, he's a customer so you have to pretend, and it's probably no help but…'

And Muller would stand propped at the bar, pulling

on his beer, his brain grinding it out – deduction being the hardest part of his job – a log would catch in his mind, his face would light up – *he was a genius, the best in the business!* – and he'd drain his beer, give Berthold a little tug of the brim, saying 'Le Havre, eh? The States?', slap down a little tip and say 'Thanks Berthold, you just gave me an idea', and he'd hit the road to get home and pack his bags. Least, we hope that's how it played out: Muller stomping up and down the quays at Le Havre, checking every hotel, steaming under his hat at every Gallic shrug and blank face. *Non, désolé Monsieur, jamais vu cet mec...*

I looked at my watch, then at the clipboard guy, on his own today, chewing his lip, scratching his helmet.

'Alright then, I'll be seeing you,' and I cast off the steps and headed up to Potsdamer, stopping at the bank to draw out the last of my money, my payment for the book, enough still to live on for months and months. I peeled off about two or three weeks' worth, folded the rest into a fat wad and, darting through the traffic, made my way towards the steps to the U-Bahn. I stopped at the fruit cart – the sign on it demanding I *Eat Only the Best Fruit!*, bought a bunch of bananas and a bag of *Brazil's juiciest!* oranges, and made my way over to the shoeshine boy, slumped against his customer chair after the morning rush.

I held out the fruit and he climbed to his feet, his watery eyes staring up at me, his legs bowed like a reject ballerina, a nervous gummy smile spreading over his face. I reached into my suit and handed him the great wad of Reichsmarks, left him thunderstruck and made my way towards the soaring slender arches of Potsdamer's neoclassical facade.

Nothing to worry about now – apart from Ingrid, apart from us.

• ◆ •

Montségur looked a picture from on high – what time of year doesn't it? – and I leapt from the Monasix, hurled Raymond his francs, thanked him for bringing me up to date with the state of the civil war in Spain – 'Such detail, you should be a reporter!' – agreeing that the Austrians were probably no better or worse than the Germans on the whole, that 'Franks' refers to both western Germans and Frenchmen in those days but, fine, whatever, Charlemagne was probably a Frenchman not a German, and good day to him, safe journey back to Foix.

I made my way down the switchbacks, swinging my case, a little trepidation in my guts until I turned the second bend and there it was, the giant Mercedes, parked in the little yard just up from the Trencavels. I came around the final bend, whistling some Handel, and Poilu was over the terrace wall like there was a house fire, and bounding up the lane.

'Ingrid says you're leaving tomorrow! Why so soon? Can't you stay a while?'

'That's the plan, Poilu, I'm afraid.' I put my arm over his shoulder, and we ambled towards the village and the row of homes above the great stone wall of the lane. 'It's not safe to stay here right now. But we will back, I promise. Once everything has quietened down.'

'Can you take me?'

'To Montevideo, Poilu? Your parents would never forgive us. Besides, Montségur would grind to a stop without you. Who'd milk the cows, tend the bees, wash the elderly, say Mass?'

'Fine, but you'll write to me and you promise you'll come back.'

'You have my word.'

'Your *verbum honoris*?'

'My *verbum honoris*, Poilu – now stop showing off.'

They were sat around the terrace table, a gathering of the people most dear to me, and I held Poilu back to take it in for a moment. Mother clearing plates, Beatrice pouring some wine – the two of them engaged in a voluble exchange across the table – my father and Father Pietro leaning towards each other, legs crossed, cupping their chins, deep in some great discussion, Raymond up a stepladder tying in his vines over the pergola, the swallows darting in and out of the house.

And Ingrid – her forearms on the table, head down, her face heavy with thought.

'How is Ingrid, Poilu?'

He shrugged and wobbled his hand. 'Comme ci, comme ca. Says she's just tired from the drive but, you can tell her mind is all over the place. Like mine when I'm translating something in my head.'

'Did she mention anything about her plans? By the way, your German accent is even better. Have you been practising?'

'She says she can't make up her mind what to do. And yes, I have been reading Goethe aloud, except around the bees – I think they get agitated by the glottal stops and uvulars.'

'Hmm, does she? But, sorry, I'm afraid German is regrettable for the harsh gutturalism of its consonants. Try Spanish. It's more breathy.'

Raymond turned, shouting 'Otto!', grabbing the cross beam of the pergola to stop him tumbling from his ladder. The heads turned and they all stood up, Ingrid leaping and covering her mouth with a fist, her eyes sparkling, maybe even tearful. I came up the steps and she was waiting for me, arms outstretched, and gave me the tightest embrace, whispering, 'You did it! You did it! But your face, what happened? What did those bastards do?' And she laid a hand on my swollen cheek.

I felt quite the conquering hero by the time the weeping hugs and handshakes and back-slapping were all done, and I was bundled into a seat, a plate of breaded veal and potato salad and a great glass of young red wine laid before me. I set about it in a crossfire of questions from a circle of eager faces.

She had explained everything to my parents, she said, when finally we broke off from the table, leant back in our chairs, spinning our glasses of wine. She had persuaded them too, she hoped, about the wisdom of getting out of Europe for a while, wait till it all blew over and it was safe to return to Michelstadt.

'Well, that's as well because I have our tickets of passage right here and Raymond the cab driver is booked to drive us to Bordeaux tomorrow. *The SS Sud-Atlantique* sets sail the morning after next.'

I clicked open my valise and took out the envelope of documents, laid it on the table. I placed my palm over it, let out a heavy sigh.

'Ingrid, I know we haven't had a chance to talk about it, about us. But look, there are four tickets in there.'

She dropped her head, folded her arms tight over her chest, a lick of jet-black hair hanging over her face.

I laid a hand on her arm and smiled. 'I have made sure you're in one of the best cabins. You even have your own balcony! And there's a jazz band every night. And Montevideo is wonderful, I hear. We can take a boat up the Amazon and ride over the Andes. We can have an adventure, Ingrid... Can't we?'

She reached for a cigarette and the book of matches, looked away and blew a plume of smoke into the vines.

'I just don't know, Otto. I just don't know!' She slapped her hand on the wrought-iron table hard enough to rattle glasses and make my father and Pietro look up from their discussion.

She smiled an apology and took an enormous heave on her cigarette, then to me, quietly, 'And I have my father to think about in New York and, you know, perhaps I could come and visit you in South America.

Once we're settled and it's all... you know, clearer.'

I looked away, trying not to say anything upsetting or final and absolute. But then said it. 'You know it's now or never, Ingrid. You know what will happen – a few months go by, I'm in Montevideo or wherever, you're in New York or Switzerland. I'm not asking you to marry me, just...'

I didn't know the end to that sentence, to that thought, and it hung there in the silence like a bunch of the grapes above our heads, Ingrid flicking her ash, me swiping imaginary muck from my thigh, my father and Pietro sneaking looks at us from under their brows, Raymond up his ladder snipping and binding, throwing glances and forced smiles our way, everyone in on the tension. We may as well have held up a placard reading, 'Will they, or won't they?'

Poilu broke the awkwardness, shooting up the steps onto the terrace, waving a little telegram envelope. He hurried over and passed it to me, Ingrid and I making knowing eye contact as I peeled it open and pulled out the message. From London. I unfolded it.

Ingrid said, 'And?'

'He's paid. All ten million marks.'

She shot her hand under the table. I reached down and clasped it, both of us squeezing and kneading.

She said, 'It's strange times when ten million marks can't bring a smile to the face.'

We both laughed but not very well and I pulled myself to my feet.

'I suppose I better go and do the honourable thing

and call off the lawyers, rescue Heini's career and his reputation for wholesome German living.'

'You don't have to, you know.' She arched her brows and tilted her head. 'You never know – sit back down and you might just be doing Germany a great favour. Destroy him before he does anything truly terrible.'

I took my wallet and address book from my case, slapping them in my palm, thinking about it. I stopped and looked back at her. 'What do you reckon?'

She shrugged, 'What's the SS motto – *My honour is my loyalty*, something like that? You have no loyalty to him, to them. They almost killed your father then dumped him in a camp.'

I stood staring at her, chewing a thumb. Beatrice and my mother emerged from the house under a stream of chirping swallows, and laid out a board of cheese, a bowl of grapes and some bread.

'No, it's not right. I made a deal, I gave him my word. My honour is my honour, my business, not some meaningless slogan. I want to show him that there is still some honour.'

She shrugged again. 'Fine, your decision.'

'Come on, Poilu. To the Post Office. Oh, and Raymond, I forgot. It was much admired, but it didn't fool the experts I'm afraid.'

I unfastened my case and unwrapped his chalice, placing it in the centre of the table. Raymond sprang from his ladder and poured himself a glass and raised it above his head.

'The Holy Grail – to all our Holy Grails!'

We lifted our glasses. Father Pietro gave me a wink and tapped the side of his nose.

·◆·

The sun had long since dropped over the horizon, away to bring its midday strength to bear on the Atlantic and then the New World, and I was staring at my distant image in the darkening window, running the cloth around the copper pan. I pictured our ship, cutting through the swell in a couple of days, the promise and uncertainty of an unplanned life – a life without Ingrid. No point forcing the issue either – it would entrench her doubts, push her further away. Maybe she was right – maybe we needed a period to gather ourselves after all that had happened, our lives turned upside down so quickly, so utterly. Besides, who can ever know what's going to happen? Could I have ever foreseen the events of the last four or five months??

Who's to say in a year or so – I smiled at the thought of it – that I might not be farming livestock on the pampas of Uruguay or the Argentine, with Ingrid, my wife, on the long wooden porch of our ranch-house, mulling motherhood or a career as a photographer? You just don't know – and it was the not knowing, that hope, that spark of faith that was going to keep me going in all the months we might not see each other, years perhaps.

A heavy September dew had cleared the terrace and

filled the living room, and I stood in the archway from the kitchen, turning to gaze down at her. Her head tilted to one side but the face still fraught with thought, the light from Raymond's great log fire caressing her peach-pink cheeks. My mother and father had the sofa, her head on his shoulder, their hands entangled – and Raymond, in the other armchair, head back, mouth open, cognac listing in his giant hand, noises coming out of him like a pig in an abattoir.

I turned back to the kitchen, Beatrice took the pan and cloth from me and gave me a kiss.

'Thank you, Otto, our work is done. I'm away to bed – get myself some sleep before Raymond joins me.'

'Have you seen Poilu? I promised I'd do some German with him.'

'God knows – tucking in his bees, taking confession? But he always turns up when you need him – he has a sixth sense, you know. Good night, Otto.'

She gave me another kiss on the cheek and then, turning back, said, 'How's it going with…?' and she flicked her head towards Ingrid.

I shrugged, grimaced and held out my palms, French-style, and she squeezed my arm and pursed her lips. I made my way onto the terrace, then around to Raymond's stone yard and up the little flight of steps, skirting the vegetable plot and into the lightly sloping orchard. A near-full moon in a clear sky burnished the fresh white paint of Poilu's slatted hives, frogs croaking in the long grass, the last of the crows circling the treetops further up.

'Poilu? You there?' In the stillness, I did not need to raise my voice. Any louder and the other half of the village would hear. 'Poilu?'

I sat on the stone bench against the wall, apples bending the boughs above my head, the fragrance filling my senses, the beauty of the moon weighing down on me. I had not drunk wine like the rest of them, knowing how maudlin I can become when I have too much, but my eyelids were heavy and, when my head fell, I startled.

And saw the headlights.

They were making their way down, flicking over the silent rooftops and then back over the valley, sweeping the fields, then back, back and forth. I hurried down to the terrace and leant against the upright of the pergola in the shadow of the vines. On the final bend, the auto slowed almost to a crawl, the driver cut the engine and then the lights and it was gone – the driver understanding that a motorcar in Montségur was an event. I went to the end of the terrace and pulled back the tangled shoots of the climber, my sightline obscured by the curve of the wall.

I crouched, my breaths quickening, running through the options. I heard it before I saw it again, the gravel cracking and popping beneath its tyres, then its heavy silhouette, the windshield glinting in the moonlight, and the frenzied barking of the dogs at the foot of the village.

I pressed myself into the climber, and it came to a

halt by the yard where Ingrid had parked the Mercedes. I pictured his yellow broken teeth, the smile breaking over his hog's features. It rolled on, creaking and squealing beneath me, and I craned forward for a view. Had he come alone? It came to a gentle stop at the steps, the bonnet crackling from the heat of the engine, the fumes of a long journey filling the windless air.

I was almost behind it now, looking down on its roof at an oblique angle. An elbow emerged from the window, then a hat, shifting from side to side, straining for an angle. I could not make out the face beneath the flattened brim – then he looked up to the top floor of the house. Yes, it was him. It was Muller alright, his face no prettier in the moonlight.

He took his foot off the brake and the car plunged and whined towards the heart of the village. I hurried into the house, springing up the stairs and into my room. Throwing out my clothes, I prised off the panelling of my suitcase and yanked open the drawstring of the cloth bag. I weighed the Walther in my hand, ran the slide back and forth, checked the safety catch and palmed a magazine up into the well of the grip. Easy as walking once you've learned it, just as Ingrid said. I wrestled into my jacket, slotted the Walther in the inside pocket, pulled on my fedora and darted down the stairs, slowing as I reached the bottom. I crept past, their four heads all at angles, the logs cracking and spitting in the great hearth.

I eased the door shut and trotted down the steps,

whistling, head down but eyes up. At the first bend I saw it without moving my head, down to the right, four houses along, pointing back up the hill, the orange pulse of a cigarette behind the wheel. I leant into the light to check my watch and dropped to a knee, untying my shoelace then tying it back up, then straight on into the shafts of dim light in the alley leading to the square.

A Monday in harvest season and not a soul to be seen. But the lights were on in the tabac and there was Father Pietro, on his corner stool, and Michel behind the counter, whipping a dish towel over his shoulder and yawning.

Pietro was adding a dash of water to his Ricard when he looked up at the tinkle of the bell above the door. I took the other stool and nodded to them both, pushing back my hat.

'Good evening, mein Führer.'

'Very funny, your Holiness.'

'You look distressed. Sad about leaving us?'

'Another Ricard?'

'Twist my arm.'

I signalled to Michel and squirmed around, scratching my forehead, squinting through the reflections on the wall of window. Michel laid down a fresh carafe of water and two glasses in front of me, tossed up and caught the Ricard bottle from the sink below the counter and placed it between us.

Pietro served himself a shot and mumbled something. I turned back to face him. 'Sorry?'

'I said, you go tomorrow, yes?'

'That's right, tomorrow. Afternoon.'

'I'll come and see you before you go. Remember I told you I may have something that may be of interest to you.'

'Oh yeah? Great, thanks.'

I slid from my stool, an idea emerging from the fog of panic, and idled towards a window table, picking up an ashtray, peering up from under the brim of my hat, scanning the square. I wouldn't have spotted Muller but then he moved, in the bottom left corner, the moonlight just catching him before his shadow dissolved into the darkness. Pietro was still talking. I laid down the ashtray and pulled out some coins.

'... so I can tell you everything now, now you're going. In fact, it's perfect, you going to South America.'

'Sorry, Pietro, what?'

'You're not listening, are you?'

I poured the coins into the change tray, took the carafe of water, filled the longer glass and, half-twisting towards the window, drained it slowly. I refilled, tipping my head right back this time and slapped down the glass, wiping my mouth with my sleeve. Hands on hips, I arched my back and crashed forward, catching the counter at the last moment, looking down at the floor and shaking my head.

'Otto, what the – ?'

I glanced up at Pietro, winked and said, 'Yes, I'll see you tomorrow.' I threw the door shut behind me, knocked into a cane chair and skirted the fountain, gave him a little stage sway for effect. My hat right down, but he was in my side vision, in a doorway to my left just down from the square, playing the cunning Gestapo agent, thinking the drunk pansy idiot's got no idea, it's going to be a nice easy hit, back on the road in the hour, no one the wiser, maybe stop and have a good drink before turning in.

On the bend of the street I paused, patting my pockets and adjusting my hat and set off back up the hill, singing 'Thoughts Are Free', the old German folk song, the kind of song you have to be really drunk to even think about singing. He'd know it well and hate it – it's about the freedom from oppression.

'Thoughts are free, no one can guess them,
They flee like night-time shadows…'

Coincidence or my bad singing voice, it was hard to say, but the village dogs struck up with a chorus of howls and a barrage of barking. I heard the car door shut and I slowed a little, ambling back past the house, Beatrice on the top floor closing the shutters. The pack came panting up behind me, a stampede of paws on the cobbles, and they were past me.

'No one can know them,
No hunter shoot them dead,
So there it is:
Thoughts are free!'

I clambered over the gate, catching a glimpse of him sidestepping into the shade of the shack by the Mercedes. The dogs shot back down the road and darted under the fence alongside, racing away into the field in pursuit of their leader. I made for the stile, clear as the day under the fierce moonlight, the dogs lapping around me a couple of times in a perfect circle.

The path steepened from the narrow field, coiling through the stunted oaks and tangled thorns that draped the lower half of the castle hill. He would run while I was in the thick growth and I stopped in a gap a few bends up to watch him. It wasn't graceful but I was surprised by the pace achieved by a man of his bulk, like a happy old bull set loose after its winter confinement.

Craning over a bough, I might have spat on his head as he lifted his raincoat to negotiate the stile, shooing away the dogs swarming and wagging at his feet. He loosened his tie, unknotted the cloth belt of his coat and pulled out a shotgun. Breaking it open, he rested the barrel in the crook of his elbow, slid a pair of fresh shells into the barrel. He snapped it shut, shot a look upwards and strode into the trees.

The shotgun altered the situation only a little. I knew enough about guns to know he now had a huge range advantage over me – but he'd be a way better shot than me anyhow. I'd need to get close up either way, even if he was holding a pop gun with a cork on a string. Very close to make sure. But maybe he didn't want to kill me? There was an ugly thought.

I heard the crunch of his steady tread, the theatrical breathing, three or four bends below now. It would have been easy to kill him there and then – there's no way he'd suspect I'd have a gun. But then he'd never have suspected me of springing my father from Dachau. I could just wait behind the boulder then shoot him point blank in the back. No, if this plan was going to work – no repercussions, no reprisals for the village – I needed to keep drawing him up and up, get him over to the north side of the castle.

I moved off, humming some Mendelssohn. He'd hate him too – if he knew who he was. Up we went, the dogs too, scrambling straight up, almost vertically, leaping from rock to rock and crashing through the low brush, one or two coming on a little slower, working their way around rather than over.

On the final bends, the battlements of the eagle's nest castle rose sheer above me, blanking out the sky, his boots grinding the gravel below, the lights of Montségur no longer distinguishable from each other, now just a pocket of haze in the pit of the valley.

You cannot see the castle entrance until you make the final turn through the rock, and suddenly there it is. I climbed the few steps to the archway, heaving for breath myself now. I pulled out the Walther from inside my jacket and tucked it into my trousers under my shirt, the steel of the barrel cold against my skin.

I took off the jacket, hung it over the wooden railing and rolled up my sleeves – hey look, just shirt and braces, no concealed weapon just in case you were wondering, no need to start blazing away, Helmut. I leant with both hands on the railing and watched his hat twist its way through the narrow defile of rock, my mouth dry, trying to regulate and slow my breathing.

When he was just short, I sat down against the curtain wall – the cold a shock against my wet back – knees up, arms folded, head tipped back, eyes closed and I yawned loud as I could. His step slowed and quietened, then he stopped. Through half an eyelid I watched the barrel of his gun poking from the wall of rock, waving up and down in rhythm with his lungs.

He swung around, butt in his shoulder, treading lightly, barrel straight at my head. He was on the third step about five metres away when I opened my eyes, stared in astonishment, then sprung to my feet, hands above my head.

'Muller!'

'That's right, Eckhart. Thought you got away with it, eh?'

'Hey, Inspector, look I can explain, please – '

'Shut up.'

The dogs burst out of the rocks into the gulley below the path hugging the castle wall. His eyes flicked right over the long barrel, and I span on my heel, through the arch, leapt from the steps, weaving through the fallen masonry. It was no more than twenty-five metres across the bailey, and by the time I reached the little postern gate in the northern wall he was only just emerging into the interior. He stood, shotgun hanging at his side, taking in the surroundings, attitude of a man who had all night.

I passed through the opening – the arch not much larger than a house door, the whole point of a postern being to allow covert access for besieged occupants. I pulled out the handgun and leant against the outer wall right by the entrance, the gun in both hands, stub barrel against my nose. Not even I could miss from that range.

To my right, the north, the dark hills rolling down to the lights of Lavclanet on the plain. Right before me, a short skirt of uneven rock and then the great drop, sheer for 100 metres into an unpassable ravine.

He would come gun first, making no effort to disguise his arrival, but he was making me sweat on it. After a couple of minutes, ear pressed to the stonework, the dogs were back, haring around inside, panting and snuffling. A flat-coat tan hunter – Fournier the blacksmith's, I think – shot out of the archway, nuzzled my groin and shot back in.

My fingers were stiffening on the gun, and there was a twinge of cramp in my calf. Come on, Muller, let's get this done. Where the hell are you?

'Move, you die.'

He rested the barrels against the back of my head.

'And drop your little toy gun. Probably got water in it, yeah?'

I lowered the Walther from my face and tossed it inside the postern gate. He didn't ask but I raised my arms all the same. Bastard came around the wall, not a sound.

'Not as dumb as I look, Eckhart. I've spent a lifetime creeping around after little shits like you.' He stabbed the gun into my head, I took a step to correct my balance – and almost cried out.

Poilu – on all fours in the dark of the postern arch reaching out for the Walther. I wailed, 'Please, Muller, please, I will do whatever you say!' As I did, Poilu seized the gun and his hand shot backwards.

'Bit late now, Eckhart. I have my orders: bring you back to Berlin with your traitor father and your traitor whore girlfriend – or I blow your head off. Know what I'm going to do?'

I shrugged.

He pushed the barrels into the small of my back and said, 'Walk, hands on your head. Then I'll tell you, put you out of your misery.'

I turned away from the castle, stepping between the rocks, gun jabbing me to the edge, the light of the moon illuminating the full depth of the drop. He'd only have to push me from here.

'So, this is what happens. I'm going for the jackpot. I blow your brains out in about five seconds' time, and *then* I'm going down to the village, grab your father and – '

Poilu coughed and Muller swung around, taking a step to the side, swinging the shotgun between me and the postern.

'Come out of there, or I'll shred you into the other side.'

Poilu said nothing. I kept my eyes on Muller, his eyes darting back to me. I watched Muller's thumb slide off the safety catch – and that's when I realised. I hadn't readied the Walther.

Poilu sprung up from behind a rock on Muller's blind side, gun in both hands.

I yelled, 'Safety!'

Poilu pulled, Muller pivoted and pulled. Poilu flew backwards, Muller staggered under the report, his heel catching a rock, turning the gun at me. I threw a leg, knocking the barrel, the sole of my boot connecting with his flank. He didn't so much fall as plunge, his cry fading as I ran to Poilu.

'Poilu! Poilu!'

His head was slumped over, cheek to the dirt, the Walther lying in his open palm. I put two fingers under his wrist, then under his nose. The upper part of his shirt was sticky. I unbuttoned it and peeled it back. There was so much blood, so much hair, it was hard to say, but the right shoulder was the wettest. I gave it a light prod and Poilu yelped, his head springing up. He laid it back down, groaning.

'Poilu, Poilu!' I patted his cheeks and blew on his face.

CHAPTER FOURTEEN

Keep busy, distract yourself – that's what they tell you to do when you're distraught or grieving. I was glad there was so much to do that morning, because I was close to out of my mind with despair, while trying to make sense of all that had happened, what was coming. And her sitting right there taunting me with her silence and her beauty as I hurried about, preparing for the journey to Bordeaux and the voyage to Montevideo.

I swung the case through the double rear doors of Raymond's big van – there was not enough room in the little Monasix – and I glanced up at her on the terrace. At the table still, serene as you like, reading her boring Maupassant, in her gorgeous olive-green silk shirt, looking more beautiful than ever, just to torment me that little bit more, keys to the Mercedes next to her empty coffee cup. I hate farewells – they are like miniature deaths – but this one was almost unbearable.

It was difficult to hold the lid down on this boiling cauldron of thoughts and feelings. There was some genuine happiness, some relief down in there and a great deal of gratitude welling up too – even some pride

– but it wasn't going to spill out quite yet, it couldn't. Not with her so close I could smell her, soon to go her own way, wafting a trail of that damned lavender.

I mean, six months earlier, a fully-grown adult for ten years, I was the selfish idler, my life drifting nowhere, gorging on the self-pity, loving my role as the superfluous man in a world that just didn't understand me. Thanks to, well, thanks to Heinrich Himmler you'd have to say, that had all changed. I had been feeling that transformation very keenly and it was still coming on. I had shed the skin of that feckless slacker. Yes, I would be a better man from now on, there was no going back, and whether they knew it or not, every last one of them up there in the house had made a charitable donation to the cause of turning around my life. Friends and family – I get it now. You have to do the hard miles yourself, make that journey, but others show you the way. We need each other.

But I was not complete. I lacked her. I loved her. It ached. And now she was leaving.

I made my way back up to the terrace. We glanced at each other, both of us quickly looking away. I wanted to say, to bark at her, 'Why don't you just get in your car and go? Switzerland, New York, London, wherever, just go.' It was cruel just sitting there, me filing back and forth, weighed down with luggage, weighed down with her.

I made sure my sigh was audible and hurried into the house, exchanging friendlier looks with Beatrice – now there was a truly kind-hearted woman. I stepped aside on the half-landing as the doctor emerged from Poilu's bedroom.

'How is he this morning, doctor?'

'You'd think the lad had just nicked himself shaving. He was a lucky fellow that's for sure – a few more centimetres to the right and, well, there but for the grace of God we go.'

'It's not the first time he's taken a barrel-full, but I sincerely hope it's the last. He's a special boy that one.'

'I still don't understand what a huntsman was doing out at that time of night.'

I scratched my head and looked away. 'Yes, it was a bit odd but then again it was almost as bright as day, doctor. These hunters just can't sleep if there's prey to be downed. Anyhow, if you'll excuse me, I have to get a move on.'

I shot out my hand, we shook, him giving me the side-of-the-mouth smile, and I bounded up the stairs to the second floor, shouting my thanks after me. Mother was arranging her hair in the looking-glass, Father sitting in the armchair at the window, his hands in prayer under his chin, gazing towards the Pyrenees.

My mother said, 'Your father is in a bad mood. I think he wants to go back to Dachau.'

'Ill temper must be contagious, or congenital maybe. Me too. But this is our best option for now. Father knows that deep down, don't you, Father?' I looked at my watch, adding, 'We leave in fifteen minutes for

Bordeaux – we can't miss that sailing.'

I put my arm over my mother's shoulder and walked her to the door. 'Why don't you go and pour some coffees – it will be two or three hours before we stop – and I'll bring the cases down.'

When I turned around, Father was standing up, smiling.

'I am not in a bad mood, Otto. A little sad of course, a little apprehensive, but no, I am a very proud father today. That's what I was thinking about this morning – what you did. Incredible. It may have taken some time, but, good heavens, you have come of age.'

My father was not a man for tears but I detected a slight glistening and, feeling my own, I went to him and we embraced, slapping backs.

I stepped back and held him by the shoulders. 'I don't need to tell you what an inspiration you have been, do I? You'd hate that, wouldn't you?'

'Yes, I would.'

'But you do know it, don't you? Your courage, your example to me, I mean.'

He smiled and bounced his head, neither affirming nor denying.

'Good, let's get you a coffee. I need to get out of here.'

'Ingrid?'

I nodded.

He said it quietly. 'Never give up hope, Otto. For her, for Germany, for yourself. You believe something will happen, you will it to happen, then you're halfway to its realisation. Keep hoping, keep willing it.'

'It's a feeling that's not going away fast that's for sure. But, come on, coffee. See you down there.'

I heaved the last two suitcases from the bed and made my way back down. Poilu was standing in the doorway of his bedroom in his pyjama bottoms, arm in a sling, a great bandage wrapped over his shaved shoulder. I sat the cases down.

'Poilu! You should be in bed. You were shot, remember?'

Poilu bit his lip and dipped his head, scuffing his foot over the floorboard. I laid a hand on his good shoulder.

'Not you too, Poilu. This house is like a funeral cortège today.'

But he kept scraping away at the floor. 'Come on, Poilu, chin up. It's not like you to be lost for words. And look, you wait, we'll be back to Montségur like your bees to their hives.'

'*Curae leves loquuntur ingentes stupent.*'

'Very good. Seneca is right – great griefs are speechless, but this is a light one that deserves to speak a little.'

'It's not my grief – it's yours. I want Ingrid to go with you.'

'Poilu, if you weren't in such pain, and I wasn't suffering from such a fatigue of embracing and such high emotion this morning, I'd give you a hug too. But let me worry about all that, alright?'

He smiled and reached for one of the cases.

'Don't be daft, I'm taking that, Poilu – now back to bed, doctor's orders. Read some Goethe or something.'

I tramped down the stairs, Poilu following, straining under the weight of Father's books and Mother's favourite crockery – 'Something to remind us of home in the darker moments'. Raymond was in the kitchen, arms out at his side, defending himself to Beatrice.

'The man was a Nazi! And the village needs another car. We're keeping it! We'll paint it whatever colour you like.'

I turned around and dragged the two cases through the front door, scraping my hand on the stone and cursing, the swallows shooting over my head. Ingrid laid her book over her chest, smiling at me.

'Otto?'

'You may have noticed I'm quite busy at the moment, Ingrid.'

'Otto?'

'Has something exciting happened in your book? Someone spilt their champagne?'

I bounced the cases down the steps. Father Pietro was standing at the back of the van, clutching a soft leather pouch, his eyes a little puffy but wearing a kindly smile.

'How's the lad?'

'Sad but fine.'

'You?'

'Sad but fine.'

'This will cheer you up.' He held out the pouch. 'Go

343

on, take a look.'

I heaved the cases into the van and took it from him, feeling the smooth leather for clues. I pulled open the drawstring and lifted it out.

'The Chalice of Tomar.'

'The Templar castle in southern Portugal?'

'Correct.'

I turned the alabaster chalice in my hand. It was small, the size of a spread hand, shaped like a poppy head, with a slender stem widening into a circular base, the stone a mottled grey and brown with some flecks of black. Four crosses had been cut in bas-relief, set equally around the bowl.

'You're not going to tell me Raymond made this, are you?'

Pietro smiled. 'Actually, he could have done – had he been alive about two thousand years ago.'

I looked up at him, arching my brows. 'What are you saying?'

'It is believed the Knights Templar took it from France to Tomar, their last stronghold, when their order was suppressed at the beginning of the fourteenth century. Story goes they took it when they fled Jerusalem during the Crusades.'

Ingrid's chair scraped over the gravel and I looked over my shoulder. She was still smiling at me, beckoning me with her finger. I nodded, frowning, holding up a couple of fingers.

I turned back to Pietro. 'And?'

He took a deep breath, exhaling as he spoke. 'There are dozens of chalices out there claiming to be the Holy Grail, *the* cup from the Last Supper but…'

'But, what? You're not saying – '

'I'm not saying anything. Just that, well, if any chalice can make the claim, it's the Chalice of Tomar. Everything adds up.'

'But what about the crosses? He hadn't been crucified.'

'The Knights Templar had them carved.'

I turned it in my hands. 'My God – and how did it come into your possession?'

Ingrid coughed a stage cough. I spun, grimacing now, and held up a finger.

Pietro's grin had spread. 'Let's just say, I wasn't entirely honest when I said I took nothing from the Relics collection when the Vatican threw me out.'

I laughed, and he added, 'But don't worry, I may be the only one in the world who knows what you're holding. And now you. They don't have a clue. I doubt anyone even knew it was down there in the vaults.'

'Christ, what am I to do with it?'

'Whatever you like. Safer with you there, than me here. Just look after it, keep it hidden. You never know who will come looking for it.'

I slid the chalice back into the pouch. 'Forgive me, father, for I must get on. I guess I may as well embrace you too. Thanks for all you've done for me.'

Pietro made his way up the steps to the terrace

where my parents had joined the Trencavels for the *Grand Départ*. I leant into the van and wedged the pouch between two cases. Raymond – driver Raymond – leant from the cab window and clapped his hands, shouting 'Come on! It's six hours to Bordeaux.'

I rested my hands on the floor of the van, the emotion churning in my guts. Stabbing a few breaths, I pulled myself up and spun around.

Ingrid was standing right before me, smiling sheepishly, case at her feet.

'Otto.'

She said it very softly, real feeling in a croaky voice, fidgeting with the key for the Mercedes.

I wanted to throw myself at her and bury myself in that swan's neck, draw in all that lavender for the last time. But we had an audience above us, and besides, I was too upset and I needed to be a man about it. For God's sake.

'So, you're off right now too, are you?'

'Yes, Otto, I am.'

'So, this is it then?'

'Yes, it is.'

She picked up her case. I said, 'Here, let me give you a hand with that. Where's the Grosser?'

'Otto, I have spoken to my friends in London.'

'Oh good, so you are heading there, are you?'

I picked up her case and she stepped towards me.

'They say they can find me plenty of work in Montevideo.'

346

'What? So – '

'Yes, Otto. Yes!'

She turned to the terrace, flung the car keys to Raymond and pushed me inside the open door of the van so that we were out of view. She threw her arms around my neck, I wrapped mine around her waist and our lips met in a soft collision.

ALSO BY THE AUTHOR

Niall Edworthy has written over forty books on a wide range of subjects, some under his own name, some under a pseudonym and many under those for whom he has ghosted.

Bound by confidentiality agreements, he cannot reveal the acclaimed titles he has ghostwritten. Below is a selection of some non-fiction titles to which he must own up.

Planet Darts
The Optimist/Pessimist's Handbook
Main Battle Tank
The Second Most Important Job in the Country
Badger's Cricket Compendium
Badger's Golf Compendium
Badger's Football Slang and Banter
The Curious Gardener's Almanac
The Curious Bird Lover's Almanac
The Curious World of Christmas
England: The Official FA History
Lord's: The Home of Cricket
Football Stories: Bad Boys & Hard Men

ACKNOWLEDGEMENTS

If I wore a hat like Otto Eckhart, I would spend much of my time tipping it in the direction of Izzy Barrett, the brilliant illustrator who has produced the lovely covers for this book.

I would also tip it towards the superb husband-and-wife team of Andrew and Rebecca Brown of Principal Publishing. This is the fourth book they have produced for me, and once again, they have proved to be exemplary professionals, champions of their craft and a pleasure to work with.

Finally, I would doff in the direction of Ian Strathcarron of the Unicorn Publishing Group, who first published this book and, after its brief moment in the sun, was kind enough to revert the rights, allowing me to publish it myself and give it a second life.

Printed in Great Britain
by Amazon